THE
Silent
Partner

Also by Judith Greber

EASY ANSWERS

THE
Silent
Partner

JUDITH GREBER

CROWN PUBLISHERS, INC., NEW YORK

With special thanks to Arlene Bluestein of "The Pampered Cookie" and to Saida and Susan Tuteur.

Published by Crown Publishers, Inc.,
One Park Avenue, New York, New York 10016
and manufactured simultaneously in Canada
by General Publishing Company Limited

Printed in the United States of America

LIBRARY OF CONGRESS CATALOGING IN PUBLICATION DATA

Greber, Judith.
  The silent partner.

  I. Title.
PS3557.R356S5   1983   813'.54   83-26183
ISBN 0-517-55295-7

10 9 8 7 6 5 4 3 2 1

First Edition

For Matthew and Jonathan,
with love

THE Silent Partner

1

THERE WAS A MIDDLE-AGED WOMAN IN THE MIRROR again.

Every morning, Molly showered and envisioned the day ahead, running images through the stream as if previewing a film. She saw herself with people—her children, her husband, her customers. She saw herself alone—planning, organizing, thinking. But she always saw herself as lithe, young and unlined, a small woman with dark copper hair and gold-brown eyes. What she saw was what she considered "Molly."

She never saw The Face.

The Face belonged to someone else, an aunt in a faded photograph, perhaps. A stranger. Certainly not to her.

She was sure an impersonator had learned her gestures, taken her name and then enclosed her like the worst of science-fiction monsters.

You could tell if you looked closely. That wasn't Molly Hawthorne Michaels' skin. This one had been measured for someone larger, and it was slipping loose. There were faint tracks next to the mouth, puffs under the slightly crepey eyes, a hint of slackness at the jaw.

It was too soon for this. Molly had fallen out of sync. Inside, she was still young and buoyant.

The woman in the mirror tapped on the glass. "Hello," she said.

"Get lost," Molly muttered.

"I'm sick of this!" The woman's voice became testy. "Every morning I say hello, politely, and you answer rudely and then you bury me under layers of junk. Do you think you can ignore me forever? Do you think I'm some kind of option?"

"I'm sorry," Molly told the matron in the mirror. She'd been taught to be polite to her elders. "I don't mean to be rude, but I—I'm not ready for you. I, ah, wasn't expecting you, actually."

"Not expecting me! *Why not?*" the woman demanded. "Did they suspend the rules of the universe for you, cookie?"

"I knew that you'd come sooner or later," Molly said. "But *later*, that's when. Very *much* later. This feels too soon. I feel too . . . ordinary."

The woman arched her eyebrows. "You of all people are suddenly avoiding the ordinary? Why, Molly, you've spent nearly forty years in the middle of the road. You never strayed, never explored, never rebelled. You *loved* ordinary. What's happening to you now?"

Molly was embarrassed by raw truth so early in the day. She had indeed always cultivated the ordinary. She thought it had something to do with her timing. She'd been born too late for the serious revolutions and too soon for the fun ones. She came of age in the sagging center of the century, years that rocked in place like a hammock in summer.

Stuck-in-the-middle Molly. The middle of the century, the middle of its morals, the middle of its wars and philosophies.

And now she was middle-aged to boot.

She sighed. Certainly, she'd followed the road more traveled, but there'd always been time to change course. Time for the dramatic act, the significant contribution, the leap into the history books. Endless time. Until now.

Was it possible, then, that Molly never would become a legend most? That she wouldn't star in a movie, have a dish named for her, be interviewed on "Sixty Minutes," cure cancer or be precocious?

Was it possible she wouldn't escape death?

Was it true that she, Molly Pearl Michaels, née Hawthorne, descendant of genius—the Molly of scholarships, bright promise and lasting patience; Molly, who'd done what was right, marrying, raising children, waiting her turn—that she had *had* it? And hadn't even noticed it?

Wasn't there something exceptional and exciting left?

Maybe the future had already come and gone and Molly, too busy with diapers and school lunches, with moving and managing, had missed it.

Molly pressed her fingers against her temples and pulled, gently, to see if tight skin returned her future. Then, feeling stupid, she released her hold and watched her face jelly down.

"Clay!" she called from the bathroom. "Time to wake up!"

Time was, she would have kissed him into day. But now she was no more eager to see her husband's face than her own.

He made her nervous lately. He was part of the general dissolution of the world. What had happened to him, to them, to their sense of a shared life and the joy they derived from that sharing?

Lately, he was always exhausted, even when he slept. He avoided her, his eyes settling on air, not her face. Their conversations were brief and in bed he sought sleep, not her.

Not only his hair had turned gray.

It was getting late. She'd have to put on her makeup after breakfast. But how awful she looked without it. Lots of good things gone, she told the mirror. And in their place, wrinkles. Some rotten trade-off.

"Cut that out," the mirror woman said. "You should be ashamed of yourself! You have everything, Molly. You're the all-American success story, the full flowering of evolution.

"It's for your sake we climbed out of the swamp. For you we stood up, put on shoes, invented combs and made fire. For you, the wheel, computers, birth control, polio vaccine, dry cleaning and hair color. For your pleasure, mass production, the stock market, plastic, democracy and trash compactors. For you, continuing education, aerobics, take-out Chinese and free libraries."

"You sound a lot like my mother," Molly said. "In fact, you look a lot—"

"Don't interrupt. The point is, all that and you stand there whining? You have everything you ever asked for. A loving husband—not some illiterate digging for grubs, not some lout smacking you around, not a sheikh shoving you into his harem. Your three babies all lived, with not one lost to plague or seized by the lord of the manor or deformed by work in the mines or enslaved. And look at you! You have your health, a business of your own, a cleaning woman and a microwave.

"Cookie, you have the best deal in the last thirty-six thousand years. I ask you, when else in all history and where else on all the globe could you have the gall to complain because your skin isn't as tight as it used to be? Because life isn't perfect? Who ever promised, who ever considered, perfect?"

"You're right," Molly said softly. Privately, she added, "So what?" The truth made no difference except to add guilt to her litany of woes. She sprinkled cleanser and scrubbed down the vanity.

"I mean you're an educated person," the mirror woman said. "You should have some sense of perspective. You should—"

Molly took out the Windex. "You talk too much," she said. Taking careful aim, she nailed the critter in the mirror, right between its middle-aged eyes.

2   "JOANNA! BEN! TONY! YOU'LL BE LATE!" MOLLY waited at the bottom of the stairs, saw no one, then stomped back into the kitchen. No matter what the mirror woman said, no matter what business or worldly success might be ahead, Molly Michaels had failed at her first endeavor, that of creating the Perfect Family.

Just as Marie Curie spent her youth dreaming of science, or young Pavlova dreamed of dance, Molly Hawthorne had dreamed of families. She had reveries of warm, closed circles, wide smiles, holiday gatherings, shared memories and smoothly solved problems. Most of all, she dreamed about Ozzie and Harriet Nelson's family and how she would one day re-create its perfection.

She had done a good job on the settings and props. The cobalt-blue and white kitchen was inviting with its dark polished woods and tile floor. The size of the room and its possibilities had been the reason Molly picked this house, and her muscles and mind turned it into a splendid backdrop.

But she was not doing as well with the cast of characters.

"The Michaels Family Hour" was not a hit show, and as its producer-director, Molly had to acknowledge failure.

Gray rain slid down the patio doors negating much of California's justification for existence.

"Hurry up!" she shouted. Only the dog, refusing to go outside in the rain, heard. Molly mixed batter.

She knew her children were ignoring her, dawdling on unmade beds, playing records, reading comic books or fighting. Anything that would help them miss breakfast and the bus. Just like yesterday.

She clenched her hand into a fist, ignoring the egg she had just put there. She felt the crack, slip and slide and heard the splat on the Mexican paver tiles.

Cords of egg white dripped from her hand. "Damn it all to hell!" she shouted.

"Way to go, Mom," Joanna said, slumping into the room.

Ben, right behind her, clicked his fingers and said nothing. He also heard nothing, except what played in a small black box attached by earplugs to his body.

"Where's Tony?" Molly demanded. "Why is he always last?"

Ben drummed on the table.

Joanna shrugged. She'd known one hundred words by her first birthday and now, at fifteen, remembered five. Silently, she slumped, limbs all over the place, her fingers raking her auburn hair.

Molly squatted behind the center island. It was comfortable, like a secret clubhouse or a foxhole. She confronted the egg. The tenacious, gelatinous essence quivered, grew and slithered from her touch.

"Tony!" she shouted, because it was embarrassing to shout directly at an egg. "Hurry up!"

"I'm *here*." Molly bobbled up to verify that the blonder of her twins was indeed in the kitchen. He had on one sock, no shoes, rumpled hair and a misshapen T-shirt that reached his knees. She was positive he hadn't brushed his teeth. "Wanna see a trick?" he asked, spreading cards across the table. He knocked over his juice en route.

"Way to go," Joanna said.

"Clean it up." Molly ducked behind her wall.

Those children were not what she'd had in mind while buying layettes.

The Michaels weren't the Nelsons by a long shot.

They'd been rehearsing for years and years, and they still stumbled around, missing cues, improvising.

Molly had been so excited as a child when she realized the Nelsons were an authentic offscreen family, living in Hollywood, California, sharing phones, cars, bathrooms and lives even when they weren't sharing it all with Molly.

She had hugged the quartet to her soul and tried on their lives for size. Her own life felt cut-rate, like an imitation. She was half of the tiniest possible family. One mother, Thea; one daughter, Molly. Period. A phony family of ones. Molly knew it would have been different—normal—if her father hadn't died.

In her mind, Joseph Henry Hawthorne, alive, moved his wife and daughter into a real house. After work, he read the paper and talked about international events, particularly about England, where he'd been born and raised.

But those daydreams were difficult. Her father's face was unclear and blurred, like the photographs she had of him. Molly had never heard his voice, never seen the shape of his hands on a newspaper.

The Nelsons, on the other hand, were easy and accessible, and she let them teach her to daydream clearly. Theirs became the way it might have been and theirs the way, for certain, it would be for Molly when she grew up. After all, the Nelsons were real. There was no disclaimer as there was inside books that the people she watched every week were fictitious and bore no resemblance to people living or dead.

But they certainly bore no resemblance to the Michaels.

For starters, the Michaels weren't always crinkling up with laughter and almost never resolved domestic crises with humor and grace. Furthermore, the Michaels family was given unimaginative, repetitive scripts. For example, she had played this scene before. A thousand times or more she'd begun her show stirring something. Eggs, baby cereal, pancake batter—whatever. Stir she did and say her lines from the stove.

The cast changed, however. First there was only her co-star, Clay—so much younger then, with so much more to say. Then there was one, then three tiny things with tight fists in infant seats, replaced by loud, spoon-banging high-chair-wobbling maniacs who threw pudding and slapped palms in spilled juice and rubbed mashed potatoes in their hair.

And then she turned her back to stir the soup and Clay was half gone and her babies were all gone, replaced by three gawky creatures.

She cracked a new egg in the batter. She was flying away the next day and one never knew about planes. She'd make a special breakfast, leave a good impression, just in case. "Swedish pancakes," she announced in a bright voice. "Lingonberry jam. Coming right up."

Nobody said anything.

Nobody said, "Wow, Mom, you sure do enhance the quality of our life by exceeding minimal parental standards by a mile."

Nobody *ever* said anything. Not even just plain "Wow."

Molly wanted praise for another day's crisp bacon, hosannas for the healthy houseplants, bravos for tables free of dust. She wanted hallelujahs, cheers, congratulations and maybe a curtain call now and then.

Or why the hell should she keep doing it, over and over and over?

She dropped her spatula, bent to retrieve it, then squatted back down near the floor. She liked it there with the thick center island separating her from Them.

If she stood up, she'd see Joanna's slump, Ben's earplugs, Tony's cards floating in juice and the California dog, crossing his four legs until sunshine returned. So she stayed crouched in her cavern, listening to Joanna refuse to pick a card, any card, from Tony. She sniffed. The pancakes were burning.

"Damn." She popped up, flipped them over and went back into hiding.

Clay Michaels stood in the kitchen doorway. His wife was squatting behind the range, cursing. One son drummed on the table, eyes glazed and ears plugged. The other, an unkempt mess, asked the deaf one to pick a card. His daughter, disguised as a migrant farm worker, slouched over the table, her head on an open book. Their lumpish dog whimpered and a parakeet squawked from its cage.

It was a goddamn zoo.

He sat down without a word. Molly surfaced. She looked unfinished, the way she usually did in the morning. He saw her at the frayed ends of her day—before it was together and after she'd used most of it up.

It used to be better.

The phrase cut through his consciousness before he could stop it. He heard it too often lately, felt it about almost everything. And it was mostly Molly's fault, for whirling away like a dervish, just when he needed her most.

Not that he wasn't supportive. For God's sake, he'd given her the loan. And it wasn't as if she'd paid back a cent yet. Her place was still losing his money.

Okay, he mentally corrected. *Their* money. But all the same, her store wasn't expected to stop costing them money for another six months. Meanwhile, it was destroying them.

From the moment he'd met Molly, her specialness had been apparent. She was like a volcano with a bubbling core that insulated everything against the chill. She seemed endless, never measuring her attention and love.

But now she hoarded herself and begrudged all of them their intrusions. She had changed.

Maybe it was true what they said about women in mid-life.

Molly popped up. She busied herself with pancake turning and the pouring of more batter. She barely glanced at Clay.

What the hell was happening to her? Jesus Christ, it was bad enough feeling an outcast at the office. Bad enough realizing that the move to L.A., to headquarters, meant he'd become a marked target, not a star. Bad enough not understanding why or how it had happened.

"Well, Clay," Dom Campiglia would say. "Correct me if I'm wrong. I don't have your Ivy B-school paper. I studied in the school of hard knocks—old Street Smarts U. So I could be wrong about your fancy theory, but . . ."

Clay was the unforgiven butt of Campiglia's grudge against life. His sins of Protestantism, good schools and an Anglo-Saxon name were not forgotten for a moment.

Clay wanted to talk to Molly about it, the way they used to.

"What happened about the memo?" she once would have said at dinner. "Did Campiglia say any more about it?" She would have leaned forward eagerly and poured more coffee.

Now, when they talked, it was about her store, her customers, her orders, her products, her ideas. And just before standing up to leave the dining room, Molly would remember. "And you, Clay?" she'd ask politely. "Anything new?"

He missed her. He needed her. He had no idea of where to find her again.

"Pick a card, Dad," Tony said.

"Bug off," Joanna muttered.

"I didn't ask you."

"Dork."

"Stop it." Clay settled in. "I don't want a card, Tony. I want to come downstairs and find you fully dressed and eating. No bare feet, no cards, no tiny boxes, no ropes, no—"

"I bet Houdini's father didn't—"

Clay turned to Joanna. "And you, young lady. Why don't you ever finish your assignments at night?"

Molly realized she'd have to leave hibernation. Clay was sinking into his least lovable paternal act, Imitation Conversation, or, The Patriarch Asks Rhetorical Questions. It set her teeth on edge. She was positive that sentences beginning "Why don't you ever," or "If there's one thing I can't abide," had long-term and damaging effects. Addressing one's daughter as "young lady" was punishable with complete inattention. Clay had inherited the disease from his overbearing, pompous father and if not checked would pass it on like his tendency to high cholesterol.

"I did my homework," Joanna said. "But my teacher hates me. She won't like my poem. She only likes her pets and she treats the rest of us like—"

Molly stood up. "Janna darling," she crooned in her sweetness-and-light voice, an award-winning Harriet Nelson imitation. "How could anyone hate a poem?" Mother, the peacemaker, waltzed to the table with a trayful of slightly charred pancakes and bacon and, for Clay, bran cereal. "Read it to us."

Joanna watched Molly through a fringe of bangs. "No offense, Mom, but—"

Every one of Molly's muscles tightened. "No offense, Mom, but—" was Joanna's equivalent of "banzai!"

Did her child lump her with an insensitive teacher? "Don't be silly." Molly's voice tinkled like Glinda the Good's. "I love poetry. I was a literature major, remember?" Poetry over pancakes had such a fine and gentle sound.

"A poem?" Tony looked in pain.

"What do you want instead? Pick a card, any card?" Joanna snapped.

"Come, come!" Molly liquefied and coated her ailing family with a healing balm made of her flesh. "I want to hear your poem," she said in her glossy voice. "As for you, Tony, keep an open mind. You might be pleasantly surprised."

Tony rolled his eyes. "Moon, June, swoon. Terrific."

"Forget it," Joanna said. "I wouldn't read near him."

"Families used to read out loud all the time." Molly tried to pull them into one of her beloved sepia hazes. "Maybe we've lost something fine. Read it, Jo."

Jo shrugged. "It's called 'Love's End.' "

"Love!" Tony wailed. "Moonjuneswoonkisskiss—"

"Shh." Molly was comforted. "Love's End." She remembered an adolescence filled with Edna St. Vincent Millay's sad sonnets and she felt a bond with her daughter.

Joanna cleared her throat. "Are you ready?"

Molly smiled and nodded.

"Sperm, ovum, cock and cunt, fucking in a—"

"JESUS H. CHRIST ON A CRUTCH!" Clay's face turned a dangerous purple. He stood up.

"Sit down, Clay," Molly said quietly.

"No daughter of mine is *ever, ever*—"

"Wow!" Tony said. "Poetry."

"—such foul, such disgusting—no daughter of—"

"I knew you wouldn't understand." Jo slumped even farther.

"I can't believe you!" Molly no longer twinkled. " 'Love's End,' you said. I thought—and at breakfast, with your brothers and all of us—"

"You asked me to read it."

"Not a— What is that thing?"

"A poem. We're supposed to find one that means something to us, and this one does. It's about abortions." Jo looked defiantly at her family. For once they all paid attention to her. All except Ben, of course, who hummed to music only he could hear. Joanna suddenly felt very hungry. She reached for the butter and added another pat to the top of her pancakes. She poured syrup on the stack. While she cut and chewed, she watched her mother reach for the anthology *Womanscreams*. She couldn't wait to see how she handled this one.

Her mother was into calmness lately. She used to be normal, blowing up, then saying she was sorry and talking it over. Now she was weird. Shaky-nervous underneath, but with this heavy calm pressed on top.

Joanna knew why, too. Her mother was afraid they'd all get mad about the store and say it had changed her, which it had, but which she wouldn't admit. So she tried to do everything wonderfully. Like being Aunt Jemima with the pancakes.

"Jo?" There was a frown line between her mother's eyebrows. No wonder. It made Joanna sick herself to think about what the poem described. Shredded bits of almost-person. Gross. But her mother wouldn't say so. She'd try to *understand*. If she'd only be honest, then maybe Jo could talk to her.

Molly's tongue couldn't clear a path through her thoughts. Why did her fifteen-year-old daughter find a poem about cheap sex and dead fetuses the one that meant the most to her? Why did that same daughter never want to talk to her mother about anything except when she next needed a ride somewhere? Why did crucial issues always erupt just before Molly had to leave town?

"Yeah?" Jo stared with no expression.

"I, ah, think its view of life is, well, the language is—crude, and although I'm sure there are aspects of it I'm missing, still I think maybe another poem for your class might—and maybe we can talk about it sometime soon?"

"And Remember," Clay said, his voice capitalizing every word, "If I Ever Hear You Use Words Like That Again Young Lady, I'll—I'll . . ."

Molly waited. What would Clay do? Cut off her lips?

"Well!" Clay said emphatically. "Maybe it's good that we're taking a breather from each other tomorrow."

The two senior family members were flying to Nassau for an

enforced weekend of fun. A perk of the corporate officer. Also, a way for Great Harvest, Clay's employer, to gather in its far-flung employees and pep them up. It was supposed to foster camaraderie—and just a bit of competitiveness. One couldn't help but notice how well Joe X was doing with his division or how many young go-getters had joined the firm. It was a guaranteed strain, a drainer of small talk, a horror of a time for Molly. But just as the woman in the mirror had said, some things weren't options.

"Oh, Grandma's coming to watch us," Jo said. "Lectures and lessons. Her facts. Did you know, children, that one-legged hippos were worshiped in A.D. 723? You didn't know? What on earth do you learn at school?"

"Mom!" Ben pulled the plugs out of his ears. His eyes were wide.

"Praise God, the boy can speak." Clay put down his coffee cup with a thunk. "I thought his tongue had atrophied."

"I have a concert at eleven. Can you come?"

"Today? This morning?"

Ben nodded. "I forgot. Sorry."

The room became dark. Molly couldn't generate any more energy. They threw too much at one time. Demands, yearnings, requests and emotions. She was only one middle-aged catcher. "I have to work, Ben," she said. "I've already swapped time so I can leave tomorrow. I can't switch again."

"I have a s-solo."

Molly crumpled. She couldn't withstand the pressures of the too-much life. Everything converged—Clay's moodiness, her daughter's interest in abortions, her mirrorside view of mortality, her trip to nowhere tomorrow—and Ben, who asked almost nothing, suddenly needing her at a concert.

And the day had barely begun. But the scoreboard was up, waiting to see who won—the Businesswoman or the Mom.

It was never a victorious tie, hard as she tried. Her life was always either-slash-or. Very much was never enough and every day was a new beginning. Over and done with were all the yesterdays of schedule juggling so that orthodontists and pediatricians and shoe stores and libraries and friends across town and theme parks were visited. The brownies, cupcakes, cookies and granola clusters baked for endless classrooms had been eaten long ago. The costumes she'd sewn were ripped and outgrown, the plays she'd attended had closed. Everything was part of yesterday and didn't count and her past efforts had only built a high platform that propped up her family's expectations. She was breaking her back trying to leap up to it again and again.

Clay waited. Would she try that snotty new number? Would she say, "Why don't you ask Daddy to come to your recital? I work too, you know."

He could hear himself in Nassau Saturday. "And how did the meeting with the Japanese go?" Campiglia would ask as they played golf.

"Had to skip it," Clay would say. "My son sang in his seventh-grade concert." Campiglia would swing his club into Clay's head.

For God's sake, Campiglia was already annoyed about Clay's delayed appearance at the conference. Clay, giving in to Molly's work-crazed demands, had agreed to arrive two days late. Then he had to move fast and make the decision seem necessary by becoming host to the visiting Japanese.

At least he hoped Campiglia thought it was necessary. The man confounded Clay, alternating between low-level anger and disinterest. Two months earlier, Clay and Art Baum had presented an idea that really excited them—the consolidation of all Great Harvest's subsidiaries under one recognizable label. No more Pasta Presto or Summer Creek Lemonade or Best of Breed Kibble. Instead, one strong image representing a truly great and endless harvest.

Campiglia had daydreamed, yawned and said nothing through their presentation. A month later, he referred casually to the idea as impractical and best forgotten. Again he retreated into irritated silence, emerging weeks later to invite Clay to a golf game in Nassau, Saturday afternoon. They never played golf together here in Los Angeles. Nothing made sense. Nothing was working out the way he had once been certain it would.

Clay looked woefully at his low-cholesterol bran cereal, then at the pancakes and butter and lingonberry jam, and then, at Molly. Where had all the good things gone?

"I can't," Molly said, her voice loud. "I cannot attend your concert, Ben." She felt breathless and nauseated, as if she'd run too hard. "I'm sorry you didn't give me more notice. I love your voice and your concerts, but it isn't possible today."

Ben looked down at his hands.

Molly looked down at hell. She was a failure. She had betrayed her own son.

Ben sighed.

Molly felt a headache begin.

"Then, Mom," Ben said, "can you come next week when we do it again?"

She considered killing him. Instead, she took a deep breath and nodded. "If you give me fair notice."

The morning was almost complete. The three lunches in their sacks, the five breakfasts eaten, the dog forced into the rain, the stray cat given food, and the kids tackling the bus just as it pulled from the stop. Down to Clay and Molly and the coffee dregs and getting dressed and made up and the final house check and lists of things to do, food to buy, stops to make and the—

"Molly?" Clay poured himself another cup of coffee. "I couldn't help but notice how tense you became when Ben—"

"If you noticed, why didn't you help ease it?"

"That's what I'm trying to do now, Moll. I—"

"Why didn't you remind him that I work? Why don't you ever do that?"

"Because you say it so often nobody else has to!"

Molly slammed down her cup, leaving a slosh of coffee to join Tony's orange juice. "What does that mean?"

"What I said. You're tense and overworked and it's time to rethink the problem."

"I am. I'm trying to get the kids more involved in the—" She understood. "You don't mean that, do you? You mean rethink the idea of working."

He smiled as if at last she'd said something clever.

She couldn't believe it. After countless talks, after a year of day-in, day-out doing it, after everything—how could he still not understand?

"You put so much unnecessary pressure on yourself. Maybe it wasn't such a great idea after all. It was worth a try and you've given it a fair shake, a year of really hard work. You have nothing to be ashamed of. But Moll, you drag in every night, complaining and more irritable than you ever were before. Frankly, I think it's affecting all of us. The children are entering a difficult stage, and, well . . ." He nodded, agreeing with himself. It was the Father Michaels nod. The one Mother Michaels never disagreed with.

Molly couldn't absorb the reality of her husband. So handsome, so impressive with that premature shock of silvery hair, those navy eyes and that face you wanted to trust. So loving, so bright, so quick, so funny.

So stupid, so self-centered, so blind.

He didn't know a thing about her. He didn't want to know because she'd been trying to tell him for over a year now. What kind of loving was that?

For years she'd followed him around the country. Whither he wentest went Molly, bumping along, deferring, adjusting, giving his needs and the family's priorities her wholehearted attention and support. But now, surely, it was her turn. Now they were permanently settled in the lap of Great Harvest headquarters. They were no longer migrants. And now her skin was signaling that time was running out. It was now or never for Molly Michaels.

Was Clay really asking her to choose "never"?

"Give it up?" she asked with real wonder. "If you can say that, Clay, then you really don't understand me at all, do you?"

He stared at her. He didn't even understand the question.

3

MOLLY HADN'T SET OUT TO BE AN ENTREPRENEUR. Females of her generation were not directed toward business. "What do you want to be?" the school counselor had asked. "A teacher or a nurse?"

She chose column A, majoring in literature until Clay Michaels appeared. Then she chose Clay, leaving college to be with him as he took his first job in Chicago. She tried to complete her degree there, but moved again, had babies in Connecticut and St. Louis, picked up some credits in Boise, tried both a part-time job and school in Houston and Atlanta and then, still without a definite career path or a degree, she moved to Los Angeles and accidentally discovered her ideal occupation. All the years of Harriet Nelson domestic dreams, all the cooking, planning, entertaining, designing and organizing became a long and thorough preparation for the store she now partly owned and wholly loved.

Even with rain dulling its colors, the sight of the building soothed the sore places Clay had left. The store made sense. Clay didn't. The truth of both these statements hurt her deeply.

She smiled at her second home, at "Sinfully Good." It was an anomaly, a yellow clapboard Victorian in the middle of the L.A. fast lane. A fiction, generating nostalgia for the never-known good life. For long summer evenings with crickets and lemonade and neighbors whose histories you knew.

The place might have migrated from Disneyland to this turbulent piece of West L.A., but it was instead an original occupant, a stubborn remnant of a lost neighborhood. The streets had once held middle-class homes, but in this new America, streets didn't need to be paved with gold. They became gold, too valuable to sleep on. No one even looked back to see his home swallowed and regurgitated as a professional building or condominium. With the exception, that is, of the stubborn owner of the curious Victorian who liked it and wanted it to last.

Molly and her partners, Ellen and Nan, had been depressed by the impersonal, rigid malls, the ersatz Spanish or Tudor villages and the high-tech complexes. Then Molly saw the bedraggled house. Years of fixing and decorating the Michaels series of houses had trained her to see the possibilities of a structure.

The yellow Victorian, reborn as Sinfully Good, sat like a genteel reproof to its concrete-and-glass neighbors, and did a brisk business almost immediately.

Probably none of the dental technicians, paralegals, accountants and tennis ladies who filled it daily had grown up in a house where fresh bread was a regular feature. But now, when they selected food at the counter, facing the copper-and-oak kitchen, they dreamed back to an idea of home, to a sense of what someone had once wanted for them.

On fine days they carried lunch to small tables on a wide veranda circling three sides of the house. Bougainvillea colored the air fuchsia.

On rainy days such as this, people clustered in the dining

room, sometimes sitting on the staircase, taking home contain-
ers of food like portable memories.

Molly walked into the old parlor where dark wood shelves
held preserves and spices, cellophane-wrapped fruit and
nut breads. There was a case of desserts and one of im-
ported cheeses. There were glass canisters filled with bright
candies and another case of fresh homemade dinners. There
were tins of chocolate, and fresh pasta drying on wooden
racks.

Nan, as usual, had lit fires in the parlor and dining room.
"Morning, honey," she said, readjusting a display. "The cheese
bread just arrived and Violet McCreedy will be by later with
the mocha brownies she wants you to try."

When Molly first met her, Nan appeared a ditsy divor-
cee with only her property settlement to recommend her.
One of her long red nails had a small jewel imbedded in it,
and on the strength of that, Molly wanted to veto her as a
partner. Molly had since learned not to judge a woman by her
manicure.

"I'm so sore today, Molly honey. Last night was a marathon.
Maybe I'm too old for more than one man a night. But look
here—Goldilocks was back." Nan held up a tiny jar of garlic
pickles. "We'll run out of cornichons soon if that thief's not
caught."

"How many more than one man a night?"

"Well, honey—"

"No. Don't tell me. It's too early." Instead, Molly looked at
the depleted cornichon display. Nan had pulled out four empty
jars. She held a fifth in which one diminutive pickle floated in
liquid like a specimen. This was the second time someone had
secretly munched up their cornichon stock.

"How does she do it? And why? And who? A gourmet,
pickle-loving, pregnant kleptomaniac? And why doesn't anybody out here ever notice what's happening?"

"The kid working the front is strange, Molly. She says shoppers go into a trancelike prepurchase state that we should never interrupt."

"How about interrupting the sound of pickle-chomping?"

The front bell jingled. Ellen, the third partner, entered silently, nodding and wiping her feet on the little carpet near the door. She hadn't been taciturn until recently.

When Molly first met Ellen, she was struck by the extravagance of the woman's gestures, by the generosity implicit in them and by her all-embracing warmth. Ellen was the fastest new friendship Molly had ever made. And not only did that friendship work but, more unusually, so did the friendship of the two couples.

"This is John." Ellen had touched her husband's arm and leaned toward him with delight as she introduced him. But nowadays, the drama was gone from her voice and gestures. She seemed to take up less space. The couples didn't see each other anymore.

"That John," she would murmur. "I don't know . . ." Vagueness dusted everything she did. "Want to know what John-the-bastard did?" she'd ask, sounding resigned.

John-the-bastard excelled at low-grade sadism. He forgot that which was important. He ignored that which was painful. He admired that which was not Ellen.

Much of his behavior was written off to the peculiarities of men in mid-life. "It'll pass," Molly said. "He's really afraid of having a heart attack or going bald."

"Or of not getting it up," Nan added.

Ellen's difficulties began to seem chronic, but Molly wanted feverishly to believe that they would dissipate and that Ellen would have a happily-ever-after finale.

Molly was sick of statistical reality. Her address book was a mass of crossed-out halves, of condominium addenda for relocated partners. Once, she'd found an old address book from Connecticut and realized that out of forty-three couples therein inscribed, only two were still coupling with each other.

It was lonely being an exception. Molly wanted troops to march under her banner, wanted reinforcements to swell their ranks. Instead, like the cheese, she and Clay stood alone. Sometimes she wondered whether they were admirable survivors or dummies who were the last to catch on to the truth.

Or worse, whether they were only lucky. She saw them standing on the same smoking battlefield as their friends, liable with their next step to hit a live mine and be destroyed themselves.

Now, Molly followed Ellen into their kitchen offices, thankful for work that kept her from thinking about her marriage.

The three women had a loose division of specialized labor. Ellen enjoyed record-keeping and had the ability to understand governmental requirements. Nan loved organizing the kitchen, working out shopping lists and creating desserts. Molly was the artist, the one who'd birthed Sinfully Good because she was so clever with her hands. She designed their packaging, ads and window displays and continued to create the "basket cases" she'd originally invented.

There were four orders for baskets today. Two new mothers, one new house and one new marriage. She started with the easiest, the wedding. This was a relatively expensive order—seventy-five dollars—so she decided to line a willow basket with a silvery silk remnant and then fill it with goodies for a newlywed's feast. Champagne, pâté, pretty goblets, flaky cheese straws and wine sticks tied into a bouquet and— She thought about Ellen, locked into her morning's marital misery. About herself, flushing with anger if she thought of Clay. About Nan, the happy one. The divorced one.

Maybe she should change the contents of the wedding baskets. Put in antacid and aspirin for the morning after the fun stops, when life isn't a picnic anymore. For when you explain and explain your dreams and your husband is as responsive as a loaf of pumpernickel.

She walked into the storeroom, passing Ellen, whose brown hair and olive skin had deepened into the colors of mourning.

Perhaps the baskets should hold warm compresses and bandages for the insults and injuries the couple pledged to endure.

Instead, she found eyelet ribbon with embroidered turtledoves. Then she selected more baskets, ribbons, fabrics, and chose special cups and saucers for the new mothers. They'd receive a basket of self-pampering—exotic teas and miniature cookies and a single cup and saucer for private, delicious moments.

Molly found herself comparing the new mothers' bundles of baby promise with the ungainly reality of Joanna, Tony and Ben.

It was newness, then, that was special and the unknown that was intriguing. It was beginnings—babies and weddings and brand-new houses—that excited.

But what of old? What of ongoing and enduring? Where were the celebrations for that?

She returned to her worktable with her supplies and realized Nan was in mid-monologue.

"He's an artist at lovemaking." Nan talked while she checked the oven and set baskets of napkins and implements on the counter. "I do wish that girl—that Marylou—would take care of this before she leaves for class." Nan had absolutely no problem keeping her life's categories distinct from one another. Only her listeners had the problem as she bounced from beds to business and back again. "There's no way to explain without sounding dumb or like a porno film's narrator. He's just fabulous. He loves it all and he spends so much time on loving me. It's like I become more than me—like I'm two people sometimes."

"I thought there were two of *him*." Molly smoothed out the ribbon with the turtledoves.

"Not at one time. Not last night. One after the other. This is Stefan. The second one. Where was I?"

"Like two people sometimes." Ellen didn't bother to look up from her calculator.

"Right. It's like being there and watching, too. I can't explain. Anyway, last night, well, he has this silky thing he draped over the massage table in the bedroom. . . ."

Molly tied the ribbon full of doves into a large bow. She was moving very slowly. Last night, while Nan enjoyed her serial lovers, Clay shouted about his misplaced golf clubs and Ben and Tony fought over a *Mad* magazine.

"Last night was special. 'Nanny,' he said, 'don't do a thing. Let go. Lie back and experience what can happen. You're so good, Nanny, so giving. Working, cooking, feeding people all the time. You make me so happy, you do so much. Now let me do you. Tonight, you just take.' "

Molly smoothed the ribbon, again and again.

"He has this view of the city from the canyon and there I was, naked on this pale peach silk, looking through the eucalyptus trees across millions of lights while he oiled me, slowly, with these circular motions. . . ."

Maybe Nan shouldn't share quite so much. Some things were supposed to be private. It wouldn't hurt to listen to the radio instead. It wasn't healthy or fair hearing about off-limit treats. Not that Molly was interested, or wanted to experiment, or was dissatisfied with her lot. Things hadn't been incredibly exciting lately, but that was irrelevant, a blip on a long film. Molly was a thoroughly contented, domesticated woman.

"And he has four speakers in his bedroom, so the music was all over the place. Felt as if it were vibrating inside me half the time." Nan pulled a dozen loaves of quick bread out of the oven and set them on wooden racks on the counter. "There was just the dark and his hands and the oil and the stars. This incredible perfume and the music inside me and . . ."

Nan's children were emotional wrecks, their time split between a rigid father, a flighty mother and a housekeeper who spoke no English. You paid prices for your games. Molly would never put her children at risk. Not for pure, mindless sensation. She wasn't even tempted.

"He brushed his hands all over me, with light, light touches, starting at my feet, up inside my thighs, around, under my stomach—he drove me so crazy I begged him to stop, but—"

Nan's Olympic lovers were emotional and intellectual paraplegics. Not the sort you'd acknowledge in the daylight. Not nice people.

"—but he said hush, Nanny, we're going to hold back and hold back so when it happens it'll be like never before and we did and it was, over and over again, and . . ."

It wasn't worth it. Not even for nights dedicated entirely to making love. Not even for surprising hands gliding up the insides of her well-oiled thighs or for incense and music, or for learning secrets and unsuspected possibilities. No. She wasn't interested and didn't want it.

But all the same—even so— *Even so!*

Her sigh was so loud, Ellen looked up, broke her dark scowl and giggled. "Me, too," she said.

"Something I said?" Nan asked.

"Everything you say." Ellen shook her head.

"Have pity on the married," Molly added. "Speaking only for myself, I haven't seen many massage tables or much silk lately, and as for incense—"

"Golly, John-the-bastard *always* provides peach silk. What on earth's wrong with Clay?" Ellen punched out numbers on the machine.

"You can't compare single with married," Nan said. "It's apples and oranges."

"Or pommes frites and greasy french fries," Ellen said.

"Or vintage wine and wine vinegar." Molly surprised herself by saying that, and felt uncomfortable.

Oh, the marriage bed, she thought as she worked on her basket. That comfortable, familiar frame for her days. That tumbled nest of bedclothes and history and reversals. Nights of wild couplings and nights turned back to back, staring into the dark, completely alone. Pulled blankets and groans as pregnancies started there advanced into insomnia and backache and 3:00 A.M. feedings and whispers so as not to wake the babies and loud, late conversations about where those now-grown babies were at such an hour.

She had no desire to leave it. But lately, after so many books and movies and friends like Nan, the marriage bed seemed a sheltered workshop for the chronically timid. King-size or not, it sounded small.

"Is someone tapping on the door? Where are the part-timers?" Nan broke into Molly's reveries. "I'm stuck at the oven, Moll, can you get it?"

Outside, dressed in matching transparent raincapes and hats stood Edna and Sally Rae Harris, dubbed the Hoover sisters by Ellen for the way they sucked up every loose morsel in their paths.

The ancient, pension-poor sisters were Sinfully Good's in-house charity, but neither side would embarrass the other by admitting it.

"Time to open up, isn't it, Mrs. Michaels?" Edna, of the tiny ringlets, spoke.

It was not quite 10:00 A.M., but the Hoovers were waiting in the rain. Molly ushered them in. They made their way to the dining room serving counter and then, as they did every morning, they sampled each entrée, accepting tasting spoons of salads and soufflés, trying slivers of cheeses and the special of the day, a Middle Eastern platter featuring falafel.

"Delicious, but a bit salty for us."

They moved on, inquiring about the Emmenthaler and wondering how much mint was in the tabbouleh. "Delightful, but a bit acidic for our temperamental tummies."

The front bell rang. Molly excused herself. The Hoovers would soon give up their search for the perfect entrée and settle for a twenty-five-cent chocolate tidbit, which each would purchase. Then they could exit, a little less hungry, faces saved as bona fide customers.

Anastasia Bell stood in the parlor, poised to make a selection or a pronouncement. Molly's money was on the latter. The only truly appealing aspect of Anastasia was the circumstance in which she'd become suddenly single. Driving home from their daughter's wedding reception, William T. Bell stopped for the light at Wilshire and Veteran and, taking advantage of its length, said, "I promised myself I'd wait until Patty was married. Now she is. Good-bye, Anastasia." And he left the car and walked off and that was that. Molly always expected to meet him, still wearing his tuxedo, wandering around the city.

Now Anastasia sold real estate. "I just saw it, dear," she told Molly. "Your house."

"Has something happened to it?"

"Not that one—the one meant for you. In the Palisades."

A customer entered. Anastasia graciously gestured permission for Molly to attend to her. Anastasia would wait out whatever interruptions fate sent her way. There are elemental forces too strong to resist or fight, and a determined realtor is one of them.

The customer chose a brie studded with pine nuts and left.

"It's you," Anastasia said. "Your family. An executive's house with potential."

"Anastasia, I keep telling you, we aren't in the market."

"Now, Molly, you can't stay in that adorable dollhouse forever, so why not move up now?"

Anastasia's high card wasn't subtlety, but she had a certain effectiveness. Molly's overpriced, sufficiently large house shrunk until it was suitable only for Munchkins.

"There's interesting financing," Anastasia said. "Five bedrooms. His and hers master baths. A man with Clay's future, a man in his position, needs an image. Think about it. I'll be back." And she left. Molly expected the woman to lift off, flapping wings and cawing.

Ellen ushered out the Hoovers. She and Molly watched the women help each other down the front steps.

"Business is going to stink with this weather," Molly said. The good people of Los Angeles did not consider rain or death parts of the natural order, and they avoided both.

"At least you're getting out of here," Ellen said.

"And into forty-eight hours of nonstop smiling and stupid talk. Not to mention the fun people—women who spend the rest of the year floating in formaldehyde."

"If you hate it, why don't you stay home?"

"Can't. It would be an embarrassment to Clay. The company's obsessed with the sanctity of the family. Wholesome food from wholesome folk. Both those ideas are lies, but they insist on them all the same. So they have these meetings, kind of like Halloween. Only we dress up as the salt of the earth."

"Maybe it won't be so bad," Ellen said. "Don't the ads claim it's better in the Bahamas?"

Across the street, a woman parked her battered car, then emerged with a newspaper-wrapped bundle.

"You think they mean 'it'?" Molly asked. "As, for example, Nan's lovers might mean 'it'?" She thought, briefly, of Nan's nights and felt a surge of emotions flood and ebb, leaving a wash of nostalgia, envy and fear. She censored herself. She had to stop thinking of wild things. She was tame.

"There is only one universal 'it,' " Ellen said.

The woman put the bundle under her raincoat and pushed the car door closed with her rear. She looked pregnant and clumsy with the newspaper projecting under the coat.

"I always wondered," Ellen said, "how the Bahamas made sure it was better there. Is there a sex clinic at the airport? Right after customs, you get therapy?"

The woman paused in front of the building and checked a piece of paper. She was very young.

"Guess it looks a bit overeager, both of us standing here,

waiting for her." Ellen left for the back room and Molly opened the door.

"Thanks!" The young woman shook her rain-soaked hair like a puppy. "I hope this is the right place. You make baskets?"

Molly nodded.

"Special orders? Like including special things and all?"

"Long as it's legal," Molly said. "Come on back and tell me what's on your mind."

The woman followed her. She wore no makeup and had clean, pretty features and an earnest expression. "See," she said, "I have to give a gift to this guy. We're kind of engaged. He's a doctor. A shrink." She accepted the benevolent nods of the trio of women. She had, after all, become almost engaged to a doctor.

"But he's like really hard to buy for because he has like everything. He's older, you see, and he's really been around and like has it all already."

"Well, but with food, it doesn't really matter if he—"

"Well, like he won't touch sugar, you know?"

"That limits us a little."

"He's like pure. Doesn't do drugs, or coffee, or tea, or alcohol."

"Then perhaps herbal teas, or nuts and dried fruits, a book, a dish, or—"

"Well, see, there's one thing he really loves, so I brought it." She pulled the newspaper bundle out from her raincoat. "What he really likes—what he loves is"—she put the package on the table and ripped open the paper—"fish."

The three women peered down at several dozen slim, silvery corpses.

"Smelts," the girl said. "Forty-six. One for each year."

Ellen suddenly became busy with her bookkeeping and Nan rushed to the parlor to help someone.

"Well," Molly said, "this is—I mean fish have a rather short —ah, we'd need ice and I don't—we never . . ." Molly searched for a polite way to shoo the girl and her smelt collection out of the store.

The girl beamed with pride. "I think he'll love it." Her voice dropped to a reverent whisper.

She loves him, Molly realized. As in L-O-V-E! Technicolor, fresh, unjaded, nutty and probably doomed, but horribly, painfully new and sincere.

It had been forever since anyone she knew talked that way, blushed that way, felt that way.

"It has to go to Twenty-sixth and Wilshire," the girl said. "The medical building."

"I'll deliver it this afternoon," Molly said. "Before it—ripens. I'll deliver it myself."

"You'll make it beautiful, won't you?" The girl's whisper was urgent.

Molly looked at her, a child, really, in her oversize raincoat and cheap skirt, spending too much money on a gift of fish for her psychiatrist love. She hoped he deserved something this special. She hoped the girl wasn't a deranged patient. She wanted all of this to be real.

"I'll make it beautiful," she promised.

At four-thirty she delivered a basket filled with lures and trout flies and a book on the art of fishing, with a loaf of crusty bread and a wedge of cheese, a tin of golden caviar and, of course, forty-six smelts on ice, wrapped in cellophane.

The doctor came out to receive it himself and he seemed bemused and delighted by his birthday smelts. Molly couldn't stop smiling. Hurrah, she thought. Hurrah for us all. It felt good being close to fresh-caught love.

She made a detour on her way home, stopping at the pharmacy to investigate what they had in the way of scented oils and incense.

4   JOANNA STARED AT THE CEILING. MAYBE IT WASN'T true what Caroline had said. Joanna had heard that you could tell when a girl wasn't a virgin because her eyes looked different, but Lisa's looked just like everybody else's.

Then maybe everybody else did it, too. Jo felt the now-familiar panic, as if something had jumped onto her lungs. She couldn't breathe right.

Was she the only virgin in the tenth grade? Was she the only one not ready to grow up? Was something wrong with her?

Caroline had called last week. "Anybody listening in?" she asked. "Positive?"

Jo explained that her parents were working and that her brothers were watching reruns of "Gilligan's Island."

"Do you swear not to tell?"

Caroline was Joanna's most obnoxious friend, but the unpleasant relationship felt unbreakable, like a Mafia contract.

"If your parents walk in," Caroline said, "mention a math theorem, okay? Then I'll know they're—"

"I'm hanging up."

Caroline continued, her voice low, like a spy's. "You know how my mother does volunteer work?" She never asked questions and went on like other people. You had to answer.

"Yes," Joanna said dutifully.

"Well, one of her places is the Woman's Place. And today, she was coming out of the bathroom, and she saw this familiar face, you know?"

"Yes."

"So my mom asked the other volunteer for the name. Marion Gregory."

"That's your big news? Somebody I don't know named Marion Gregory was at your mother's club?"

Caroline hooted. "Club! The Woman's Place! And Marion Gregory's the other volunteer."

"Caroline, what's the point of this?" "Gilligan's Island" was looking good.

"Lisa Blackstone."

"What about her."

"That's who was leaving. Lisa and her mother."

Joanna let that percolate into her brain. Lisa. Whose hair never frizzed or went lank. Whose teeth didn't need braces. Who never got zits. Who all the boys in the entire tenth grade and probably the world had crushes on. Who Joanna envied more than anybody.

She also envied Lisa her mother. Mr. Blackstone lived in Arizona with a new wife, and Lisa and her mother shared a townhouse with big pillows on the floor and funny posters on the wall. Mrs. Blackstone wore running shorts and halters and drank Coke out of the can and talked about boys and dating and stupid teachers.

Lisa was lucky, no doubt about that. Maybe that's why she always seemed more comfortable than anybody else. Joanna had never seen Lisa sweat. It was that kind of comfortable and lucky.

Still, so what?

Caroline laughed nastily. "And why was she there?"

"I don't know. You called me, remember?"

"Lisa Blackstone had an abortion," Caroline said. "My mother would kill if she knew I told you. She doesn't know I heard her tell my father. She was upset. She approves of it, you know, but she doesn't approve of my friends needing it."

Joanna felt the thing jump onto her lungs and stop her breath. That was a week ago. The thing kept on jumping since then. Joanna thought about Lisa and abortions and little else. She felt as if somebody had stuck a broom handle through her ears and was carrying her around, her feet dangling over something horrible. She felt as if she'd been taken apart and put back together the wrong way.

She thought about the abortion and the almost-baby. Whose was it? Was it right or wrong to get rid of it? She thought about that horrible poem that had freaked her parents and her.

But mostly, her mind pulled back to before the abortion, to one theme over and over. If Lisa had had an abortion, then Lisa had had sex.

And if Lisa had sex, was Joanna supposed to, also? Now? Was she staying a baby while everybody else grew up? Was she retarded in some way?

It felt way too soon. The idea made her break into a sweat and no matter how she varied it, it always sounded disgusting.

Sure, she'd kissed boys, even though it was usually boring or painful, with them pressing so hard her braces cut at her lips. She suspected that someday she'd find out why it was supposed to be such a big-deal thing.

But she never even *considered* having any of those boys put their—that *had* to be horrible!

How would it be to have a piece of somebody else actually inside her own private body? Have something *strange* and *foreign* and *stupid-looking* and *huge* be *inside*?

She was so *little* there—God, her *finger* could just about fit, so a boy's *thing*? How could they possibly say it felt *good*?

She considered finding out with knockwurst or salami, then nearly threw up when she realized she was becoming a *pervert*.

If only there were Protestant nuns. If only she'd been born a hundred years ago when girls didn't have to be this way this soon.

Maybe she was a lesbian. How did you know? She liked boys, though. But liking them wasn't the same as doing *that*.

She had thought she didn't have to think about it for years. Her mother said she'd just know when she was ready, but her mother was wrong because the time to be ready must have passed.

She was angry with Lisa for forcing the issue. Now Joanna couldn't think about anything else, and she was sure she was going to think about this for the rest of her life.

Who could she ask if she was normal?

Not her mother. Her mother would say of-course-you-are-normal-dear. She'd say someday-when-you-are-ready. She'd say let's-talk-tell-me-what's-bothering-you.

Who could she ask what it felt like?

Not Lisa. She wasn't going to let Lisa know that she, Joanna Michaels, didn't know.

Maybe everybody else already knew. Maybe they were all doing it all the time between classes or after games or behind the taco stand.

How? How did you even do it? Did you lie down and wait? Did you take off your own underpants? When? How about jeans, or leg-warmers? How about his clothing? Zippers and socks and things? Did you watch while he took his off?

Why *bother*?

Did you *have* to do it to be popular or normal?

God.

Lisa had done it.

Lisa had been pregnant. She could have been somebody's *mother*.

So could Jo.

Her body was a traitor, ripening at its own pace. She hated her breasts, her pubic hair, her period if they meant that important changes had to be made right now.

She sighed loudly. How would she ever find out if she was normal or a freak? She sighed again and continued to stare at the ceiling.

5

"Face on *you!*"

Molly tried not to listen. Obviously, Ben had done something Tony perceived as humiliating.

"Yeah, yeah, face on *you*, Ben!"

Molly walked into the kitchen where the boys, in theory, were washing dishes. Ben was plugged in, staring at a loose mosaic of pottery shards that had once been a plate.

"Leave it," Molly said. "I'll get it later. I'm in a rush—Grandma's plane is going to land soon." She unplugged Ben and repeated the message. "Don't cut yourself," she added, then gently replugged him.

"How about if I come along?" Clay said.

Clay's offer felt significant. Only a masochist requests an unnecessary trip to LAX. But once in the car, his silence sat between them uncomfortably.

"Is something bothering you?" she asked.

He shrugged.

"A rough day?"

"Baum was fired." Clay's voice was drained of inflection. He kept his eyes on the road.

His words didn't register at first. Molly thought of sports stars, headlines she'd missed. Then she realized what Clay meant. "Art Baum?" she asked. *"Art?"*

Clay nodded.

"Fired?" She shook her head. Fired was for bigger-than-life athletes who chose high risk, or people who made news in large, sad groups, like steelworkers, or for anonymous, lone incompetents. Not for their friends. Not for sweet-smiling men past fifty with executive-level jobs. Art Baum had been Clay's first friend at Great Harvest, in many ways his mentor and guide.

"Campiglia gave him the glad news, then put himself on the plane to Nassau. Nice, isn't it?"

"Why?" Molly asked. "Why on earth would anyone fire Art?"

"How would I know?" Clay sounded gruff. "The economy. New theories about how top-heavy in management a firm can be. Things are changing all over and there's always a victim."

"But Art? Come on, Clay. Art?" She could hear her own fear and could sense Clay's annoyance with her. But Art was a good friend—a person just like them.

"He was a budget cut," Clay said.

Molly breathed deeply, waiting for Clay to say something more. "How can you be so cold about it?" she finally blurted out. "Calling him a budget cut? You're talking about Art, your closest friend at Mother Megaslop."

"I wish you wouldn't call the company that name."

Her panic rose and she wasn't sure anymore of its cause. Of course, she told herself, Clay's position was secure. Clay was Mr. Marketing—hadn't someone called him that? Oh God, had it been Art who called him that? Anyway, the company would always want Clay, she was sure.

The Great Harvest Family, it called itself. Mother Megaslop, Molly called it. But families and mothers didn't shove you hither and yon, demand they be first in your affections, then toss you away.

That wasn't how the story went. First you worked hard, then you were rewarded. *That* was how the story went.

She reached for Clay's hand on the steering wheel. It was damp with perspiration. She didn't dare inquire whether Art's fate was to be interpreted as a warning or whether it had an iota of relevance to their future.

"How's Art taking it?" she asked instead.

"How would anybody? He isn't dancing. Honestly, Molly—"

"I didn't fire anybody. Don't talk to me that way."

"I'm sorry." He breathed deeply. "It's just—I can't stop thinking about it. I mean, he wasn't the most aggressive, and maybe he messed up with the fruit bread mix a few years back, but he's bright. Even if Campiglia didn't like our project, he could certainly tell that Art's bright. Jesus, he's fifty-three years old and it feels so—it feels—"

"—so unfair," she finished for him, sympathetically.

Her words seemed to startle Clay into reverse. "Unfair? It's business, Molly, not some game or social welfare arrangement. It's dollars and cents and bottom lines. Art wasn't producing, so it was time to let him go."

"Wrong," she said. "Why don't you admit that Mother Megaslop—oh, pardon me—Great Harvest—is fallible and sometimes downright lousy?" She moved closer to the window. She tried to feel sympathy for the silent man on the other end of the front seat. He was as frightened as she was, and she knew it. He didn't have well-developed resources for handling fear; she knew that, too. To protect himself, he rinsed away all emotions, sought safety in jargon and moved himself squarely onto the side of the decision-makers. She knew that, too. It still didn't make him lovable.

She tried a new tack. "Let's have Art and Joanie over when we get home from Nassau. Let them know they still have friends."

"Give it some time, okay?"

"Oh, Clay!"

"For Christ's sake, we don't see them every day. If you call them now, isn't it going to seem ghoulish? Like a creep who appears when there's something ugly to feed on? Don't act as if I'm backing off from them or something."

"Funny you should say that," she muttered.

They reached the airport and he said nothing as he found the right parking garage and slowly navigated the ramps. He was a stranger, yet an uncomfortably familiar one. She disliked the way he snapped closed his armor, covering every vulnerable spot with heavy metal.

She disliked the way he refused to look at what he didn't want to see.

She disliked him.

No. She erased the thought. You've had eighteen years with the man, a billion moments. This is only one of them. The picture's been good, rolling along forever. This is one of those little flaws on the film. A glitch. You love him. You do. Except for this part.

She wished she could love him completely again with that dizzying totality she remembered. She had once been as smitten as the girl with the smelts.

Clay parked the car and sat behind the wheel. "Okay," he said. "Okay."

She felt like a spectator watching a battle.

"Don't ask me to explain, Moll. I'm afraid Art will talk and I'll find out he didn't do a damn thing wrong—except maybe work with me on that labeling project. I'm afraid somebody will remember I'm pals with Baum and decide I'm like him—a loser. I know it's irrational. Everybody already knows I'm friends with him, but still, I'm afraid to talk to him. I'm afraid it'll be interpreted as political. I'm ashamed of how I feel and I'm sorry I wasn't straight with you right away, but I can't see them now because I'm so afraid."

End of glitch.

They walked to the elevator hand in hand, protecting each

other. Funny, Molly thought. We don't look like people fleeing in terror. Mr. and Mrs. Middle-Class Middle-Age. A chunk off the solid old establishment. Shaking with fear.

The concrete ramps above them felt very close. "Sky's falling, Henny-Penny," she heard in her head. Molly cringed from a growing sense of the imperfections and loneliness in the closest of bonds.

What was happening with everything? With her family, her friends, her body, her marriage—with the Mollyclay base line of the structure of her life?

Sky's falling.

If it's unthinkable, don't think it. When specific fears became too enormous, when sleep wouldn't come, when a child's fever became alarming, when she had to wait until morning to have the doctor check the lump in her breast, when finals loomed or Clay was hours late and unaccounted for, Molly hauled in the worst and most impersonal—fear she could think of.

What if an 8-point quake on the Richter scale happened right this moment?

Death. Cars crashing through concrete, crushing her, crushing Clay. No time for panic. Over. Maybe one moment, the rumbling, the swaying pillars, the final clinch, the shout—"I love you!" Zap!

It was a pleasure dealing with such uncomplicated problems.

6   MOLLY KNEW ABOUT REAL LIFE. SHE KNEW ABOUT actuarial tables, about mortality and geriatric probability and how it was.

But it was still a low pull like a labor pain when she first saw her mother. Thea Hawthorne had never been tall, but she'd been solid. Now, while Molly hugged the short, white-haired woman, she heard the early rustle of ghosts. Thea was nearly eighty and gravity was calling her to itself. Her back was starting to curve. She was shrinking and becoming translucent. Beneath the coat, Molly could sense no flesh. She hugged and kissed weightless, hollow bird bones.

Thea pulled back to study her, and Molly wondered whether the sight of her own face was as much of a shock to her mother. How did it feel seeing wrinkles on your baby's face?

Neither woman chose to comment on time and its meaning.

"We had a lovely meal on the flight," Thea said. "Shrimp. I made a new friend because I told him how the poor Chinese called grasshoppers 'brushwood shrimp' when they ate them."

Molly grinned. She'd grown up with her mother's grab bag of facts.

"Also ate rats. Called them 'household deer.' "

Molly grimaced.

"You didn't know that? And you in the food business. Anyway, he hasn't a cent."

"Who?"

"My new friend from the plane."

Of course. Thea's friends never had a cent. Molly glanced around, looking for the likely buddy. There had always been men dropping into the apartment for food or talk or the loan of a book. They were interchangeable with their stubbly chins, nervous tics, obsessive interest in issues nobody else cared about, their shabby clothing and insatiable appetites.

Molly had once feared that her father had been one of them.

"Oh, no," Thea said. "Joseph Henry Hawthorne was an elegant man. He wore soft shirts and was handsome. You have his jawline, a little. And of course, his hair and eyes."

Now Thea asked, "Do you think we can give my friend a lift? He's going to Venice. As I recall, it's on the way."

"No problem," Clay said.

Molly spotted the likely new friend puffing on a cigar. He had a battered duffel bag between his legs and his jowls hung like a bulldog's. Molly knew he would talk nonstop, waving the cheap cigar for emphasis.

"Daniel!" Thea cried. "Daniel, do you want a ride?"

The smoking bulldog continued to stare into space. Instead, one of the most beautiful human beings ever created walked gracefully toward Molly Hawthorne Michaels, who had trouble keeping her balance as the airport crash-landed.

In a city where beauty is not only commonplace but possibly dictated by law, this young man was still exceptional. Heads turned and stayed aimed in his direction.

Molly's jaw slackened. She wished for poetry, for something more adequate than the discordant babble of the terminal. A symphonic swell of music, perhaps, to herald perfection.

Daniel smiled and shook Clay's hand, then hers, in greeting.

He made polite noises, thanked them for the lift, and she said polite things in return and then, dazed, walked beside her mother, behind Daniel and Clay as they retrieved the luggage and made their way to the parking lot.

Molly knew she was having a conversation with Daniel because she saw his mouth move and he seemed to be receiving answers. She hoped she made sense, because in her head, only a long and garbled "Aaaahhh" resounded.

She tried not to stare at the curve of his rear or the shape of his thighs and shoulders. Or at the way his ears lay so close to his skull. Or at his lips which were sculpted in a manner which made it difficult not to look at them.

She was stunned by her own reaction. Never, never had she felt this way before. When she had felt this intensely in the past, she had not been this mature, had not had the wealth of images or such well-trained sensory apparatus.

She had thought herself beyond—or apart from—this sort of thing. Of course she listened to Nan's stories with interest. Of course she read books and watched movies and sometimes daydreamed. But things like this only happened to people ready to receive them. Which she certainly wasn't.

But this certainly was happening.

She valued people as individuals for a wide range of attractive, human aspects. For exciting minds, for achievements and beliefs and poetry and daring. Certainly not for baseless, mind-bending, lust-inducing beauty and nothing more? Not for cheeks balanced on high-wire bones and a curve to the jaw that was achingly clean and sweet.

Oh, and the shape of his hands and the way he sat in the back seat, leaning forward slightly, an eager energy propelling him—these things did not make up Molly's value system.

Then she'd forge a new system. Because if she could ascertain his price and find the fee, she'd buy Daniel, mind or no mind, values and achievements or not. She'd buy the boy and tuck him into her purse and keep him there until everybody left home. Then she'd take him out and play with him.

The freeway slipped by while she thought about the ways she could play with Daniel, touch him, manage a closeness the thought of which made her lean back and breathe deeply.

She stopped hearing everything except the crimson roar in her ears. This must be how women felt before they swooned, she realized.

Daniel said something, but she lost the words as she found the shape and sound of his voice itself. It was low and melodic, like a warm bath, but with a floor of raspy pebbles. Inviting and slightly dangerous.

She wanted him to say things to her, for her, alone.

She nearly burst into tears.

"—film," she suddenly heard Clay say. Her hearing activated in spurts, like a radio in the country, picking up signals, then slipping back into static. "—difficult. Have you experience?"

She strained to pay attention to Daniel's answer. "High school . . ." His drowning pool of a voice pulled her under.

Her throat tickled as if she were about to cry, or sneeze, or laugh loudly. She was short of breath and what was happening between her legs was unthinkable. But she felt so much better, so much more whole and alive than she had for a long time.

She swiveled around to face him and searched for a sentence that would justify so direct a stare. "And, ah, who do you know in Venice?"

He smiled and she choked, coughing and turning halfway back, crossing her legs.

"A friend from school. He's at USC now, for film."

I will have him over for dinner. No, for breakfast. Everybody will leave. I will hand-feed him delicacies. Strawberries in sugar. Naked. We'll lie in front of the fire and oh, God, I'll do —everything. Anything.

"Then," he said, "when my sister graduates this spring, Mom 'n' her are moving out and we'll find a place together."

He was a good person. A family person. We could walk to the beach when it's empty. We could run, come home flushed, and . . .

"What's that last name?" Thea asked. "So I'll recognize it in the movie ads." She patted his hand. Molly was consumed with jealousy.

"Allard. Some people think there are too many 'l's' in Daniel Allard," he said.

"It's fine," Molly answered. "I'm sure you'll make it." She looked directly into his heavily lashed eyes, sending frantic messages.

Daniel looked solemn. "Everybody talks about cattle calls, auditions and rejections. Being treated like something less than human. Being real lonely."

"If I can make it less lonely," Molly crooned. "I mean, you could come stay with us, have dinner, spend time, any-thing. . . ." She felt Clay's sudden and full attention. She re-fused to look in his direction.

"That's really nice of you," Daniel said. He leaned closer to the front seat and touched her hand where it lay on the back-rest. It burned and became a brand on her flesh. "And when my mom gets here," he said, "I'd like you to meet her. She's a lot like you—friendly and all. You even look a little alike. I bet you'd be good friends."

"Your mother?" Molly heard her voice thicken. She cleared her throat. "Mother. Oh yes." She turned and faced the front. Her cheeks burned. His *mother*. He wanted her to *meet his mother*. Because she, Molly, was friendly and all. Motherly. Not burning with heat. Not sexually alive at all. Not even worth a graceful waltz out of the ring and a kiss-off because Molly had never been in the ring for starters.

Daniel was young.

Molly was the lady in the mirror.

And there it was. All of it.

"I think this is the address." Clay stopped in front of a minuscule clapboard duplex.

Molly watched Daniel lope away in a glow so bright she could almost see its reflection in the wet driveway.

Clay shook his head with suppressed anger as they headed toward home. "Sometimes I cannot believe you," he said. "Have you lost your common sense?"

Had her emotions been that shamefully public then? "What —what do you mean?"

"Inviting him over like that. A stranger from the airport."

"Mom knew him. She felt good about him, right?"

"Right," Thea said. "He made me feel very very good. Has to be the sexiest thing I've seen in eighty years."

"That's the point," Clay said. "I don't want him in my house."

"You find him—threatening?" Molly began to enjoy herself again. Clay was rushing to her rescue, saving his woman from the glorious stranger. Jealousy and possessiveness were secondary thrills, but she was ready to accept anything.

"Of course he's threatening!" Clay snapped. "I don't want sexy unemployed actors around my daughter!"

Molly folded her arms across her half-worn body and shivered. "Face on *you*, Molly," a chorus of unmet expectations cried. "Oh, Molly, face on you!"

Well, then, what if a tidal wave rose from the Pacific floor this very instant and all the houses from Ocean Park straight through to Brentwood were lifted and carried away . . .

"I love what you've done here," Thea said later as they had tea together. The children were upstairs and Clay was in the living room writing a report. "It's a happy place, this house."

"Thanks." Her mother's approval of her domestic talents always surprised Molly. Thea Hawthorne had wanted to remake the world, but never to make a home. She supported and stayed with her child, but always with the air of a wild creature allowing itself a short spell on a farm.

"Why, then, do I sense something less than happy?" Thea asked.

"You're amazing. A friend of ours was fired today. It—it makes everything feel wobbly and suspect. God, Mom, I just remembered Jack Aronson, when he was fired. I must have seemed like the most insensitive, most smug—"

"Most normal teenager. I never wanted to let you be one. That was the problem."

Molly had often been exasperated with Thea's focus on what she called the real world. The adolescent Molly believed she had teachers for history and a mother for subjects closer to the heart. The night of Jack Aronson had been based on the conflict of what Thea's role should be. Thea had sipped tea, tapping her fingers on a letter.

"You remember Jack, don't you, Molly? Heavyset man. Teaches English in New York. Make that *taught* English. Brilliant. You should have seen him do Shakespeare years ago."

Molly remained lost in her own thoughts. According to her mother, everyone had once been brilliant. Along with Thea, they'd been on the fringe of the theater twenty years earlier. They were part of the past. They didn't matter.

It was raining, a hard rain threatening sleet, and Molly was desperately in love with Hank Nestor who talked to her every day and then betrayed her by inviting Susan to the Valentine's dance.

"Do you understand what McCarthy is doing to the political process? To our basic freedoms?"

Molly decided that Hank had succumbed to the combined size of Susan's breasts and wardrobe.

"How can we ever take risks if twenty years later we lose our jobs for what we honestly believed? This country's so afraid of foreign dictators it will create its own!"

What was Molly supposed to do? Pretend she didn't care about the dance? Go to a movie that night?

"Maybe I should get rid of my scripts. I work in a public school, too. What if the red-baiters—"

"Mother, nobody cares about *Courage House* and the rest." The old script was interesting only for being evidence of an earlier, more exotic Thea Mueller. But it was a dreadful political play that had one short run in a town hall somewhere. "And you're a school secretary. Nobody's going to know about it. And besides, Hank invited Susan to the dance!"

"That's nice, dear."

"No, it isn't nice. It's horrible. I told you I like him and you don't listen and you never do and you just don't care!"

Thea was stunned. "Of course I care! I care about how Jack Aronson and his children and wife will live now. I care about this country and what's happening to it. I care about—"

"Everything except me!"

"Most of all I care about you! I care about the world you're going to live in. I'd hate to think you're a self-centered, materialistic, bourgeois—"

"Why can't I have a normal mother? A normal house and family? Why?"

Molly finally realized that her mother wasn't going to change. Instead, she herself did. She became the resident domestic expert. She sanded and painted, wallpapered and sewed. To her mother's horror, she borrowed decorating magazines and cookbooks from the library. Jack Aronson was probably largely responsible for the direction of Molly's life.

Joanna walked into the kitchen. She wore an oversize T-shirt and fuzzy bedroom slippers. "I nearly forgot, Mom," she said, "Mrs. Baum called." She rummaged in the refrigerator, examined the pantry, then picked up a banana from the copper bowl on the counter.

"Oh, dear." Molly glanced at the clock. "Was I supposed to call her back tonight?"

"Anytime."

Molly scowled, thinking about how difficult that phone call would be. And when would she make it? It was late now and tomorrow she was leaving for the Bahamas.

"Why do you look that way?" Joanna said.

"It's just that—well, Mr. Baum—you remember him, don't you—he, uh, lost his job."

Joanna peeled the banana. "That's rough," she said with no particular inflection.

She doesn't care! Molly thought. She knows those people and she doesn't care. What kind of insensitive, self-centered—

"Joanna!" she said sharply.

"Shades of Jack Aronson," Thea said loudly. "Now it's time for the lecture, right? Can I do it, or will you this time?"

And Molly, feeling foolish, had to laugh.

"Now what's so funny?" Joanna asked.

"I am," Molly said.

"We all are," Thea said. "All so different and all so much the same. Sometimes I get the feeling we're on rerun."

"What?" Joanna said.

"It has to do with what interests grown-ups and what doesn't interest teenage girls. Tell you what *will* interest you, though. I met the sexiest man on the airplane. Oh," Thea said, "if I were only sixty years younger. I don't know if I've ever felt as—and your mother, too."

Joanna no longer looked confused. Now she looked uncomfortable.

"You would have loved him," Thea said. "He would probably have loved you, too. In fact, your father was pretty worried about that."

"Yes," Molly said. "You'd better watch out for that father of yours. He's going to protect your purity like a dragon—whether or not you want him to." Perhaps, if she gentled around the topic of sex, Joanna might open up a bit and explain the revolting poem she had read that morning. "Has he asked you to be fitted for a chastity belt yet?" she asked.

"Oh, *Mother!*" Joanna was across the room from her, but she backed up nonetheless. "I'm not—I wish you wouldn't—you just don't . . ." She scowled and resumed eating, almost angrily.

"You know," Thea said, "your own mother used to say 'Oh, *Mother*,' the exact same way. And she'd say, 'You just don't understand me!' But of course, the problem was that I *did* understand her. That's why I annoyed her so much."

"I give up," Joanna muttered.

Molly suddenly envisioned a young Thea in a Victorian country kitchen, heard her say "Oh, *Mother*," or think it, if such words were forbidden. They all felt completely new and misunderstood creations. As they all were. And as none of them were.

"I don't think parents today understand their children," Joanna insisted. "It's different nowadays. If they did understand them, they wouldn't act so—so . . ."

"That's just it," Thea said. "They do understand, but they don't want to. It's too painful, all that remembering."

"Why? Why is it painful?"

"You'll have to grow up yourself before you understand."

"That's *just* the kind of answer a grown-up would give." Joanna sighed dramatically, but the subject wasn't bothersome enough for a scene, so the sigh was mild and untroubled.

It was when I felt most misunderstood, Molly thought, that I began to make myself up, to become me. She looked at her daughter, wondering which of the abrasive moments between them had or would become Joanna's starting line. And which of the good times would become the glue that kept her from coming unstuck?

"The thing is," Thea said, "we survive it and turn out to be amazingly alike in the important ways. And meantime, that's why there are grandmothers. We understand, too, but we don't carry on about it."

Joanna tossed her banana peel into the disposal. She smiled, her braces glittering in the overhead light. "Fact is, I don't understand either one of you," she said. "But I wish you understood geometry instead of me, because I don't understand that, either." She kissed each one of them good-night and left to do her homework.

Thea watched the doorway for a long while, as if afterimages of her granddaughter were still there. "It's good to be around young people," she said. "Convinces me I'm not missing anything. Even though it does make me realize how old I am."

No, Molly thought. Not now. Here they were again, alone together in a kitchen. All their history was sitting right at this table. There had been no others. No walk-ons, no extras. No grandparents, no aunts, uncles, fathers, brothers or sisters.

Only Thea and Molly and spats and teacups and Molly's homemade curtains blowing at the kitchen window. Thea was *it.* She was memory and meaning and she had to last forever. Molly looked at the maps and lines on the translucent skin and hoped they were only distant early-warning signs.

"Sometimes I forget about age, living in Adams Wall," Thea continued. "I know everybody, see the same people over and over. We're all getting there together, you know. I don't see the schoolchildren since I retired. Don't remember anybody under sixty still exists."

"Mom," Molly said gently, "stay with us. For keeps. We've asked so many times. We'd love it, and—"

Thea shook her head. "After forty years, I can't just up and leave Adams Wall."

In the past there had always been indignation, a laugh or lifted eyebrows, a resounding "No!" This was feeble. This was really an admission of ultimate defeat. Molly felt the oldest, smallest part of herself rise in protest, cry out for time to stop. It hurt too much to be this linked and have the future advance like a buzz saw. "Well," she said, "if you ever change your mind . . ."

Her mother nodded. "But not yet, Molly," she said, and she grinned.

7   WHENEVER MOLLY APPROACHED FLIGHT, SHE became restive and superstitious, finding portents in the atmosphere, in newscasts, in the tea leaves in her cup.

With airborne death a certainty, she put her affairs in order. She made provision for her children, for the store and for her community commitments. She left notes ensuring orderly procedures following the crash of her plane.

She tidied her underwear drawer and ironed everything that had accumulated since her last flight. She was particularly loving and patient with her children, wanting to be remembered fondly, not as one who had orphaned them for the sake of a good tan.

She mailed birthday and anniversary cards and purchased baby and graduation gifts ahead of time so that when The Worst happened, there'd be an extra ration of tears for the lovely, thoughtful woman who was gone.

Once aboard, she chewed antacids, studied exit charts, and listened intently, trying to memorize the logistics of oxygen masks and inflatable life vests. She wondered whether flight attendants repeated instructions in real emergencies or whether the dummies, like Molly, flunked and were doomed.

Mostly, Molly read. She flew with a small library, because without someone else's words in front of her, she'd shape her own and they'd all have the sound of hysteria.

She had precise requirements for the combination of sleaze and swiftness that kept her from considering the altitude or the pilot's mental health. She always flew with a thriller, a sexy best-seller and one serious tome, the last item to appease God, who surely had high literary standards.

Now, she sat reading in the air. Next to her, Clay turned the pages of a magazine and waved smoke away. She endured flight for him. He endured the smoking section for her. She sighed loudly and closed her book. The steamy best-seller was annoying her.

Jessica, its heroine, had just been raped in the soft-core supermarket version of that act. A macho man ignored her protests and took her against her will. And bingo, Jessica decided that rape wasn't that bad. By the time the lout stomped off, she was addicted to his abuse.

Molly bridled at the idea. It was wrong. Women's bodies didn't work that way. If sex was against the will, it was painful, criminal, dreadful. If it felt good, it wasn't against the body's will. That was gynecology as Molly knew it.

"I don't think any mentally healthy woman wants to be raped," she said. "*I* certainly don't."

"Is someone attacking you? Someone very small?" Clay closed his *Fortune* magazine.

"It's this book, and lots of books, and TV and movies and even psychiatry—all those myths about women dying to be raped. And no way to disprove it because screaming, kicking, *anything* is called denial. Makes me furious."

"Hmmm," Clay said. He had saved his foil bag of peanuts and he now carefully ate its contents, one nut at a time.

"I mean women enjoy seduction, but that's different." Molly

thought again of Nan's voluptuous nights, of Nan's men. She heard echoes of their whispers, felt their fingers on her skin. "What do you think, Clay?" She wanted to hear something seductive, hints of dark private pleasures ahead.

He shrugged. "Never thought about it." He ate four more peanuts. Plunk, crunch, swallow. Plunk, crunch . . .

He never thought about it. Wouldn't now. Nan's man had. Lots. Lie back, he said. Let it happen. He'd seen it first in his mind like an erotic film, then he'd made it come true.

Clay leafed through his magazine again.

"Don't you see?" she said. "Seduction takes intelligence, time, charm. To realize what somebody else wants. To make it match what you want. To kind of ease it out of them." Lie back, he'd said. Enjoy. Experience. Feel. Oh.

"Guess so," Clay said.

He made her uncomfortable with his disinterest. Made her old. Maybe she was being prurient or unhealthy. Maybe at her age she wasn't supposed to sit in the sky suggesting sex. God, but it still sounded lovely to be petted, catered to, led into a new world of sensation.

However, she apparently had not struck a mine of interest. She changed tack. "Well, why do you think women are that way in novels? So innocent and uninvolved in their own bodies or destinies. Maybe rape saves them from ever having to feel responsible for themselves or their sexuality. God, but that's so Victorian, so outdated—why is the idea so popular now? Maybe all these books are really written by twisted men. What do you think?"

Clay was engrossed in an article on business software.

"Clay?"

"Hmmm. Oh, you're right. Completely."

She lit a cigarette and blew smoke in his direction. Why condemn Jessica? Molly was just like her. Molly in the sky, taken against her will to an imitation of pleasure. Molly raped.

Perhaps, she hoped, perhaps tropical weather and sumptuous beaches could become seduction, not rape.

The wet heat of Nassau slapped against her. She'd lived in the Los Angeles desert long enough to have forgotten humid sunshine, and by the time she reached customs, she felt sausage-swollen and nauseous.

The customs inspector appeared annoyed. No drugs on these capitalist swine, no interesting smuggling to ferret out. He pulled apart Molly's clothing like a destructive, bored child, snapped shut the suitcase and waved them on.

Instead of air conditioning or shocks, the taxi had loose stuffing, an overpowering smell of exhaust fumes and a surly driver who hurled their suitcases into his trunk, tied it shut with rope and set his meter belligerently.

"How long a ride is it?" Clay asked, once under way.

The driver took a long while before he deigned to speak in a rusty voice. "Half hour. Not much traffic."

Clay changed his watch to Nassau time. "Not rush hour, eh?" Clay had a compulsion to endear himself to cabdrivers. Molly suspected a basic male need to be one of the guys who knew his way around.

"No rush hour here, mon," the driver said.

"Are you lucky!" Clay answered. "We're from L.A., and—"

"No rush hour here *ever*."

Molly felt scalded by the man's boiling rage.

Clay ignored it. "Guess it's true that island people take life easy, huh?" Molly grimaced, begging him to ease off before the driver turned around and took their lives easily.

"Don't take it easy or hard," the driver said. "Nothing to *take*, mon. People here is *poor*. Black people is poor. Only people here with money is *tourist*. The *people* is *poor!*"

"We're not exactly tourists," Clay Michaels, cabby conversationalist, said. "We're here for a business conf—"

"I know. Food people. Lots of you here two days already. You late."

Molly stared out the window. The scenery didn't lift her spirits. The travel brochures hadn't featured this part of paradise where the road was lined with tin-roofed shacks and lean-tos on hard-packed dirt. Here and there a ragged woman sat, lost in a humid stupor.

They entered Nassau proper. The scene became depressing in a new way. Half the hotels were vacant-eyed and abandoned, relics of plusher days when Brittania ruled these waves. The shops they passed were boring with glassy displays of china and perfume, not the local crafts that would have made them worth investigating. She tried to doze.

Clay frowned. Look at her! Just look at her—a lump, sitting with hands folded and head bowed. Was she praying? Couldn't she try just a little? He was sick and tired of being the only one who tried. Couldn't she start a conversation? God knew she talked enough other times.

So the island wasn't beautiful. So what? Did she have to look condemned to death? This was part of the job, dammit. Would she rather be Joanie Baum, freed from conference meetings and from an employed husband, too?

Well, he'd be good and goddamned before he was going to feel guilty about working hard and taking his wife to the Bahamas!

He, too, folded his hands in his lap and studied them.

Molly's legs were slippery with sweat as she walked toward the white stucco hotel. She comforted herself, as if speaking to a baby. Shh, calm down. You're overheated. Inside, it's cool and quiet and behind the building there's sand and an ocean. You'll swim and return to your cool room and shower and relax on clean sheets and shh—it'll be fine.

But it wasn't fine or quiet or cool.

"Sorry about the air conditioning." The girl at the front desk tried for perkiness, but her blond bangs were stuck to her forehead and her uniform jacket had perspiration stains. "We're working on it."

"How long has it been broken?" Clay asked nervously.

"Since, um, gee, a while, but as a token of our appreciation for your understanding, the management offers this voucher for two free daiquiris on the oceanside terrace." The girl's voice was heavy with moisture and repetition. The drinks token looked well used, as if they often had need for apologies and placation.

Nonetheless, Clay Michaels accepted it along with a key for room 1407.

"The casino's air conditioning is functioning," the girl said. She smiled a weary dismissal.

"Excuse me," Molly said, "I'd like my own room key. My husband and I will be at separate meetings, and—"

"We don't give duplicates." All sugary sweetness was gone. "Guests are requested to leave keys at the desk when not in use. This reduces the problem of lost keys and—"

"But I—"

"That is our policy."

Molly turned—slowly—toward the exit. She wanted her house, she wanted rain-soaked Los Angeles, she wanted her children, odd as they were. She wanted, more than anything, *out*.

"Clay! Hey, whatcha say?" A couple who looked as if they might wear madras underwear approached at top speed. Molly remembered the man's florid cheeks, perpetual smile and too-hard handshake. But not his name, which was one reason her grade as Corporate Wife was less than A +.

"You remember Bill Burchard, don't you, Molly? Our man at Mother Lancaster outside of Philadelphia?"

"Of course." Molly winced under Burchard's sadistic handshake. She had tried to associate his flushed cheeks with the make-believe health food division he headed. The association held, but not the name. She remembered also his knotty wife who appeared made of macramé, remembered even that she'd evolved from the sort of wealth wherein nobody had bought furniture or paintings for the last three generations. But her name?

"And Eleanora," Clay said, and that was one more reason he was a success. Molly shook Eleanora's hand.

"Hello, Margie," Eleanora said.

"Molly."

"Yes." Eleanora's eyes traversed the lobby, unwilling to settle for Clay's little wife until positive there wasn't more significant GH prey around. "Heat's awful, isn't it?"

That was the way of conversation at these functions. Like a verbal square dance, you changed partners and do-si-do'd. How's the weather? How's the new job? How's the new city? Nothing significant because any piece of yourself that you let drop could be held for ransom later.

"Awful," Molly agreed. Sweat trickled down her stockings. Her wrinkled skirt was glued to her thighs.

"Guess you sunny Californians are used to the heat," Bill said, smiling as he spoke.

"Well, the humidity is—"

"They'll never fix the air conditioning," Eleanora said. "You know how these people are."

"Electricians?" Molly asked.

"Oh, Margie, you're such a card!"

One of the most astounding aspects of corporate wifehood was the way Molly was expected to share prefabricated prejudices. No one ever questioned her political stance or view of life. Instead, they made pronouncements about the inherent laziness and inferiority of minority groups. They ranted against the horrors of governmental interference in the private sector. They took hawkish positions and called protestors riffraff and suggested where else they should go live.

They never asked whether Molly agreed. She was a Great Harvest wife, one of the world's privileged, and she was therefore expected to believe what they believed.

"Take a minute for a drink with me," Bill said to Clay. "Let Molly freshen up."

If, Molly instantly decided, if Clay has that drink, if he sends me to my room like a punished child or a corporate wife, then I will go home right now and goddamn Clay's image.

"Can I have a rain check?" Clay said, saving their marriage with six words.

"Oooh! Don't even mention rain!" Eleanora said. "They're predicting it, you know."

The Michaels rode up in the elevator in silence until Clay broke it. "It isn't so terrible," he whispered, following the bellhop down an enormous hallway.

"What isn't? The carpeting? The heat? Eleanora?" Molly shuffled along. The hallway was a windowless tunnel sending up hot memories of feet.

"Here we are." The bellboy opened the door onto a large airless room done in Standard Tropical. Aquamarine-and-white lattice print on the chairs, a white spread on the twin (not king-size as per request) beds, prints of orchids and birds of paradise on the walls. A small bouquet of roses and baby's breath and a large fruit, cheese and wine basket on the dresser, both gifts of Great Harvest. There was also a plastic packet with the corporate cornucopia logo. It contained itineraries, directives, time schedules.

"Nice," Clay said, pulling grapes out of the basket.

"Odd how you don't offer your own products, isn't it?" she snapped. "Why not a basket of Doodle-drops or Whammy-Candies, or Froth, the drink you love to lick, or—"

The bellboy cleared his throat. Molly went to the window and saw the surf on the horizon. It was sapphire and irresistible.

"During this unfortunate breakdown," the bellboy said, "you

can check your valuables in the hotel safe. Then, if you leave the terrace windows and the hall doors open, you'll get a little breeze."

Molly turned to him. "Leave the doors open at night?"

"Keeps it cooler," the bellhop said. His face was blank. It did not suggest that the woman in front of him should, rationally, be thinking about closed doors or sex. He accepted his tip and left the door open behind him.

Molly kicked it shut. "Get me *out* of here!" she said. "Where's my bathing suit?" She rummaged through her suitcase.

"Listen, Moll," Clay said. "The cocktail party begins in an hour. We don't really have time to go to the beach, swim, change and be there."

She held her bathing suit close to her. She opened her mouth to speak, then closed it.

"Molly?"

She took her bathing suit to the dresser, opened the middle drawer and put it inside. Then, silently, she methodically hung up her dresses and saw the navy blazer on his side of the closet. "Your uniform arrived in time, I see." She slammed the closet shut.

Her mind screamed so loudly she feared and hoped Clay heard it. What am I doing here? What have you done to me? Why am I in a flowery slum with mean drivers and boring people and a suffocating room where they won't give me the key but it doesn't matter because I'm supposed to leave the door open so I can breathe? Why?

Because I love you, that's why, and it's becoming more and more an unfair love. Just as I cook sauerbraten because you like it or take your suits to the cleaners or remember your parents' anniversary, I'm here. Another little act of love, but a ridiculous one. I shouldn't pervert my time off, my playtime. Not for anyone.

Faking a vacation. Of all the stupid—What would Masters and Johnson say about this one?

Clay put his hands on her arms. He bent close and kissed her cheek. She stiffened even though she wasn't sure that's what she'd intended to do. But for starters, it was simply too hot. She was too old and Clay too familiar and she didn't want to touch anything—least of all, warm flesh.

"Is it that bad, then?" he asked. "Or is it me?"

"It's—everything. It's—"

"But I didn't—"

"It doesn't matter who, it—"

"Only for two days and—"

"That Eleanora is such a—"

"You don't have to—"

"That driver—"

"Once we cool down and—"

"That clerk!"

"I'm sure we'll—"

"Well, I'm not!"

She pulled away and went into the bathroom.

Clay ate a pear. I'm blamed for everything, he thought. For heat waves and broken equipment and corporate policy and the personality flaws of cabdrivers. Wonderful. She's become a bitch. It's definitely true what they say about middle-aged women.

Molly waited for the shower to blend hot and cold into a bearable whole. So. He's disturbed because I'm not skipping around, chortling with glee at sharing this fabulous vacation experience. To hell with him! He's so used to being in control of everything, he forgot it doesn't include me!

Clay stood at the open window. There was no breeze. She hadn't even asked if he'd like to shower first or anything. Just charged in there. God, she used to be different. So giving. So much of everything he'd ever wanted. He smiled, remembering how she'd been.

It's no fun anymore, Molly thought, shampooing her hair. Not even vacations. The shower curtain rustled and she wheeled around, a scream on her lips, perpetual victim of a Hitchcock movie.

And then she smiled. Begrudgingly, but a smile all the same. A slightly wilted rose was proferred to her and behind it, Clay, in his unbuttoned white business shirt and nothing else. He carried a bottle of wine taken from the gift basket into the shower, then leaned out and brought in two glasses.

"It may become diluted, so don't judge the vintage by this tasting." He poured the wine. "To us. I can still drink to that, can't I?"

She was reluctant to give up her anger.

"Am I your enemy?" he asked softly.

She bit at her bottom lip and shook her head. Of course he wasn't. He was dear, beautiful Clay, her best friend. But still, there was something he was guilty of. What was it? Consorting with her enemies? Signing agreements without her consent? What?

"And besides," he said, passing a glass to her. "Do I have a cute cleft in my chin, or what?"

She gave up on the anger.

Water poured over his wonderful silvery hair, over his young face and navy eyes and onto his shirt. "I'll do your back," he said.

"This is fraught with danger," she answered. "As your helpmate, I have to warn you that we could be late for cocktails."

"We're having them now," he reminded her. "My dear, my dear, a man has needs and they are not to be denied."

She giggled again. "B-movie time, is it?"

"Here, near the waterfall, native woman." He worked the soap into a lather, then ran his hands over her upper arms, her sides, her breasts.

She succumbed to the quiet movements, the smooth slide of his hands and the soap over and around and behind her, on top and under her. She loved his hands, loved how they knew their way around her. She loved soaping him as well, the slippery smooth trip around his strong legs and broad back. She loved touching him and feeling him spring into life. It was magical how years and years later, a touch and a look and a turning to each other brought a response. She felt powerful as she pulled close, pressing on him, soaping his back and buttocks and rocking with him while the shower poured over them.

They were backing against the wall, sliding slowly down and onto the tub floor. "A person could drown," Molly said idly. She loved him and she'd been wrong. It wasn't a choice between wine or wine vinegar. It could be familiar and wild and sweet, all at once.

His hands were on her breasts, her belly, between her legs. He pulled back a bit. "Here's the plan. We stay under the waterfall until the last possible moment, but then we find the bed, avoid the orthopedic surgeon and stay there until we evaporate. Got it?"

"I have it. I have it."

"You do indeed."

She did. It was simple. She wanted to live and die and evaporate with him all the time. She loved him. The only hard part was remembering it sometimes.

"Well," he said after their second shower. "Did that qualify?" He brushed his teeth. She stood beside him, sharing the mirror, carefully applying eye makeup.

"As what?"

"Did it show intelligence, charm, salesmanship? Weren't those the requirements?"

"For what?"

"Seduction." He turned and faced her. "Are you telling me that wasn't a prime example of seduction? The seduction of the furious spouse? Sounds like grand opera."

"I think you're making me furious again."

"Fair is fair, woman. It wasn't rape, correct? But it wasn't exactly your idea for starters, so give me credit where—"

"I didn't think you were paying any attention."

"I always pay attention. You don't pay attention to my way of paying attention."

He smiled at himself in the mirror, checking out his glorious clean teeth. His smile made the cleft in his chin more prominent. It had gotten her the first time she saw him. That and the eyes and the smile. They still did.

She dressed quickly and watched him button up a clean blue shirt. She felt wonderfully still and pleasantly light and full, like a feather pillow. Through the open window she heard the sounds of a nervous new cocktail party. She glanced toward the grassy bluff below. She was too far away to make out faces, but she saw the soft gauzy colors and the navy mass of men.

Months ago, Clay had sent his measurements to some obscure corporate official and tonight, the Great Harvest blazer waited for him. The dresser-top instructions suggested wearing it to all evening functions. Clay adjusted his tie and put on the jacket. It had a stylized cornucopia embroidered on the pocket. There would be lots of cornucopia gifts this weekend. Mother Megaslop devoted an entire department to finding sites for its logo. Molly owned key chains, silk scarves, charm bracelets, stickpins, beach towels, a shawl, two wraparound skirts, a dozen glasses, a desk set and four bookends all with the Great Harvest gold cornucopia as a motif. One year there had been a diminutive branding iron with the ever-present cornucopia. Molly still wondered what the corporate officials intended that she do with it.

She turned back to the room and watched her husband disappear. Gone was Clay Michaels who brought roses and wine to the shower and carried her to bed. In his place, Clay Michaels, company man.

He buttoned up more than a shirt, knotted more than a tie and, brushing an imaginary speck off his blazer, withdrew. She could almost hear the visor on his armor click shut. She was not such a fool as to deny that he had to protect himself, that the night and day ahead were jousting matches. She simply mourned the truth.

He was so much more lovable when he was undressed.

"Very handsome," she said. "Anybody ever tell you you look like Cary Grant? When he was in his prime, that is."

"What's that?" He looked startled. "Oh, thanks. You look lovely yourself. We'd better get going now." He double-checked his watch.

The man in the shower hadn't been her enemy. She wasn't as sure about this fellow.

8

"REALLY?" MOLLY SAID WITH A DELIGHTED SMILE. "That's so *interesting*."

Eleanora beamed. "Wait, there's more." She checked the circle to be sure everyone was still paying attention.

Molly passed muster. She cocked her head, smiled, ate canapés, smoked a cigarette and drank her Perrier, all at the same time. Her body tilted in a pose of acute interest. Clay would have been proud, had he been around to see her.

"And so," Eleanora continued, "because of that—"

Molly smiled even more broadly and nodded encouragement.

"I've come to believe—" Eleanora paused dramatically.

"Really?" Molly said with a delighted smile. "That's so *interesting*!"

Eleanora's mouth hung half open. The rest of the circle became heavily silent. Jesus, Molly thought. What do I do now?

What she did was cough. Choke. Gasp for air, hold out her empty glass and point toward the bar, to which spot she escaped.

She took a deep breath. Even if her smile had long since

gone into spasm, the evening was still young. There were miles to go before she slept.

The bartender handed her a fresh Perrier. She never touched alcohol at a Great Harvest function. Like an evil curse, office gatherings thickened her tongue, obliterated her vocabulary and tightened her brain. And that was when she was sober.

Molly couldn't find Clay in the wide pool of navy blazers and clean cropped heads. She was sure mother penguins could spot their chicks, and she was ashamed that she couldn't find her mate when he wore the same jacket as other men.

There were several hundred blazers on the lawn. Great Harvest men, she thought. Great Harvest *is* men, she amended. No matter what they said, no matter how many token females they sprinkled through their ranks, GH was an international fraternity, slapping backs and wearing, if not the old college tie, then surely the new firm jacket.

There were also pale silks and feathery chiffons on the green tonight. But given that these pragmatic males had limited uses for women, and given that they paid very little attention to what was of limited use, they were now at a loss as to what to do with the mass of females sharing the trip. If you were already married to one of them and you had said just about everything to her long ago, and if you were forbidden this weekend to screw any of the rest, then why bother with them at all?

So, after a courtesy round of mutters and grunts, the men, like lemmings, herded themselves toward the sea.

Molly climbed a short path to the bluff, welcoming the sunset breeze that rearranged the heat and colored the terrace dusty rose. A band played songs of several generations past. The softness of the music, the air and the colors, the dresses blowing, the well-kept bodies in their blazers evoked afterimages of F. Scott Fitzgerald. His spirit hovered, festive and fevered and doomed.

Like primitive organisms, the groups below split and regrouped, finding their own kind. Navy clusters grew and issued basso tones as they became a single instrument. Around them, skirts, scarves and sparkling gems combined and sounded with high gasps.

Molly remembered the year before, in St. Kitts. She'd had a wonderful time with Joanie Baum who shared her jaundiced view of these trips. Joanie created a menagerie of the people around them, aptly discovering giraffes, hyenas and foxes.

But the Baums were gone, erased from the books in industrial revisionist history. None of the men Molly watched was mentioning Art Baum, she was sure.

The sky grew more purple, the pink easing into blue streaks that fell toward the horizon.

"Mrs. Michaels! How *are* you?" This said with desperate jolliness. "May we join you?" Two women were suddenly beside Molly on the bluff. The one who'd spoken smiled broadly, but the expression was forced. She had a face that surely cried often and easily. "I haven't seen you since you left Houston! Mrs. Michaels, this is—"

"Please. I'm Molly."

The woman nodded several times. She was painfully thin and tenuous looking. "*Molly*, then, this is Roberta Bryant. Her husband Philip is with the Snackers Division in New York State. Mrs., oh, *Molly*, is in Los Angeles, lucky thing. Roberta and I were roommates at Northwestern, isn't that incredible? To meet again after ten years—here?"

Molly now had a great deal of biographical information. Only the identity of the speaker remained a mystery.

"Their daiquiris are *delicious*, aren't they?" the thin woman said. "I *love* them." She peered at Molly's glass, then hooted. "Oh, boy, you can always tell a Californian. Perrier with a twist —or is it with a sprout?" She shook her head. "*Nobody* in Minnesota drinks Perrier." She sipped her drink, holding up one finger to prevent interruptions and keep her turn as speaker.

"But then, maybe I'm wrong. What do I know about Minnesota? I've only been there two years, and I sure don't know what it is that Minnesotans *do*."

"How *is* Minnesota?" Molly asked. It was a required question. The answer was also required, no matter what the truth might be. Because how could Minnesota be? For a Great Harvester, Minnesota was a vast processing plant for livestock feed. It was the company's equivalent of the Gulag Archipelago and not a spot where promising executives were sent. The daiquiri lady and her husband were in exile.

"Minnesota?" she said. "Terrific, of course. And Claude—of course Claude loves his job."

Of course. She was a little weavy, a little heavy on the blood alcohol, but she remembered her lines.

"I hated leaving Houston, didn't you? The people were—I had friends who—I used to play tennis all the time and well, then we were in Cleveland for a while, then to Minnesota, and God . . ."

Her companion, Roberta, looked at her warily. She was improvising, leaving the script and making everyone nervous, but she continued to speak. "Minnesota winters are tough, and meeting people is—I mean, you know how this warm weather feels after—You think I mind no air conditioning? Where I live you could freeze your—"

"It's *interesting* getting to know so many parts of the country, don't you think?" Roberta said, covering her friend's gaffe. A good corporate wife never complained. She was a chameleon, moving from subtropics to near-arctic, from metropolis to backwater, blending her hues with whatever local color was offered. She never told other corporate wives that she minded the process or found it difficult because they had corporate husbands who would be interested in such negative information. Nobody wanted to move a whiner into another town where she'd spread bad will and a poor company image.

"Sure." Daiquiri woman got hold of herself again. "How

about you, Mrs.—Molly? I know you went to California after Atlanta."

How was it that Molly remembered nothing of this woman? "We love it," she said out loud. "It took time, though. It was rough at first." She could admit what she had triumphed over.

It had been more than rough. She had hated moving again, hated leaving Atlanta and an exciting new job, hated L.A. and briefly, intensely, hated Clay most of all. It felt one move too many, even if it was the final one, to headquarters.

The Michaels sold their five-bedroom "executive" home in Atlanta and were barely able to afford a "fixer-upper" in Santa Monica. They moved into a house in such disreputable condition, it could have qualified for urban renewal in less bizarre real estate country.

Within days, Clay was at his new office, the children were in school and Molly was lost on the freeways with a city map that was a hundred-page book.

When she wasn't on the freeway or working on the house, she was searching for doctors and dentists and hairdressers and other necessities that can't be packed in a Bekins box.

"And what illness does your child have?" the recommended pediatrician's nurse asked on the phone.

"None. My children are very healthy."

"I'm sorry, then. Doctor is only accepting new patients with rare diseases."

Eventually, she found a doctor willing to see healthy children. She found electricians, butchers, sources for wallpaper and fabric. The house began to look as if people lived there. Molly didn't get lost every single trip out. Her hair stopped looking mangled and, most important, she found a real friend in Ellen and, then, work that she loved.

Now she described the city in terms of blue skies and easy living. "I love it," she said with real enthusiasm. She regarded the experience like childbirth: incredible pain followed by blissful amnesia. "How about you, Roberta? Have you been in Albany long?"

Roberta shrugged. "Three years. But we're moving to Orlando in June. I'm looking forward to more sunshine. Or maybe we shouldn't mention sun in front of Vera."

Vera. Jackpot. A label. A skinny, nervous girl in Houston. "I guess they play tennis indoors in Minnesota, Vera," Molly said, feeling devious and brilliant.

Vera shrugged.

"Don't you still play?"

She shrugged again. "When we moved there, I tried to find —but—oh, who cares? It's only a game." She drained the last of her daiquiri, peered into the glass, then forced a smile. "Minnesota is interesting in its own way," she said.

Give her a gold star for effort. She wanted so much to drown that fury and be the right person, the right wife.

"How about you, Mrs.—Molly?" Vera asked. "Are you still busy running everything like you did? Honestly, Roberta, this woman can do *anything*."

Molly felt uncomfortable. "Oh, that isn't—" she began, but Vera waved down her protest.

"Everything! You wouldn't believe what she did!" She held up one hand, ticking items off by raising fingers as she spoke. "—and the school fair, and the book sale at the library and, oh —who knows? She was so efficient and God, we admired her so much, but I'd get tired thinking about it all and having babies and moving, too, but Claude admired you so much and when he was promoted, well, I had this image of how I had to be, and—"

"You're exaggerating," Molly said. "I never did all that much and I don't do any of it anymore."

Vera wasn't listening. She swayed in the breeze, gesticulating with her Tinker-toy arms. The evening had not yet begun and Vera was already sinking, intentionally heading for deep waters. "Oooh, and those beautiful parties where you made everything, and I said Claude, that's well and good but I can't—"

"You're embarrassing me, Vera." Molly immediately regretted the coolness of her tone.

"But I'm complimenting you!" Vera looked drunk and confused. "I wanted to be like you."

"Better to be like Vera," Molly said softly.

"How is it that you aren't doing any of that anymore?" Roberta said brightly.

Vera turned her back to them and stared out to sea. "Oh, what I wanted to be, what I wanted to be . . ."

"I work full-time," Molly said. "I'm a partner in a food business and I can barely find time to brush my teeth, let alone do much volunteering. Listen, why don't we start back to the party?"

Vera seemed to be having a vision. She lifted her glass like an offering to the horizon. Molly and Roberta turned away from the sight, as if they'd noticed an undone zipper.

"We're dying to know how you wound up in business," Roberta said, as if Vera were actually still with them on this planet.

"Accidentally," Molly answered. "I loved making special baskets as gifts. A new friend saw one and asked me to make one for the PTA president, who'd just had a baby. Then PTA members saw the basket and asked if I'd make more, and well, things started happening. My friend became my partner."

"So you have a gift basket business! Imagine that, Vera," Roberta said.

"Imagine, imagine, imagine." Vera stared seaward. "Claude thinks she's perfect."

"Actually, it's become more than gift baskets." Molly spoke very loudly.

"Everything becomes something else," Vera intoned.

"I really think we should go back to the—"

"How's that?" Roberta asked. "It grew? Into what?" She leaned toward Molly, desperately intense.

"Strange happenings," Vera said. "Strange changes."

"People asked for the ingredients in the baskets—cookies or breads or herbal teas, so we began stocking them. Then we acquired a few corporate customers, we outgrew our houses and found a little Victorian place, and somehow then it made sense to sell lunch also and have take-out and oh, it grew. It's really still small, but it feels enormous. Now let's go back down."

"I moved seven times," Vera said. "Seven times in twelve years."

"I, too, have always been intrigued by retailing," Roberta said. "I was assistant buyer of hosiery when I married Philip. Someday I'd like a little shop with hand-painted fabrics and handmade clothing. When I know where we'll settle . . ."

"Not in Minnesota, I hope." Vera turned and faced them, tears streaming down her thin face. "Minnesota *sucks.*"

"I'm going to find Clay now," Molly said firmly. "Dinner should be any minute." She took Vera gently by the shoulders. "Don't cry," she said. "Don't give up this way."

Vera sniffled and stared at her feet, then walked down the hill with Molly and Roberta.

"Seven times," she mumbled. "Seven."

Oh God, what am I doing here? We have no ties except that we're members of the Great Harvest Ladies Auxiliary. What do you want us to do with one another? Say to one another?

Hi, I'm Molly. What do you do?

Do? Do? I move. I cry. I drink. I screw around. Then I move again. Why?

She hated this game. Hated the system built on the backs of passive women. She felt so lonely and wondered if every other woman here felt the same way.

The trio walked near the outside fringe of the crowd. Molly didn't see many familiar female faces. So many friends gone. Some, like Joanie and Art Baum, left two by two. But more disappeared singly, silently, like pebbles dropped into a lake.

It was easy to spot their replacements. They stayed closer to their men than did the old guard, and they were seldom of the same generation as their husbands.

A moonfaced man approached them. He didn't try to disguise his disgust.

"Claude," Vera whispered. "Ohhh, Claude." She sounded ready to cry again. She held out her arms, then dropped them as he stopped just out of their reach.

"I'm sorry, Mrs. Michaels," he said, not defining what caused his regret. Was it his wife's unhappiness? The complexities of their joined lives? His own loss of face because of her drunkenness? The need to leave the party and possibly miss something useful?

He said no more and asked nothing of his wife. Instead, he guided her to the high white hotel, avoiding her touch. Vera swayed and stumbled behind him, but he marched resolutely, staying clear of his blighted wife.

Molly was sure he blamed his soured career on Vera. She wasn't perfect. Wasn't like Molly, she'd said. How ridiculous. How sad.

What were they supposed to be, these wives? As alike as the men in their matching blazers?

The answer was yes. Too many hurdles were erected against individuality. Oh, she knew there were a few women who didn't conform, but they were avoided, made fun of. There was dark, aloof Moira Klausen who attended every year, said nothing and wore funny ethnic costumes and floppy hats. She was said to be a composer. There was Carol Merendy whose life was the Women's Movement. There were others. A few lawyers, several potters, a writer, other things, but only a handful. Mostly, the women were "formers"—former teachers, former social workers, former nurses, former office assistants, former merchandising trainees, all stopped on the first or second rung of the ladder. "Wife of" was their occupation.

Clay found her and led her through the crowd to a table.

"Harry and Ivy asked us to join them," he said. "I couldn't get out of it."

Harry and Ivy Hailey were a matched set of cretins. Molly said nothing. However, Clay looked at her and found something displeasing. The set of his jaw became more rigid.

She smiled at her tablemates. She knew Fred Winger, but not the sweet child next to him. "I don't believe you've met my wife Beth," Fred said.

What about your wife Charlene? Molly wanted to ask. I *have* met *her*. Where is she? Hibernating?

Molly stared longest at the Young Couple. They glowed and tinkled irresistibly. Once, in Chicago, in the company Clay was first with, Molly and Clay Michaels had been the official, undisputed Young Couple. Brilliant, precocious Clay with his coal-black hair and blue eyes, his cleft chin and movie-star looks, and Molly, his petite, extroverted redhead of a wife. Oh, how Molly had savored that time, tossing it like a shiny stole across her shoulders.

Molly felt the Young Wife's eyes flick casually across her face and move on, and why not? Molly was nothing more than another fading senior wife.

A loudspeaker echoed and twitted and finally found its proper range. "Ladies and gentlemen of Great Harvest," intoned the chairman of the board. "I'm not going to make you wait for your dinner." The PA system squealed and resonated. "But I want once more to welcome all of you to our groaning board and to hope you enjoyed this sunny tropical day. And I want to remind you that seminars begin at eight A.M. tomorrow. Great Harvest personnel in the Green Room on the sea level and spouses in the Whitman Room next to this patio. And tomorrow afternoon, for all interested spouses, a sightseeing and shopping tour of the island. Please sign up if you—"

"You going on the spouse tour?" Ivy Hailey's voice was one tone deeper than a dog's whistle.

Molly shrugged.

"I'm going to buy the rest of my china," the Young Wife whispered. "They have terrific bargains here."

"—finally, again tonight, we honor the beautiful half of Great Harvest, those patient, long-suffering"—he paused for the laughter that turned the truth into a joke—"partners we honor on this trip, our spouses who, even tonight, despite the heat, continue to work miracles by looking like spring visions. To our partners, a toast." He raised his glass and was mimed by hundreds of blue-blazered arms.

The women bowed their heads and smiled demurely, as if they did not, indeed, deserve recognition. But these were the gears that kept the men running smoothly, the maintenance personnel that provided a base. If a man wanted a career, a home and a family, then he needed to find one of them.

Molly kept her head held high and drank a toast to herself and to her more modest sisters.

Clay worked the table as if he were on automatic pilot. He prompted its men and women into their most attractive roles. Generally, Molly admired him for his gifts. Tonight she poked through the melon appetizer and into the roast beef without really listening to the conversation.

"Oh," Ivy said, breaking into Molly's consciousness. "I'm a real tennis nut now!" She laughed a tiny glass-shattering tinkle that reminded Molly of the mice in *Cinderella*. "I've been ranked an A player on the club ladder." Bibbidi-bobbidi-boo.

The second Mrs. Winger was soft-spoken. "I'm in law school. I was a paralegal, but Fred convinced me to take the big leap." Fred beamed at her.

"Figure we're in Chicago for keeps," Fred said, "so why shouldn't Beth develop her natural talents?"

Molly began to see the logic in all the marital reshuffling. Wife number one bore the children, coped with the moves, placed her power solidly behind the throne and developed her husband's interest. Because of that, he became successful enough to attract wife number two, who had only one function, to develop herself.

"You're scowling," Clay whispered. "What on earth's wrong?"

"The earth is wrong."

"What? What?"

A double question with no space for an answer was a dangerous sign. She cleaned up her act. "Roast beef's tough," she said. "That's all."

He directed his blue eyes and smile to the other diners. The Young Wife was saying, "Larry and I think of Great Harvest as *our* employer. . . ."

Molly was tempted to warn her of the dangers inherent in thinking you shared your husband's job. What happened when you were fired? Where was Charlene Winger's job now? Indeed, where was Charlene Winger?

There was, Molly suspected, a holding bin for discards somewhere. Miles of barbed wire behind which were stored first wives, early mistakes, hit-and-run victims of mid-life crises. And their children who slowly faded from Papa's busy field of vision, engaged as it was by sports cars and child brides and then, in the way of things, freshly minted children.

"—super business with two partners. *Los Angeles* magazine called them the most refreshing of the gourmet—"

Clay was talking about her, and with obvious pride. Molly felt a conflicted rush of emotions—delight that he bragged about her in public, and fury that he discouraged her in private.

"Well, I think that's terrific," Harry Hailey said. "Grand to have a cute little place to keep you busy."

Ivy squeaked. Her husband sounded more enthusiastic about the cute store than about her A rank on the club ladder. "But," she said, her mouse voice gnawing on Molly's nervous system, "don't your children need you at home?"

Molly sighed. She wasn't going to defend, explain, even admit that she lived like the rope in a perpetual tug of war.

"Don't you want to be there for your children?" Ivy prodded.

"My children aren't usually there themselves," Molly answered. "Anyway, I'm sure you've read the current theory of childhood neurosis. You know, the one that blames everything on the unlived life of the mother. Nine out of tén doctors say that if you want to save your kids from the Moonies and the booby hatch, you have to get your life together and live it out. Which is what I'm doing, as exhausting as it is. For the children's sake, of course."

Nobody said much after that until the chocolate pie arrived and provoked a chorus of overenthusiastic praise.

9

"IF WE MIGHT RISK OVERSIMPLIFICATION, THEN WE might suggest several basic personality types. . . ."

Molly tried to stop thinking about how everyone had died in the Black Hole of Calcutta. The conference room was windowless and unbearable. Two hundred women sat on folding chairs holding Styrofoam cups, sweating and staring at a silly man with a Ph.D., a Hawaiian shirt and horn-rimmed glasses.

He looked the sort who'd been beaten up a lot as a kid. And then his mother said never mind, you're smarter than they are, and he became so smug about that, they beat him up even more.

He was, above all, a neuter. It was impossible to fantasize buttocks and genitalia inside the pants that hung limply from a dress belt. His feet were shod in elaborate sandals, for the casual touch. He had written a long and difficult name on the board. "But please," he'd said in a high tenor, "just call me Dr. K. Let's keep this informal." His neck seemed to ache for a bow tie.

Molly finished her second cup of coffee. They had completed part one of the morning, a session devoted to the art of decision-making. "There are ways," Dr. K. said, "to work things out methodically, girls."

Girls! Watch it, buster, Molly thought, but she said nothing, echoing the silence and impassivity of the rest of the "girls." Sugar and spice, that's what we're still made of, she thought, and felt furious with them all, herself included.

In any case, Dr. K. described the laborious manner in which he and his wife had decided to be in Nassau rather than in Nashville at this time. He drew lists of pros and cons for each option until Molly was suffused with sorrow for the long-suffering Mrs. Dr. K. Imagine each partner writing separate lists, numbering priorities, combining them, giving weight to each factor. Why hadn't she simply said, "Shuck this crap, Doc! I want a tan, so it's Nassau, not Nashville."

The air was charged with electrical tension. Every so often, the building reverberated with distant thunder. Molly slumped. Why was she here, enduring this drivel? While Dr. K. replayed his decision-making process, she'd die of a lack of oxygen, like those folk in Calcutta. Besides, he was patronizing them with his fool checklist. There wasn't a woman in the room who wasn't used to running her home on her own, meeting emergencies on her own, making decisions on her own, but he behaved as if they spent their days in a dithering rustle of petticoats.

There were no men in the room. The meeting was called a "spouses' seminar," because Great Harvest had two married female executives along. However, it seemed wives were the only spouses who attended morning meetings.

"Here we have a quadrant," Dr. K. said, drawing an enormous plus sign. The "girls" squealed as the chalk grated across the board. "We have dominance and passivity, warmth and coolness. A person can be dominant and warm or dominant and cold—"

Or passive and hot as hell, Molly thought. Like me. What in God's name was he talking about?

"Often, a person unfortunately is passive, allowing events to—"

What was Molly doing listening to it?

"—the ideal is warm and dominant. A take-charge person who cares. He will supervise with humanity and—"

He? She sat up a bit straighter.

"—cold dominant persons may be aggressive instead of assertive; the compassionate dominant personality—"

More than heat pushed into her pores.

"—being in control, making life decisions—"

It wasn't the temperature that spun her head and blurred her vision anymore.

"—because a passive person who allows—"

Behind her, the top executives' wives sat near the coffee maker. Escape was impossible.

"We certainly don't want to see—"

Thou Shalt Not Make a Scene. There Are No Extenuating Circumstances. Molly weighed those corporate commandments against ideals she'd been taught earlier in life. Her mother used to quote Gandhi. "Almost anything you do will be insignificant," Thea was fond of saying, "but it is very important that you do it." Gandhi sounded a lot better than Dr. K.

"So in common situations of this sor-sor-sor—" He stammered at the first sight of Molly's raised hand. "—sort," he said finally, "we have people who—"

They had been told to hold questions for the end. Dr. K. of the missing bow tie was a man who needed structure. She knew an interruption would derail him. She waved her hand.

"—who have to, have to, who—Yes? What is it?"

Several dozen heads turned in her direction. "Sorry to interrupt," Molly said. She smiled, knowing her auburn hair, short stature and dimples still had power to disarm the Dr. K.'s of the world. She kept her voice airy and nonthreatening.

The lecturer made a Christlike gesture of forgiveness.

"But I'm confused. Could we backtrack a step?"

"Shoot," he said.

"Are we discussing the ideal personality?"

He nodded.

"*The* ideal?"

More nodding.

"And that ideal personality is active and dominant and definitely not passive?"

"Right you are." He pointed a trigger finger at her.

"Then tell me, Dr. K., are we discussing the ideal personality of those of us sitting here this morning?"

"Ideal is ideal. Period. But since Great Harvest is our sponsor, why perhaps I was veering toward the ideal executive, managerial personality style, so—"

"Pardon me, but are we then sitting here and listening to a discussion of the ideal personalities our husbands should have?"

"Well, in the sense that—"

"Don't you think that's pretty *passive*? I mean we obeyed a summons to be here at eight A.M. so we could sit in the heat and hear how our *husbands* should be!" Someone giggled. "Hey, Dr. K.," Molly said, "how about *us*?"

He didn't smile. "Everyone is ideally this—"

"Nonsense!" It wasn't Molly this time, but silent Moira, the composer. Molly had never heard the deep voice before. Moira stood up and waved her empty coffee cup. She wore a floor-length Indian cotton gown that was completely inappropriate in this sea of linen slacks, skirts and tennis outfits. But Moira, of all of them, looked cool. Her voice, low and commanding, was also cool, but her words were not. "Nonsense," she repeated. "If we weren't passive, we probably wouldn't stay married. How can we possibly be as you say and take charge of our destinies? Warm and passive. I'd say that was the ideal us. Do you think our husbands are listening to someone describe *our* ideal selves at their meetings? Or even thinking about us? We're beyond passive. We're comatose. Obedient. *Feminine*."

"Now, now." Dr. K. was visibly alarmed. "No cause for anger. We're discussing ideal types—"

"For executive positions!" Moira said.

Molly realized her mouth was open. She watched Moira and Dr. K. like a set at Wimbledon.

"I, sir, am a composer. I'm in no way convinced that I will create finer music if I'm assertive, commanding, passive or completely schizophrenic. Your quadrants are irrelevant to my work. The relevant item, however, is that you don't know what my work is, or that it might have been interesting to find it out. That you are discussing ideal personalities and styles without determining a single fact about your listeners. If anyone ever required a completely passive audience, that person is you, here, today. You know nothing about any of us and you don't even know it's a question worth asking. You walk in and lecture us about an ideal human being who cannot, by definition and function, be any one of us here!"

A single set of hands applauded at the far left side of the room. Molly joined it and heard another up front. "Hear, hear!" a voice said.

Moira looked as if she'd just come out of a trance. A dozen women now applauded and smiled at her.

Molly hugged herself. This was wonderful! "Comes the Revolution," her mother used to say, "watch it all change." And now, the revolution was coming, even here, in the holy sanctuary of the status quo.

Moira put up her fingers in a V-sign and sat down.

Dr. K. was rapidly losing his professional facade. "Let's clear up some apprehensions," he said. "You're not expected to be passive. A healthy person takes charge of his destiny—"

"And his wife goes along for the ride. That's how it is for us," a woman up front shouted. "Pretty passive, yes?"

"It isn't, though, because . . ." He couldn't finish the idea.

Another woman pulled free of the silent linen ranks. "What

if my husband's boss does something offensive? Shall I tell him off, be assertive, break the rules?"

And another. "What about when my husband says the company's transferring him again. Should I say, 'Not on your life'? Is that a good wife?"

And one more. "What about us? Why can't we talk about things that are real to us? Don't we exist?"

The noise spread and grew, although Molly couldn't tell if its parts were made of agreement and support or protest and annoyance. She saw a hand waving. The rebels were shouters. The hand had to be a rule-follower, an agent of the crown.

Dr. K. sensed it immediately. He nodded at the hand.

She smoothed her lavender wraparound skirt as she stood. "I want to say I'm surprised." Her voice was soft and ladylike and she was very pretty. "I've been a Great Harvest wife for fifteen years and I can't sit silently through this. I think the other side should be heard. I don't have any of those feelings. I'm my own person in my marriage and I don't worry about what I'm going to say at dinner with my husband's boss." She glanced swiftly at the row of women in the back, then continued. "My husband lets me say and do whatever I like."

"*Lets* you? Aren't you ashamed to say that in this day and age?" This from a rude rebel.

Lavender Skirt closed her eyes with exasperation. "I think happy people should be heard, too. I was very interested in the discussion because I consider myself a partner in my marriage and the more I know about my husband's responsibilities and psychology, the better partner I can be. Anything that has to do with my husband has to do with me." She sat down to a hearty round of applause. Molly swiveled around and saw the senior wives nodding and solemnly applauding.

"Where are we?" someone shouted. "I haven't heard that kind of talk since I was in a sorority in the fifties."

Dr. K. gasped air like a drowning fish. Molly grinned. What was he going to say to Lavender Skirt? That it was psychologically healthy to identify completely with someone else? To be that passive? To have no separate identity?

Sweetness triggered everyone's repressed ideas, good or bad. Women shouted to their neighbors, to friends, to God. The room became a hot and angry sea, whitecaps of indignation spuming, the tide rolling in every direction.

Molly leaned back, feeling like Lenin, Trotsky, Che, Tom Paine and Gandhi all in one. Comes the Revolution! She knew Lavender Skirt and her sisters would triumph, but nevertheless, it had begun. Molly giggled. She laughed out loud.

"Unfortunately," Dr. K. shouted, pounding on the podium, "we're out of time. This would be interesting to pursue, but—"

Chairs screeched and voices continued loudly as the mass pushed for the doorway.

Moira came over. "Glad to know you." The blonde from the front left joined them.

"I'm Carol Merendy. Let's be friends. Nobody else will have us after this."

"I've been to twelve years of Great Harvest getaways," Moira said, "and this is the first fun I've had. I admire your courage. I never would have started a thing. I couldn't have been the first."

It was dark and muggy outside. An enormous cloud hugged the horizon as Clay walked toward them.

Molly made introductions. "How was your meeting?" she asked.

"Interesting. Brainstorming for the next decade. Lots of changes in the wind. What did you talk about?"

"You."

"Me? I heard shouting. I didn't know I was that fascinating. Or controversial."

"Well, we stopped talking about you—plural," Carol said, "when your wife turned things around."

Clay's face tensed subtly. "Like—how?" he asked. Molly had

a moment's panic, waiting for him to show he was the Lavender Skirt's man, every frightened, conforming company man that ever there was.

"I started a revolution," she said softly.

"Sure as hell did," Carol said. "So understand if people shout, 'Unclean, unclean,' as she passes. See you later, Molly. You've given me the courage to skip the shopping tour. I'll read feminist tracts in the bathtub, instead." She was off, as was Moira.

"What's all this about?" Clay looked worried.

"Like I said. I started a revolution. Oh, with ideas that are twenty years old, at least—but new here. I was uppity. I made trouble. Clay, that lecturer was a patronizing, irrelevant nerd."

"But what did you do?"

Her heart accelerated with tension. "I couldn't stand it, so I questioned his premise and started a hullabaloo."

"In front of everyone?"

"Like what everyone?"

"Oh, like Dom Campiglia's wife and the chairman's wife, and —everybody?"

She put her hands on her hips. "Yes, like those everybodys. What do you have to say about it?"

He smiled suddenly, his eyes glinting dark blue, his perfect teeth bright. "Was it fun?" he asked.

She loved him with a rush that almost knocked her flat, and she was ashamed for repeatedly testing him, for always being ready to slot him with ordinary mortals.

Above them a gray cloud split a seam. They felt the first trickle of rain.

"Ah, Clay, I feel so good." She held up her face so that rain fell on it. "I'm a loudmouth my mother would be proud of, and it feels wonderful." She studied the sky. "Looks like good rain, fella."

He nodded.

"Not exactly a beach day."

He shook his head.

"Reminds me of a shower I once knew. Of how a man needs what he needs and suchlike."

"Well, I have a golf game with Campiglia, and—"

"But it's raining!"

"They have these umbrella things that—"

She felt a solid sulk begin. She was running with juices, charged by her morning, and he was talking golf. "You could skip the game," she said.

"I really can't."

She nearly turned away, then she stopped herself short. "Clay," she said, "Dr. K., our *teacher*, explained that the ideal person is assertive and warm. Fact is, Clay, I'm very warm and I'd like to assert that I want to wrap my legs around your back."

"Holy Christ, Molly!" He turned to see whether anyone had overheard.

"No need to be passive and shy, Clay." Her voice was too loud for intimacies. "Passive and shy are dreadful. Dr. K. said so. I'm working toward the ideal. Warm and dominant. Could you get into dominance? Dr. K. made it all so clear I could—"

"I think some things are private, Moll, and—"

"But a person has to take charge of her destiny—even if Dr. K. never said 'her.' A woman needs what a woman needs. I— Clay, are you going to talk about golf again now?"

"The game isn't until this afternoon."

"Well, why didn't you say so? Move it, man!"

He put up his hands in mock surrender. A pleasant-looking man came toward them. "Clay," he said, "can I steal a few minutes of your time?" Molly stuck her index finger into the small of her husband's back.

"Sorry," Clay said. "I'll catch you later." He stepped into the elevator.

"Oh, Clay," Molly said, "isn't Nassau fun?"

The rain lasted slightly longer than they did. Another sign

of mid-life, but Molly wasn't upset by it. Only aware of it. They were into quality, not quantity.

"Maybe I can get a weather forecast," Clay said, turning on the radio. They had ordered room service for lunch, and they sat by the open terrace windows, letting spray from the rain shower enter the room. Molly enjoyed the gusts of wind, the storm, her lunch and Clay. She felt comfortable with her life.

The radio static finally cleared and they listened to the only clear station. "Oliver Banny, your car is ready. Pick it up before five. Nathan Moss, your uncle Louie died in Miami. His body is at Crestwood Funeral Home waiting directions. . . ." Clay turned the radio off. "Either those are coded messages for drug dealers or the island lacks something in the way of hard news," he said.

"I'm glad we're here," Molly said. "We needed time to be alone, in a bedroom, in the middle of the day, even if we had to fly three thousand miles to find it."

"Remember, before we had kids?"

"Was it because we were young or because they weren't around to exhaust and interrupt?"

He poured himself more coffee from the silver carafe. "They'll all be gone soon. So quickly."

Molly took his hand. "That's why the store is so important to me now," she said softly.

"I know. It's not that I don't understand what you're doing or why. I get the big outlines. It's the details, the way it works out every day, that confuses me. But we'll make it. It'll all sort out." He stood up, leaned over and kissed her. "Look out there," he said, "just like in the movies, a new day's a-dawning for the two of us."

A thin line of light outlined the horizon. The cloud was lifting and the rain was now light and fine.

"We need more of this kind of time," Molly said. "It's a shame how the system works. We take care of everything else first and then, if there's time and energy left, we fit us in, too."

They stood very close, watching the sky change.

"I love you, Clay," she said. "I love you so much that it doesn't even make me mad that you aren't listening to me right now."

"I am so," he murmured.

"Halfway at best. You're thinking about the golf game, aren't you? And you're going to keep that date, aren't you?"

He sighed.

"And you never for a moment considered not keeping it. No matter what might have happened between us, you'd have kept that appointment, wouldn't you?"

"This particular game is—"

"Point is, you never once considered missing it, right?"

"Right."

"That's okay. I like real life."

He played. She read, then walked on the overcast beach, reveling in the sounds of the breakers, the seabirds and now and then a wind-scattered voice in the distance.

She walked straight and proud, feeling reborn. She'd meant what she said. She liked real life, liked where she was and the future she saw.

She pulled her sweater close. The air was chilly and gray, the sky patched over with clouds. Molly walked on hard-packed sand. She should thank Dr. K. His insensitivity had blown away debris clouding her vision.

She felt able at last to relax into herself. She'd been tense for too long, acting as if the difficulties of transition were problems she had created and must solve alone. She blew a kiss to the horizon. Good-bye all-purpose Molly. No more pancake flipping and gourmet-lunch packing and ridiculous overachieving. Good-bye Harriet Nelson. No more reruns. Good-bye black-and-white and hello full color. Including lots of grays.

She remembered how she'd felt the morning after she lost her virginity. Or the day she first knew she was pregnant. Both times she was sure "it" showed because she felt so revised inside.

She felt that way now.

She let her feet be buried as she stood in the melting sand beneath the surf. She watched the tiny air holes left by minuscule crabs whose entire lives were spent avoiding waves. I'm too old to live that way anymore, she said, surprising herself.

Maybe this was the trade-off. Maybe it took all those years of weathering to feel this fine. Perhaps they weren't a wearing down but a burnishing until your rubbed and wrinkled skin held something within that glowed.

She stood, arms outspread, like a priestess blessing her world. Then the need to expend energy took over. She ran on the hard sand, loving the sensation of using herself.

She had always been good at loving. She opened herself up and encircled everything she saw. But she had stayed in the center, the source and not its object. Now she could include herself as well.

She ran, her white pants wet and sand-splashed so they stuck to her ankles, her auburn hair loose and flying behind her.

She was part of the elements. She was energy and power and love, and she knew she would soon lift up and fly, circling and crowing and screaming her joy to the universe. It was so good to live, to be her, to be herself. She ran and laughed and thought she might do both forever.

The game was over. Clay walked through the trees that rimmed the beach. He felt ancient, a sick animal seeking a sunny clearing. But there was no sunshine, simply a late afternoon gray-and-beige seascape.

He stood on the edge of the sand and leaned on a stand of unused beach towels and chairs. There was no one else around except on the horizon, where he saw Molly.

There was no mistaking that mane of hair. He watched her, entranced by her obvious joy. She had always seemed more completely alive than other people, more touched by life's possibilities. But up to now he'd seen it in details through gestures, touches, expressions, surprises.

Now he could see it whole, her body silhouetted against a steel sky and gray water, somehow producing its own light.

She ran, but he read it as praying, cheering, delighting in. Something magical and terrifying was happening to her and he couldn't tear his eyes away.

There he stood, awkward and stiff in his shoes and socks, a withered stick, while on the horizon, his wife danced with barefoot energy and bright color. He felt a catch in his throat for the love of her, for the ways she was different from him, for the joy she produced and shared. But mostly, he felt the catch and the pain and something close to tears for the damage he knew he was about to do her.

10

"DAMN!" SHE GRABBED THE ELEVATOR DOORS BE-fore they sealed and stepped back out. She didn't have a room key.

She walked briskly to the front desk, carrying her pharmacy bag of scented bath oil.

"Please." The acne-scarred desk clerk was peeved. "Remind your husband to leave the key next time. I'll ring for a bellboy to take you up." He slammed the bell and Molly, head hanging like a shamed schoolchild, wondered how she'd tip the bellboy. Could she charge it to her room, the way she'd charged her drugstore purchase?

And then she remembered Che and Tom Paine, Gandhi and Molly. "The thing about revolutions," her mother had said, "is that once begun, no power on earth can stop them forever. For a while, sure, but not forever." She'd been right.

"No," Molly said, wheeling to face the clerk.

"How's that?"

"I want my own key. I don't wish to be led to my room. I'm a grown-up person and I'm entitled to my own key."

"We don't—"

Molly leaned closer. "I'm not interested in your little scam with the bellboys."

"Our policy is—"

"I want my own key right now!"

He handed over a key.

She marched off, whistling softly. It wasn't comparable to storming the Bastille, but it was surely something.

Clay was asleep. He still wore his golf clothes and his shoes, and his room key was in his hand. It looked as if he'd barely made it to bed, then collapsed.

She bent to kiss his forehead the way she'd once bent to her sleeping babies, as love and a blessing both. Clay looked marked and vulnerable. Then she tiptoed into the bathroom.

The new bath oil had a lemony fragrance. She felt refreshed when she climbed out of the tub and toweled off.

"Hi," the mirror lady said.

"Came all the way here, did you?" Molly dotted moisturizer on her cheeks and forehead and chin.

"Why not?" The woman watched Molly with interest.

"Because I'm on vacation. Sleeping, resting. Well, if the sun had been out and the air conditioning working, you wouldn't be here looking like that."

"I keep telling you," the woman said, "I'm for keeps."

Molly worked hard to obliterate her. She painted with a pale stick that erased nature's little coloring errors. She covered those marks with foundation. Covered that with blusher in two tones, the darker emphasizing the hollows beneath her cheekbones, the brighter highlighting their summits. She carefully lined her eyes in a rusty shade that accentuated their amber and gold. She smudged the lines until they were suggestions, then chose a smoky stick of color and carefully applied it to the underside of the bony ridge of her brow.

She penciled light strokes over her eyebrows. She applied two coats of mascara and covered her mouth with a delicate shade that was cousin to her hair and her cheeks, and then dusted her face with gold-flecked powder.

"Well, well," the mirror lady said, her voice a bit muffled. "We're a little like your husband's make-believe food, aren't we? Artificial colors, preservatives to retard spoilage. Ten percent real woman somewhere inside."

"Shut up," Molly said. "Nobody likes an aging smartass." She reached for the next potion, the one that would make the real difference and rid her of the nag in the mirror.

There was nothing left. She turned her cosmetic bag upside down, shook it, pawed through the pencils and tubes and brushes and bottles like a junkie needing a fix, but there was nothing more left.

"Gotcha," the lady in the mirror said.

Clay was quiet when he woke up. Groggy, he said. Not used to naps.

At dinner, he joked, eking a smile out of Campiglia's persimmon wife. He debated California versus Florida with an Orlando man. But still, he wasn't quite Clay. Molly couldn't pinpoint what was different, but something important was.

It's me, she suddenly felt with a shiver. Me. How did his eyes see her if she herself was so startled by every glance in the mirror? It must be me, the terrible tug of time and loss I advertise with my face.

He's noticing all the replacement wives, and I'm looking worse and worse. And I'm loud and uppity to boot.

"I love you, Clay," she said as they danced between courses.

"And I love you," he answered.

But why did she feel this terrible pressure on his part to hold back and say no more? What were the truths he was hiding?

In the casino, after dinner, Clay was less than enthusiastic, but that was understandable. He didn't like gambling. He was there because the air conditioning worked in this room and because Molly wanted to be there.

Clay was analytic, domineering. He wanted to understand systems and then control them.

Molly, on the other hand, knew the system was rigged and the odds impossible, but she didn't care.

Clay went to play blackjack, then wandered back in the direction of Molly and the one-armed bandits. His wife was jumping up and down, clapping her hands. Quarters poured out of her machine. People cheered and a loud burst of music came from the speakers around the room.

"A winner! A winner! A winner!" the snappy voice shouted on the loudspeaker.

Molly laughed as quarters overflowed onto the floor. "Look!" she cried when she saw Clay. Silver flowed, a twinkling stream in the artificial light. "I'm a winner!"

"Always knew it," he said. Then he kissed her and helped her exchange her silver for dollar bills.

But he wasn't himself. He was a low-wattage Clay.

She refused to think about it, refused to X-ray him like a mad physician insisting on a secret malignancy. She was a winner. That was all she wanted to consider right now.

In the dark, later, she walked over to his bed, again cursing the management for ignoring their request for a king-size mattress. She sat on the edge of his bed and touched him and felt his involuntary pull from her hand.

"It's the heat," he said. He rolled over on his back and looked at her. "Exhausts me."

He looked old and mortal. "Whenever you're ready, I'm here to listen," she said. "I'm your friend. Can you remember that, Clay?"

"Oh, Molly." He sounded desperate. He pulled her close. "I love you. I love you." And then he turned her and was on her, entering her, saying over and over, "I love you," and "Molly," and she was there and nothing more. Her eyes wide open, she watched his face with fear. His eyes were closed and he was chanting her name and she was far away, an idea, a familiar comfort he needed. She unfolded herself for the taking. She wanted to meet that need, but she felt maternal, not sexual. A giver of comfort, a casing for his despair.

"Molly," he said, again and again. "Oh, Molly."

She stared past his shoulder, trying not to think.

Clay waited until they had passed through customs in Miami and had boarded their second plane, the jet for Los Angeles.

From the moment they'd awakened that morning, he'd known that Molly, too, was waiting. There were politenesses in any long relationship and he acknowledged them. This was one, her realization that he had something to say and her restraint in pressing him. But it wouldn't last forever. Molly wasn't terrific at restraint.

Keeping this to himself hurt, as if he were really carrying something heavy and pointed under his heart. But when else could he have told her? Anyway, the air was a good place. Private. A capsule in space.

And Molly couldn't run away up here.

She brought it up as soon as they were airborne again. He noticed that her hand shook as she closed her book, lit a cigarette and spoke. "Time to end the dance, lovey," she said. "We have to talk about it now."

"It?"

Now her voice shook a little, too, but she stared at him, her chin held high. "Let's get it out in the open so we can see what to do about it. What is it? Another woman? A need to cut free and find yourself?" She paused. He heard a ragged little sigh. "Things happen," she said. "We're getting older and life's no simpler, and—"

"Molly? We have to move. To Pennsylvania. The Mother Lancaster division. I'm going to head it."

They were passing over the Gulf of Mexico when he said

this. She looked at his face to see if he were serious. Then she looked out the window.

Her mind curdled, refusing to process the information. Better a ravishing twenty-year-old nymph. Better a serious psychological burn-out. They would have left her intact and capable.

No, her mind said. This is not possible. We live in L.A.—at headquarters. Home base. This can't happen.

They slid through the sky. She smoked cigarette after cigarette.

"That was why Campiglia arranged the golf game," Clay said. "He's known for weeks. Decided to tell me in Nassau."

She stared out the window. She didn't care if she was unkind or offensive. She didn't want to see his eyes or his pain. She didn't want to care about him. They weren't partners anymore.

He filled her silence with explanations that explained nothing, rationalized everything. He spoke while the flight attendant placed plastic meals in front of them.

He spoke over Texas and into New Mexico and Arizona.

Mother Lancaster was reorganizing. Health foods, or the company's version of them, were too expensive to produce. The market was changing; Clay was going to work out a new approach to marketing and plant efficiency. He was going to turn the division around. A great opportunity. A promotion.

"Why you?" she finally managed.

He answered with a rehash of his résumé. The campaign for granola years ago. The way he'd gotten the Connecticut sales office into shape. His managerial expertise. He was their man.

"But why? We're at headquarters, the stopping place. I thought—you said—I believed . . ."

So had he, but the new theories challenged Great Harvest's ratio of executive workers to production workers. The Japanese were much less top-heavy with management. Corporate expenses were too high relative to corporate sales, and sales were down and times were hard and his present job was being eliminated.

Philadelphia was a good place. He reminded her of their college days there, of going home again, in a way. He knew she'd only had two years of school but maybe somebody she knew then would still be around.

She stared out the window.

He talked about how Art Baum's fate could have been theirs, how lucky they were, what with the economy being so shaky. He talked about what a fabulous house they'd buy in the East where houses cost so much less and how he knew it'd be hard on her and the kids but after all . . .

They approached Los Angeles.

Home, she thought with a silent sneer. Home.

Clay drank his third scotch. "Molly," he said. "Look at me. I can't stand this any longer. What else can I do? I can't quit. It would kill me to be a failure, a nobody, to have no job. I physically cannot do it. It would be insane, anyway. This is a horrible time. Everybody's cutting back on middle management, so how could I—and this is a *promotion*. A challenge. I want to tackle it."

He swirled the ice cubes around in the plastic glass, waiting, waiting for her. She seemed as cold as the cubes, as solid and unyielding. "Molly," he said, and felt the words come hard, "I don't have any other options."

Neither did she, whether or not anybody thought to ask her the question. She'd been asking it herself straight across the country, and she'd come up with zero every time. She had three children, fifty dollars in winnings from the night before, and a partnership in a still-unprofitable business. Those were her assets and realities. Those and the man next to her and the life she'd been building for eighteen years.

She had no options whatsoever.

11

A CHINA-BLUE CALIFORNIA WASHED CLEAN BY THE rains greeted them. Palm trees glittered near the airport and in the distance, sunlight struck snowcapped mountains. Molly was afraid to let herself look at its beauty.

She and Clay had decided to wait before telling the children the news. Like couples announcing a divorce, they needed a stance and an angle that would make the change desirable, or at least bearable.

But as soon as Molly saw her trio, she felt duplicitous for not telling them immediately in the most messy manner. Together, they should weep and moan.

They seemed younger than they had when she left. No matter how they disguised it, with plugs in their ears or magic or interminable sulks, they were hostages in the family, and they knew it.

Children were born with different strengths, and the Michaels' migratory patterns tested those of their homegrown crop. Ben lacked the gene that made being a stranger a challenge worth meeting. With every uprooting, he became more introverted. Tony seemed able to slither into whatever openings his peer group offered, but he took friendship lightly, as if it were an illusion that would, by nature, prove a trick. And Joanna had the dangerous habit of panicking and grabbing whatever hand extended itself.

Molly hugged them and listened to their tales of the weekend and ate an early dinner with her family.

"We had fun," Thea said while Tony and Ben cleared the table. "I told the children all about the Aztecs' cannibal banquets. You know, after they ripped out the living heart of the sacrifice, they divvied up the rest and made a stew out of him. Added a little maize." She left the room to find her newspaper.

"Her stories are gross," Joanna said. "She told us how vultures pee on their feet to keep them cool."

"It's Ben's turn to wash," Tony said.

"Tony's."

"Ben's."

"I'll do it," Molly said. They looked at her suspiciously, but self-interest defeated curiosity and they left the room.

Molly stood by the sink, arms in water, letting herself become liquid and drain away.

Thea returned, holding the newspaper. Under the bright kitchen light, she appeared tiny and dry.

Molly shook herself out of the numbness. "I'm going to walk on the beach. Want to come, Mom?"

"No thanks, dear. I'm reading. Would you listen to this? Hamsters ate their way through a building in England. Came through the light fixtures and the walls."

Clay, who'd sat silently through dinner, spoke. "I miss your stories when you aren't with us."

"Well, the other ones are repetitive after eighty years. Wars, poverty, bad marriages, scores, arrests—boring." She blew them a kiss and left the room.

"Beach sounds great," Clay said.

Molly said nothing. She needed to separate herself from him. It was all the places they were joined that were so vulnerable.

Clay was determined to win her back with his patience and enduring love. "Listen," he said, "how about if I come along . . ." Molly stood behind the sink, her hands on the counter, her body frozen like an animal in headlights.

She waited, allowing him to do whatever he wanted. He would anyway, she thought. He always did.

The warmth Clay had felt turned into anger. Look at her, he thought. Arms and face hanging like some abused species. Damn her.

Look at him, she thought. Is he capable, ever, of saying the one thing that would matter? *I'm sorry?* I know this is ripping apart your life. I know it's my dreams versus your dreams. *I'm sorry.* But instead, he wants to walk on the beach so he can explain more, convince more, sell me some more of his line. Well, go to hell, you oily-smooth salesman.

"You were saying?" she asked politely.

"Nothing. Enjoy yourself."

The last seaside walk seemed more than a day earlier, much farther from Molly than even a continent's width. Beside her now, the Pacific stretched lakelike, a single breaker rolling onto the sand. She didn't dance. She carried her shoes and walked, watching a low-keyed sunset. The rain had washed the sky clean. On other nights, the dying sun whirled through crystal pollutants, producing a razzle-dazzle light show.

She was going to miss even the smog.

She felt a dull pain between her breasts. Her life hurt.

"And the worst," she told the rolling surf, "the very worst is that like everything else about me, it's so ordinary. Nobody's going to be shocked, or horrified, or even interested in the shredding of my life. Happens hundreds of thousands of times every year. Why is no weight given it? No notice?" She lifted a small shell, then tossed it back into the surf.

"Ladies and gentlemen," she told the water, glittering with the sunset, "I've called this press conference to announce my

removal from Los Angeles." She heard the roar of their response, the agitated round of questions and protest. "I'd like to
say that it's not that I love my home and business less but that
I love my family more."

They fell back, mouths agape. "You'd give up everything
you've worked for for a man and some kids?" a CBS reporter
asked.

Molly bowed her head.

"But your children will grow up and leave." This from a
pushy gossip on a morning talk show. "What will you have
then, Mrs. Michaels?"

"Why Mr. Michaels, of course," Molly said sweetly.

"Throw off your chains! Stand up for your rights! You aren't
chattel!" the editor from *Ms* shouted.

"I want to say we're behind you a thousand percent, Mrs.
America!" Molly had trouble finding the speaker. He was in
back, behind the major networks, the large papers and magazines. "Here," he called. He wore red, white and blue bunting.
"Consumer Coupons and More," he called.

Aha. Her fans. The throwaway in the market. Freebies and
garage sales and tidbits about specials. For her: the woman with
nothing to do but shop.

She let them all twinkle back into dots on the water. Not for
Molly any proper rite of passage or sense of dignity. Instead,
people would say, "Again? Good thing I write your address in
pencil in my book."

One more all-American jumping bean. Today's senseless pi-
oneer, reexploring old territory. She kicked sand. No. I won't
be one. I won't go home ever. Will not. Won't live with him
anymore.

Never give up my friends, the store, good schools for the
kids, the house I worked so hard on. Won't.

But like a runaway child not old enough to cross the street,
she repeated her threats, retraced her path, and then she went
home. They were all of them trapped.

12

THE NEXT MORNING, SHE STOOD ON THE PORCH OF Sinfully Good for a long time. The sun traveled through the bougainvillea, throwing dappled patterns and a pink haze on the white floor. Empty tables dotted the wide veranda, waiting for printed cloths, fresh flowers and people to bring the scene to life.

It was going to be hard falling out of love with this.

A spicy aroma greeted her when she opened the door.

"New recipe," Nan called from the kitchen. "Called 'My Billys.'"

"Should I ask why?" Molly leafed through a small pile of orders. A wedding basket, one baby, one operation, one funeral.

"They smell the way my Billy tastes, that's why."

"I shouldn't have asked." Molly looked around the room, appreciating it. She loved all the squatty, curved, tall and faceted bottles filled with oils—almond and walnut and double virgin olive, and vinegars flavored with tarragon or raspberry or dill. She loved the packages of fancy mixed herbs, of multicolored peppercorns, of spices and cinnamon sticks. She touched a bottle of Greek olives, as if to keep it from disappearing. She felt like Emily in *Our Town,* back from the dead for one painful viewing.

"I hope they taste the way he tastes," Nan went on, " 'cause then we'll make a million."

Over. Done. Lost. Even silly, salacious one-track Nan. Who among the East Coast's Puritans would do official orgasm tallies and paint murals on her fingernails?

"Ellen here?" Dumb question. The back section was one room broken only by the center serving counter. Their three work stations were visible and empty.

Empty. Over. Leaving. Lost. Gone.

"She called. She's running late. Why aren't you tan? She was late Saturday, too. Missed half the day and didn't call. And out sick on Friday. It rained both days. It was crazy here and oh, the new part-timer's leaving. Moving to Hawaii. I don't know, everything's strange lately. Must be the rain."

"You need me?" Nan shook her head. "Then I'll start on my orders." Molly began with the funeral basket. Grieving people needed solid, unaffected foods. Fruits, herbal teas, nut breads, cheese. Things of the earth, sustenance; symbols of pendulum swings and seasons. She nestled jars and a loaf of date bread against a green paisley lining, and the sight of her hands at work comforted her.

Except.

Damn him, or it. Damn the capitalist system. International corporations. The decline of individual farming. Nations. The invention of the tin can. Freezing. People who eat food. Anything. *Something.*

Their part-time counter workers came in and began mixing the Chinese chicken salad and filling the coffee urns. At ten o'clock, still without Ellen, they moved into higher gear as the Hoover sisters entered for their daily tastings.

Molly dreaded telling her partners the news, but she would, today. They deserved a long lead time, minimal disruption. She had worked out the logical options the night before. The best was for John-the-affluent-bastard to buy Molly's share. Or, if Nan could find some more ready cash, then she and John/Ellen could buy out Molly and make the store a fifty-fifty partnership. They could train an employee to make baskets. It could work out.

She caught a piece of wicker under her nail and gasped, then sat down, tears of pain prickling her eyes. She could see Nan and Ellen a year from now, working happily, sunshine pouring through the bougainvillea, something marvelous scenting the air.

And Molly would be three thousand miles away, shoveling snow off her walk and, truth is, waiting only for late afternoon so she could turn on the soaps and have a drink.

But maybe she could start again back East. She began the second basket, tapping the hurt finger gently, testing its sensitivity, tapping and testing a picture of Molly, starting over on the other side of the country.

She had trouble seeing anything. There were too many questions and not enough money. Considering imponderables exhausted her. She stopped making baskets and instead waited on customers. She had to push against her lethargy to see and hear clearly.

"Sorry," Ellen said, so softly it startled Molly. "I'm late." She looked different—formal. Composed, and suddenly very middle-aged. She was wearing too much makeup.

"How are you? I hear you were sick Friday. I need to talk with you."

"Right. Soon." Ellen put on an apron and began to work.

Molly waited on a woman who took forever debating between Bûcheron and a domestic goat cheese. Then she turned to Ellen. "A lot is happening," she said. "My whole life just—"

Ellen hung up her apron, nodded and said nothing, as if the subject had been thoroughly covered. She went to do the books.

"Ellen's not too good at small talk lately." Nan danced around to the center divider where two part-timers filled take-out orders. Molly decided to work on her baskets.

"Ellen," Molly began, but Ellen frowned. "Later, okay?" she said.

Molly slammed lining into a basket. Time clicked on. Ellen remained mesmerized by her columns of figures. Molly finished two baskets and sold lots of food and ate lots of it, too. She munched on her anxieties until she knew she'd be a blimp someday. And who cared? Maybe she'd become a professional eater. Her life, a movable feast. She'd round out until she was a wheel of flesh. Perfect. Then Clay could roll her to their new address.

Ellen continued to check figures.

"It's hard to believe a human being can love *numbers* that much," Molly snapped.

"Grmph," Ellen said, clucking over her adding machine.

How was Molly supposed to break through to this woman? Hire a singing telegram to announce it? "Hi ho, hi ho, it's Philly-ward she goes, so kiss her off and buy her share, hi ho—"

"It doesn't add up." Ellen sounded panic-stricken.

"What? Are we being audited?"

"Not the figures. Oh, not the figures. Molly, it's just, it's *just —too—much!*" She wailed, then pulled out tissues and blew her nose, then she wailed some more.

"Ellen, I'm so sorry! I didn't realize you were—I mean I thought it was ordinary Monday upset, I mean . . ." Molly's guilt monitor clanged to the top. Mirror, mirror, on the wall, who's the lousiest friend of all?

Still, it was difficult accepting guilt on an already weighted back. This was *Molly's* rotten day. She was reluctant to share it.

"I can tell you're upset with me," Ellen said.

"Upset, yes, but not with—"

"I don't blame you. Friends should be honest, or what's it all about?" She sniffled and blew her nose very loudly. *"Oh, Molly!"* she cried.

"Psst!" Nan waved them out, a look of real alarm on her face. The etiquette of commerce was in strong conflict with Ellen's need to blow her nose and be noisy and miserable. Customers were going to think her sick or insane.

Molly grabbed a bottle of wine and some glasses for first aid, then led Ellen out the back door into the driveway.

"Did you ever," Ellen said, "feel a trapdoor had opened under you?"

"Absolutely. Just yester—"

"I feel like a fool." Ellen paced in front of the trash cans. Molly perched on one and watched. She poured two glasses of wine and worked on one of them.

Ellen's trash can loop appeared a permanent holding pattern. She walked, circled back, and wailed, over and over. This wouldn't do. Ellen was going to stick in her misery like the dinosaurs in the tar pits. Besides, Ellen should be wallowing in pity for Molly, who had major troubles. What lousy timing! When would Molly get her wallowing time? Was she supposed to give over her entire wretched day to empathy?

"Okay," she said, "if you can't say it, I will. You're having problems with John."

"Who told you?"

"Ellen, good friends can read subtle signals. Like, oh, how you hyperventilate, look like death, don't eat, react weirdly to everything."

"Somebody must have said something."

"Listen, it happens. Nobody's road is smooth. If you're in there for the long haul, you have to expect rough spots." She sounded like a truck driver's manual.

"Oh, Moll, I wish this were somebody else's story. I hate having something this awful be, well, funny." She sniffled and leaned against a trash can and gulped wine. "You know John's out-of-town trips? The client in San Francisco? They weren't real. He'd have me drive him to the airport—an overnight, he said. Hated long-term parking and we live so close, so I'd drop him off. And—this is so embarrassing!—then he'd take the fucking jitney to the fucking airport motel and spend the night fucking!"

"Jesus."

Ellen walked around, waving her arms. Anger was written on her fingertips and shoulders even when she said nothing. "And then I'd pick him up the next evening. The cheap bastard wouldn't even call a cab!"

She wheeled around and screamed, waving her arms to the heavens. *"I carpooled my husband to his affair!"* And then she crumpled and sat down hard on a trash can lid. "Tell me a bigger fool," she said.

"But how did you find out?"

"You know John. The reader. Of anything. Anyway, I gave him this great book for Christmas and he took it along, every single time. And the bookmark stayed on page seven. God damn it—it doesn't take three months to read seven pages unless you're—unless you're—"

The back door of the store opened. "Molly, Ellen, what's going on? Moll, there's somebody for a basket in there. She'll only speak to you. Could you . . . ?" She glanced at Ellen, who sat and cried quietly now. "I'll stay out here. Bring more wine, okay?"

When Molly came back outside, expecting to find more keening and tears, she found instead her partners doubled over with laughter.

"I'm sorry," Nan said, "wrong to laugh, but really—"

"And listen!" Ellen had trouble catching her breath. "He says she's special because she doesn't know a *thing.* He can *teach* her everything. I mean not about *sex,* of course, but about *life,* he said."

Molly leaned on her trash can.

"She's never read a book," Ellen said. "John finds that alluring. He has an authentic illiterate."

"This is better than the soaps." Nan leaned back and waited for more.

"She's an actress. Out of work," Ellen said.

"Trite. What else."

"She's twenty-six."

"Amazing," Molly muttered. There seemed to be a special pool, a private reserve of twenty-six-year-old women for men in their forties who were tired of their peer group. How was it possible? Where were they bred? What did they do while they were waiting? The world was full of strange phenomena. She drank some more wine.

"What are you going to do, El?" she asked.

Ellen's giddiness disappeared. "Do? I can't do a thing. What do you do when the other side quits? John's gone."

"Gone? Didn't this all just come out?"

"Friday. But today, I was dressing for work. Brushing my teeth. Everybody was gone. And I saw through the open bathroom door that John's closet was empty. He packed up while I was out running, and he's gone. Took everything he owned except his dirty laundry. I called his office. He said he didn't want any scenes." She poured more wine and drank it.

"How about talking or working it out?" Nan looked furious. "They call it a scene when we say anything! Men!"

"Maybe he left," Molly suggested, "because he was afraid you wouldn't carpool him anymore."

Ellen looked ready to cry, then she gave up and looked merely stunned.

Nan kissed her. "I have to go in. I'm the most sober, and there are customers in there. Don't fret, El. There is life after husbands. I'll fix you up with some wild men who'll curl your hair."

"I'm too old and scared for that," Ellen said.

Nan waved and went back inside.

"What does he want, El? What did he say when you called?"

"He wants out. He wants to tutor her through life. He wants to be twenty-six. I'm sick of it. I can't digest it or make sense of it. Divert me. Who was inside?" She stared off into space. She was not listening at all.

"Order for a basket based on the ten plagues of Egypt. Lice and vermin, contagious disease. Dandruff, too."

"That's nice," Ellen murmured.

"Excrement," Molly added.

"You'll manage. You always do."

"No," Molly said suddenly. "Listen, El, I won't always manage. Not for more than four months. Ellen, I've been looking for a way to tell you all day long. I know it's not the time or the day, but it's real life, so here goes. I'm moving away. Clay's transferred to a town outside Philadelphia. I'm moving again!"

Ellen was listening now. "No," she cried. "*No*, Molly. I can't bear it. Everything going at once. No!"

"Not everything. You'll still have this place and Nan." Molly started to cry.

"But I want my friend and my husband!" Ellen broke into sobs again.

A boy of about twelve whipped into the alley on his bike. "Yo!" he called to an unseen companion. "Come here! Two drunk ladies crying on trash cans!"

By the time his buddy cruised by, there were two drunk ladies laughing on trash cans. They waved at the boy and made contorted faces. He left quickly, using all ten speeds.

"We're a mess," Molly said.

Ellen nodded.

"So's our lives."

Ellen nodded again.

"A funny thing is—I had this plan for John to buy out my share of the store. I have this feeling now that he won't."

Ellen's speech was a bit slurred. "He already warned me not

to hit him for money. Know what else he likes about her? She doesn't do anything except be out of work. I do too much, he said. Too domineering. Too aggressive. Because of this place. She can't even cook."

"I have a great idea," Molly said. "Move with me. Then we'll both have a friend to talk to."

"And nothing to do. I need the store now. Please don't ask me to buy you out. I can't. It'll go under if we have to liquidate."

"I—I won't." Molly watched the idea of another store back East puff and disappear like a blown-out match.

"I have an idea," Ellen said. "Don't move. Stay here and work and just plain don't move. Let him go wherever he likes. Damn men."

Molly shook her head. "I'm not ready for that yet. I—usually love him. And, God, it's hard saying this to you now, but I believe in our marriage, in what I thought we had, and it isn't because I'm scared, Ellen, it's because I so much want the good thing we've made to last. I—am I making sense?"

Ellen nodded. They sat in silence for a long while. Then Ellen looked at her with bleary eyes. "Okay," she said. "This is how it works. The store stays. I stay. You move."

Molly nodded.

"You know what—you'll be the silent partner!"

Molly squinted at Ellen, trying to make things clear. "Silent partner," she repeated. "Funny, that's the same thing Clay has written on our contract, too."

13

"FRIGID. ONE. EXTREMELY COLD. TWO. LACKING warmth of feeling; stiff and formal in manner. Three. Abnormally lacking sexual desire. Said chiefly of women."

Joanna pushed aside the dictionary. Seeing the word explained didn't make her feel any better.

Why had he said that? And worse—how could he tell? Just by one kiss? She felt sick at her stomach.

Anyway, it didn't matter how he knew. He knew, that was enough. It showed. Everybody knew. She was abnormal. Lacking. Abnormally lacking. Now she knew it for sure.

They had walked home, both clutching their books.

"Tough luck about moving," Ricky said as they reached her house and stopped at the FOR SALE sign.

"Yeah," she said. "My dad's already living back East. We're supposed to go when school ends. Only I'm not going. I heard I don't have to go if I can find another place to stay."

"Yeah? What do your parents say about that?"

"It's the law, but they don't believe me. They don't understand. I mean it's *his* job and *my* life. I won't move."

"Good," he said, "because I'd, uh, like miss you, you know?"

She flushed. She was surprised and happy.

And then he grabbed her. Hard. Like in the movies. Kissed her. Hard. Like in books.

Except that he dropped his algebra notebook and the rings opened and the looseleaf pages fell onto the flagstones.

And except that she was scared. She couldn't even pay real attention to the kiss. She was afraid somebody would walk out of her house, that she would also drop her books, that she really didn't want to be kissed this way, now.

He pushed forward, pressing against her looseleaf binder. And then his hand, free of books now, moved around her back and under her vest, under her sweater and flat out onto the naked skin of her back.

She jumped and pulled away. Even when his hand dropped, she could feel it above her waist, each finger separate on her flesh.

His whole face pulled in tight. "It's true what they say." His voice was mean and low. "You're frigid."

She couldn't move, couldn't breathe, couldn't speak. She stared at him, then raced into the house. Frigid! She didn't know what it meant except it was bad. Frigid! She raced up the stairs, slammed her bedroom door, threw herself on the bed and cried.

Frigid. *What they say about you! Say!*

Frigid! They say! Who were they! Did everybody get together and talk about her?

She would never speak to Ricky again, never go to another student council meeting. She hoped Ricky's books were covered with mud, the lessons ruined. She hoped all the unfrigid girls got pregnant and had to have abortions like Lisa had. She hoped the whole house blew up and she died.

And suddenly, moving to the other end of the country seemed a gift from a good fairy godmother. Up until now, she'd thought it was the worst thing her parents had ever done to her. Just the night before, they'd called from Philadelphia.

"We've found it!" her mother said, her voice that fake twitty sugar. "Five bedrooms so Grandma can stay with us forever if she wants, and the boys won't have to share, and a big family room so you can have lots of parties, and—"

"I'm not moving," Joanna said. "I told you."

"Janna, we've been all over this. It's sad, but—"

"Never. Caroline said I can board at her house. I'm not moving. I'm not letting you ruin my life. You never ever think about your own children. You don't think about anybody except yourselves. I'm not moving away from here ever!"

Well, now, when her mother came home, Joanna could say she had thought about it and had decided to be a good sport. She'd never confess that the move was her only hope, her only escape from shame.

The easy part would be moving. The hard part was getting through the six weeks left before school ended.

But she would fill them thinking of a way she could be different in the new school. A way she could hide her deformity, her abnormal lack.

What they say! True what they say! They say! They say!

14

MOLLY SET THE OVEN TO PREHEAT. "NOBODY DOES A damn thing to help me," she muttered. "What effort does it take to *flush?*"

She was exhausted. Every day, before work, she scrubbed sinks, polished tiles and made charming arrangements of fruit in copper bowls. Every day she inspected bedrooms, picked up socks, threw away wadded paper and candy wrappers, folded towels, cleaned hair out of sinks, washed away toothpaste globs, and sprayed rooms.

Every afternoon, they crashed in from school and reversed the process. They dropped books and school flyers, rumpled sofa cushions, left shoes on the floor and jelly streaks on the counters.

"I could be happy here," is what house buyers had to say. And teenagers, demonstrating how thin the walls were with their loud music, and dropping pretzel crumbs like Hansel and Gretel, weren't brokers of dreams.

Molly screamed a great deal. Why couldn't they sit without wrinkling, eat without spilling, work without spreading sideways across the room?

And why didn't they flush the toilet?

"Why do you care so much?" Tony now asked. "We don't even know the people who come through."

"Nobody understands what I'm going through with Daddy three thousand miles away and me, alone here, taking care of everything about the move and my store, too."

"What's her problem?" Joanna whispered loudly, entering the room.

"Toilet," Ben whispered back.

"Every single day," Molly said, ripping plastic sealers off frozen pizzas, "I leave this house perfect so any—"

"Toilet? I don't get it."

"She's pissed about shit," Tony said.

"—body can come in and look. God knows the relocation company isn't going to pay us what it's worth, so it's for your own good to sell it ourselves, but you—"

"Shit?"

"Watch your mouth!"

"I was only trying to find out what the big inquisition's about."

Thea walked in.

"There was a bowel movement in the toilet," Molly explained.

"Goodie." Thea sat down. "Then the children are finally all toilet-trained, is that it?"

"Where do you want it to be?" Joanna asked. "I mean, what is the problem? I thought we weren't supposed to go in our pants. Or in the street, like Tony—"

"I never did!"

"Did so. When you were little."

"I want it in the sewer, that's where! Flushed away. Not floating where strangers see it! Do you think that makes them assume this is a clean, well-kept, well-run place they'd like to own?"

"They could flush it themselves," Ben suggested.

"That isn't the point. I can't handle this any longer. I feel all alone. I'm not getting an ounce of cooperation from anyone. Not even enough to flush a toilet. So I want to know who did it. I'm asking you now—who was it?"

The children rolled their eyes at one another. Molly saw three sets of shoulders shrug, three heads shake from left to right and back.

"I once moved my bowels," Tony said. "Maybe that was it."

"Mom, this is *gross*," Joanna said. "What do you want us to do? Examine it to see what the person ate last, then trace it back? I mean, really!"

"You're the oldest," Molly said, near tears. "You should understand. I'm so tired."

"I understand that I'm not going to eat pizza if we keep talking about . . ."

"About shit," Tony said. "Turds. Crap."

"Tony!"

"Oh, I'm sorry." He leaped to his feet and waved his magic wand. "Ladies and gentlemen of the jury, we have here the case of the floating *thing*. Some evil person did not flush the toilet!"

"Failure to flush!" Ben grabbed his heart and fell sideways off the chair. "Aaaagh!"

"Are you troubled by the heartbreak of flushlessness?" Joanna asked. "Do you see—bowel movements—rise before your eyes? Do you become tense approaching an open toilet? Do you—"

"I give up!" Molly said.

"Don't you want to torture us? Make somebody confess? Are you going to let the criminal escape?" For the first time in a long while, Joanna smiled at her mother.

And Molly smiled back. "Yeah."

"That's what's wrong with America today," Thea said. "Soft on crime."

"Soft on shi—"

"Tony!"

"You know what?" Ben said, "I think the realtor did it!"

"Years ago, Gurdjieff, a mystic, believed inhaling the odor of cow dung restored good health." Thea's voice always became animated when reciting one of her facts. "However, he was probably wrong. Seems to have hastened some deaths, among them the writer Katherine Mansfield's. Speaking of dung, that is."

"You certainly know how to make conversation," Molly said.

"Yes." Thea smiled sweetly. "Don't I?"

Molly put the pizzas in the oven. Somehow, with Clay gone, meals degenerated into whatever was fast and easy and pleasing to the children. Molly blamed some of their new lax habits on the fact that the house was for sale. This way she avoided the smells of defrosting fish or pots boiling over, or oil splattering onto counters and walls, or food dropping onto the oven floor, burning and smoking.

Thea, staying with them through the move, read that the aroma of fresh baking was a sales plus. She had no skill in the kitchen, but every day she baked inedible but sweet-smelling cinnamon cookies. Beyond that, no cooking was done and the house was almost always ready for inspection.

"Know what?" Tony said. "This family is crazy."

"But okay," Molly said. "Basically okay."

But they weren't quite a family. They were missing the Father. In his place, Pizza. Nobody seemed to notice.

Clay turned the key in the door of the furnished efficiency apartment. He tiptoed in like an intruder, even though he'd lived here now for eight weeks. But the room repelled and depressed him for what it said about his current life. He was sure the architect had planned this unit as a residential straitjacket for rampant loneliness.

Its striped wallpaper made him think of cells or cages, and its miserly size didn't leave enough room for the hope of companionship. The television was larger than the kitchen.

He pulled back the louvered door that hid the half-size kitchen and peered inside the refrigerator. He had eaten, as usual, at the restaurant across from his office, but something still gnawed in him. The pickings, however, were worse than slim. There was a withered, pocked lemon, one-half a Tastykake Junior, its chocolate topping stale and rubbery, and three bottles of beer.

The cupboard had a jar of instant coffee, two English muffins with the consistency of hockey pucks and an open bag of soggy ruffle-edged potato chips.

He carried the chips and beer over to the TV and flipped through the magazine on top of it, checking the night's listings. It was hard to believe there was nothing that appealed to him when his standards were so low. All he wanted was noise. He pulled off his tie, unbuttoned his shirt and checked his watch. Too early to call Molly. She'd still be at work and she liked talking after dinner, when things calmed down for her. Damn time difference meant he had to stay up half the night, and he was exhausted. But if he fell asleep or forgot, she'd be furious.

Ah, but she was furious about everything nowadays. Angry and distant on the phone. Chilly and silent when he flew in on his twice-monthly visits. Belligerent and sulky when she was here, house-hunting with him.

He took off his shoes and turned on the set, forgetting that there was nothing he wanted to see. He sat down on the sofa bed, sighed heavily and began eating chips and drinking beer. Onscreen, a precocious little girl insulted her mother's date.

Clay tried to think about Molly, but shook his head. She was too confusing. He could only hope to ride this out, wait patiently and trust that the move would change things around, that being together as a family again would make all the difference.

He knew she was upset about leaving her friends. He understood. He was upset about leaving people he liked, too.

He knew she was upset about leaving the store and he felt sorry that things hadn't worked out for the best there.

But they simply hadn't, and he couldn't understand the depth or range of Molly's anger. It seemed too large to be held in her small frame.

It would be different, maybe understandable, if he'd sprung a fast one on her, if he'd taken her by surprise. If he'd appeared at the kitchen door one day and said he'd decided to devote the rest of his life to the study of fungi, or that he was going to become some guru's disciple.

But he was the same man he'd always been, doing what he'd always done. "Do you take this man?" the minister had asked, and Molly had said, "I do." It seemed that simple. He was still the man she'd taken, only she didn't seem to like that brand anymore.

He suddenly remembered a party game played years ago when he was in seventh or eighth grade. The point was for "It" to figure out the rules of the game. Everyone else knew them.

Clay despised the game, felt awkward and thick when he was the outsider, "It." But Nikki Elsworth, whose beautiful, heartless face filled his mind when he should have been learning Latin or what the Bill of Rights was, had purred and begged him. "It wouldn't be fun without you," she said.

After a long, sweaty time, Clay grasped at what he remembered. "I know," he said, "you can't have two words that start with the same letter in the same sentence."

Nikki closed her eyes with exasperation. "That's so stupid," she said. "That was the rule the last round. It doesn't even make *sense* now. You weren't paying attention!"

The good thing about growing up was that you didn't have to play anymore if you didn't want to, not if you didn't know the rules.

Until now. Because now, Molly had rewritten the rules and Clay felt no wiser or more quick-witted than he had three decades ago.

I'm the same man, he thought. I still get up in the morning and provide for them the best I can. What's so wrong about that?

He listened to himself, and nodded agreement. Because, he continued inwardly, if you have two people who love each other, who are together, a team, for years—then how can one of them decide to change the list of what's important?

He ate the last potato chip, then turned the bag sideways to try and get out the crumbs. His lap became covered with salt, and he stood up and brushed at his pants.

It wasn't that he didn't understand that women wanted more nowadays. He'd never stopped her from whatever she wanted. He helped bankroll the place, helped with the books, he . . .

But it just hadn't worked out in L.A. That was reality. Now, Clay's job was here, so what was she shouting about? And what were their options? Her store couldn't feed a family of five or pay the mortgage.

He stood, staring blindly at the TV set. "What did I do wrong?" he asked it. He crumpled the chips bag and drained the last of his beer. He was sure that logic and reason and history were on his side.

God, he remembered how Molly used to rhapsodize about his mother. She bought similar china and planted herbs in sunny windows and sewed table cloths and napkins and said she wanted that same clean stability, that organization and calm. Wanted what she'd missed growing up. A real family. Traditions. Pretty things as part of everyday life.

And she'd gotten it all, hadn't she? Everything she wanted. But suddenly it wasn't enough, wasn't right, wasn't fully "hers" in some way he couldn't understand.

"What the hell am I supposed to do differently?" he asked the jaillike walls. "Am I supposed to quit my job? Go on welfare? Would that make her happier? Christ, this is the way the system operates. We're not some kind of exception—we're the goddamn rule!"

He went for another beer. So okay. It was hard on her when they moved. But she'd always been adaptable. "No problem, as long as it's with you," she'd said when she moved from Philadelphia to Chicago after their marriage. And she became a whiz at relocation. She took over new places—she joined and organized and entertained and hammered herself securely into place. Clay was repeatedly dazzled and amazed. She wouldn't have problems anywhere, but when he'd reminded her of that, she had just about snarled at him.

He hadn't changed, but she certainly had. The damn store had grown to be a monster. It was the store that was at fault.

He brought a fresh beer back to the sofa bed. Maybe he'd open the bed up now, and if he fell asleep, then he fell asleep. What was the point of talking to her anyway, if she only complained? He pulled the bed open, then stopped to watch the screen.

An undersized boy squashed his father's girlfriend's hat. Was this the same show? Clay frowned. The kid looked different. Then he realized the last one had been about a girl and her mother's boyfriend.

What had happened to the sitcoms of yesteryear? Where were the families—the Cleavers, the Nelsons, the bunch of Bradys?

Now, none of the shows had complete families. How come?

Were families too sad? Were they as outdated as he was?

Who had changed all the rules, and what were the new ones?

He stacked the pillows, then he stretched out on the bed, loosened his shirt, pried the cap off the beer and tried not to look at the walls of his room.

15

"PUT ON MORE MAKEUP," THEA SAID. "YOU LOOK pale."

"Aren't you the woman who spent half her life telling me that beauty was an honest and clean face?"

Her mother grimaced. "You weren't going on television then."

"Hey, Mom, they aren't interested in me. They're coming in to Sinfully Good to look at the store." But even so, she put on more blusher and rechecked her mascara.

Ellen had shouted the news on the phone. "Listen, listen! Phyllis Foley of Channel Six wants to do a special on us. On recycled skills. She's calling us, 'Still in the Kitchen, but Oh, what a Change.' You like?"

"Sure."

"We couldn't buy better publicity."

"Great."

"Molly? You're so—subdued."

"Well, I'm the silent partner."

It was difficult for anyone else constantly to remember how Molly's perspective had changed. In three weeks, Sinfully Good would be something Molly had once loved. It was masochistic to savor the goodness of what one had to abandon.

"You look beautiful," Thea said.

"But not quite an honest face. Still, not bad for a dame of forty."

"Not for five more days. Think you can lie about your birthdate to your mother?"

The doorbell rang.

"Gotta run," Molly said. "Ellen's here." She kissed her mother. "We won't be that long, but be sure the kids do their homework. Tony always goofs off and Janna—"

Her mother waved her off. "Go become a media sensation."

Once she was in Ellen's car, her nervousness erupted. "Maybe this was a bad dress to wear. And I've put on weight—can't stop eating. And the camera makes you look—well, you don't have any problems there. You're so thin."

"That's the trade-off for grief," Ellen said. "Haven't you noticed how divorcees always lose weight? All it takes is the inability to swallow both what happened to you and your food."

"No, you look better than just that. In the last three months, you've blossomed." Ellen looked years younger than she had while John was living under the same roof.

"Must be the hairdo. I decided that John-the-bastard didn't deserve extended mourning. No more Greek widow look."

"I know you've been through hell," Molly said, "and that it isn't over, but you're so alive now and in charge of your life that I—I'm jealous, El."

"Oh, Molly, I don't have any other choice. You do. You can be happy *with* somebody else. You have a terrific marriage."

"It doesn't feel terrific anymore. Or real."

"Well, you've been living apart for three months, commuting. You're under enormous strain."

"I don't feel on the same team as Clay anymore. I feel like one of those toy ducks the kids used to drag around. Clay moves and pulls me on a long string. Quack, quack."

"You're living apart, you're—"

"Under strain. Yes."

"Listen," Ellen said, "I have to make a stop at the pharmacy. We have time, so don't panic. And Molly? Take some advice. Snap out of this. You aren't thinking straight. It's just that you've been—"

"Living apart. Under strain." She waved Ellen out of the car.

Molly tried to untangle her thoughts. Perhaps every move had done its own damage, shaking Molly and Clay and weakening their foundation. But this one had leveled whatever was left to a pile of loose sand.

She was nervous almost all the time. "You're horny, honey," Nan had said. "A little playing around between conjugal visits would help. Every other weekend's not enough for a red-blooded woman."

But Nan was wrong. Molly's jumpiness had to do with Clay's visits, not his absence. With each trip, her strain increased. It wasn't sex that was the missing ingredient, it was loving.

Too much was at a remove or altogether abandoned. Talk and attention and small gestures and casual touches—all were gone. They lived a continent apart and when they were together, none of the great space between them closed. Instead, harried, disrupted, interrupted, they battled politely using technical details as shields. When should the savings account be transferred? How does one move a bird? To whom should the fish and gerbils be given?

Don't forget—Drain the lawn mower—Buy snow shovels. . . .

Should we lower the asking price of this house? Is there a swim club near the new house? Was there—should we—don't forget to—can we—if . . .

Furthermore, while he was away, Clay suffered domestic amnesia and twice a month he returned home with messianic visions of How a Family Was Supposed to Be.

"This place is a zoo!" The prodigal paterfamilias had shouted when last seen. "Listen to that damn music!"

"Come on," Molly answered. "Kids' music always sounds horrible to parents. It's a rule of the universe." She realized with queasiness that she now automatically sided with her children. Her primary allegiance was clear.

"Why isn't there any organization around this place—any plans, any controls?" he stormed.

There were controls. There was organization. The thing was, Clay wasn't a part of them. In the months he'd lived back East, the family had proven resilient. Like injured protoplasm, it had smoothed over the missing piece and redefined itself. Ellen and her children were now a complete family. Molly and her children were now a complete family. Fathers left for a variety of reasons, but in the end, gone was gone.

But how was she to tell Clay that he had become a visiting relative?

During his last visit, two weeks earlier, Thea had zipped through the living room on her way outside for a walk. "Baked two batches of cinnamon cookies. Tossed them out. Know what I read? Folks on Tierra del Fuego killed and ate their women during hard winters. But they didn't eat their dogs because dogs were useful and caught otters."

"What the hell did that mean?" Clay said as the door shut behind her. "Where's she going? Where is everybody? I fly three thousand miles so I can be *home*. And when I get there, everybody leaves. The kids race off as if they can't stand the sight of me—"

"That's so unfair. It's a spring Saturday and they're at the beach. Why don't you go, too?"

"Because I flew here to be home, dammit, with my family!"

"Don't begrudge them their beach time. God knows, they won't be surfing in Valley Forge, Pennsylvania!"

It did not go well. It did not go well.

"Sometimes," Clay said at the airport that Sunday night, "sometimes I'm—relieved to get back on the plane."

Molly was kinder than he was. She didn't tell him she shared the feeling.

She drove home slowly. And slowly, with each mile of the freeway, the Idea entered her like a secret lover.

What was so dreadful about being single again?

After all, she'd had lots of practice in single parenting. Clay had traveled in each position he'd held. Clay had been out of town when Tony needed stitches in his skull, when Joanna said her first word, when Ben played a moth in his kindergarten play. Clay had been out of town when a dear friend died, when his own father had a heart attack a few years earlier.

Clay was always being notified in the shorthand of messages left with desk clerks or in late night phone conversations. He was seldom around for firsthand cries, terrors—*living through*.

She told Clay that Ben was all right before she told him he'd been hit by a car while riding his bike. Clay missed the scream of the car's brakes. Clay missed becoming paralyzed behind his front door, rubber legs unable to face a son crushed or dead in the street outside. Clay had only to tune in the late news on the phone and leap across all the emotions that had indelibly stained her life.

She'd been a single mother most of her marriage. It wasn't dreadful to think of making the title official.

Ellen returned from the pharmacy with a brown paper bag. "Any sane woman would buy a hundred cartons of tampons in her teens, right? I mean, why is it a surprise and emergency month after month?" She started the car, grinned at Molly, then lost her smile. "What's wrong? We won't be late, don't worry."

Molly said nothing.

"God, Moll, you aren't still on that junk—about being jealous of my so-called freedom?"

Molly sighed and slumped down.

"All right, then. Make your point. Split up. Let Great Harvest do you in. You don't even need a human third party. I'd love it. We could get drunk together and mouth off about lousy stinking sonofabitch men and hang out at bars for aging singles and hope our friends can find an unobnoxious divorced man to fix us up with. Doesn't that sound like fun? Listen, divorce isn't some fad you're missing out on, Molly!" They drove in silence until they reached the yellow Victorian. "Enough said, okay?"

"How much time before the camera crew gets here?"

"A few minutes. So collect yourself, clear your mind, and baby, we'll make you a star."

Molly willed herself away from thoughts of marriage and Clay. She walked up on the porch, took a deep breath, practiced a television smile and unlocked the front door.

And the building exploded into light and sound and all Molly heard was "Happy Birthday!" and laughter, and all she saw were smiling faces moving toward her and kissing her, taking her picture, embracing her. And at the head of them all, astoundingly, impossibly, Clay.

"How on earth—?" she began, but he held her and kissed her and said, "Happy Birthday, I love you," over and over and he was really there, no matter how.

Her children and Thea had been whisked there as well while Ellen dawdled at the pharmacy. The neighbor who'd transported them winked and grinned. Everyone Molly knew had been collected and presented as a gigantic birthday gift. Early L.A. friends and Great Harvest people and favorite suppliers and neighbors and PTA members and customers she treasured, including the Hoover sisters. Molly stood, mouth half open, shaking her head and crying.

She found Ellen and kissed her. "But," she asked, smiling, "does this mean I'm not going to be a TV star?"

"Next week, okay?" Ellen leaned close. "More important is

for you to know that Clay made this happen. Only Clay. Don't be a fool."

The night pulsed around her, too large to be absorbed. She laughed, she kissed, she ate caviar and piroshki and drank champagne. She tried to catch hold of the party, to imprint its sound and textures on her brain, especially the sight of Clay, beaming, so happy for her, so loving.

"Hello again," he said a second time. "I still love you. Happy Birthday." He kissed her and smiled with his special wicked-solemn-surprise-delight blend.

She was diverted by Art and Joanie Baum, smiling like twin cherubs, happy with Art's new job with Kellogg, even though for them, too, it meant another move. She hugged the PTA president whose baby gift had started the whole business. She hugged her landlord and his boyfriend and the Hoover sisters, but all the while she saw Clay, his blue eyes powerful and clear from across the room, just the way they'd been the first time she'd seen him.

She shelved the Idea.

It was easy to track Molly. She'd always glowed for Clay, emitted a visible light. He was repeatedly surprised to realize she didn't have flame-red hair and her skin wasn't much pinker than anyone else's. He could always find her beam in a crowd.

He'd felt it the first time he saw her. He'd been studying on a patch of grass outside the student union. It was late October and warm, except for sudden gusts of wintery wind. Clay put his book down and pulled a sweater over his head. When his face reemerged, he found himself returning the intent gaze of a girl who stood nearby, glowing.

She had russet hair and a burnt orange sweater and she stood in front of winter, blocking it with her heat. He felt his life crack neatly in two. There was all the past, as pale and predictable as the even stitches on his sweater. And then there was possibility: there was this girl.

He unlocked himself from his childhood, from a house in which a set of iron-firm rules maintained the peace. He had inherited a pastel view of life and had never seriously questioned it before.

But as quickly as she'd appeared, the girl left, running into a nearby building. He followed, but couldn't find her in any of the classrooms. He returned to the grassy patch outside, waiting two and a half hours in the increasingly chill winds, but she never reappeared.

For four months he watched for her without success. For four months, he remembered the power and clarity of that glance.

Then, in March of the following year, Clay dropped in to the local chapter of his undergraduate fraternity, and she was there.

It was a big, old house with a shabby living room that smelled of beer. Music blared something about a party doll and there, in the center of the party and the music, dancing and laughing like the subject of the song, was the girl.

He couldn't stop watching her. She seemed to move in a spotlight of her own making.

He was riveted to the spot, until the music changed to a slow ballad, to Sinatra's soft-edged voice urging him, or her, to change partners. Clay knew it was his obvious, indisputable cue.

She seemed surprised, seemed to recognize him as if she, too, remembered that autumn glance. They danced wonderfully well together, the way he'd known it would be.

"C.M.," she said, nodding toward a monogram on his shirt, at just about her eye level. "A monogram man, are you?"

His mother loved embroidery. Their house was like a gigantic sampler, and when she ran out of pillows and runners and tablecloths, she began on clothing. He hadn't thought about it until this moment. Now he knew it for a monstrous aberration, a curse on his chances with this girl.

"My mother," he said.

"I didn't think you looked the type for such fine stitchery. What's it stand for? Cotton Mather?"

He missed a beat, almost tripping her as he shifted awkwardly in confusion. "Why—him?" he managed.

"You look a little fierce. Very proper. Founding father's stock and all that."

His tongue became paralyzed, his throat sealed. He had finally found her, but she found him a repulsive, dried-up Puritan prune.

"Did I say something wrong?" She blushed, making her skin pinker than ever. "I'm sorry. I didn't mean it as an *insult*. Actually, your looks are very, oh, I'm really embarrassed. I, ah, listen, are you here alone?"

He nodded. "How about you?" he asked. Another stupid line, another inept gesture. Girls didn't come here alone on Saturday night.

"I have a date. I'm Molly Hawthorne, by the way."

"Clay Michaels," he said with a small bow of his head.

"I like weird first names."

"It was my mother's maiden—I keep mentioning her, don't I?"

She nodded. Sinatra continued in the background. She hummed along with the music.

"Look, I'm not like that at all. I never think about my mother, much less talk about her."

"You're doing it again," she said.

The music swelled and began to fade as Sinatra promised that he would never again change partners. Clay inhaled and swallowed carefully. Why couldn't he remember how to talk to a girl? This girl. This all-important one girl. "Hawthorne," he said. "As in Nathaniel?"

"Vaguely. A cousin a continent removed. My father was English, part of the family that didn't emigrate."

"Was?"

"Died in the war. I never knew him. My date's very drunk.

He was also drunk the last two times I was with him. Would you walk me back to my dorm?"

"Would you marry me?"

She turned even rosier and laughed. "Possibly, but I have to use the powder room first."

He stood in a feverish daze as she walked away. He had meant the proposal and what was more, he knew he was going to keep on meaning it. He would become a fanatic and stalk her if she wouldn't agree willingly.

He knew nothing about her except that she had beautiful coloring, a ready and generous laugh, was distantly related to Nathaniel Hawthorne and didn't like monograms or habitual drunks. That seemed enough on which to build a life.

That was March. In June, Clay received his M.B.A. and they married so that Molly could accompany him to Chicago, where his first job awaited. She left behind her scholarship and early plans and they both left behind parents who were apprehensive and unsure about their children's decision.

But it had held, and for Clay, Molly never lost that initial glow and warmth. Without her, he would freeze and die.

The lights in the store flicked off and on. "Cake time!" someone shouted.

It was Nan's finest hour. She strutted out from the back room holding an enormous sheet cake shaped like the United States. Forty white candles tracked their way, each on a chocolate footstep, over mountains, plains and rivers from a red-tiled Spanish house in Los Angeles to a tiny Tudor-style home in Pennsylvania. "Happy Birthday to the All-American Girl" it said, but "Girl" had a slash through it and "Woman" was written above it.

Molly began to cry.

"Make a wish, Mom," the boys shouted. "Make a wish before the candles melt."

God but she loved them. Let me feel this way about myself

and Clay and the children and life, she wished. Let me hold on to this for a while, please?

She blew the candles out, left to right, ending with the good-luck candle on her new house.

"I'll bet you wished for something good in the new place," Ben said.

"Well, no, I . . ." Molly became silent. She had forgotten all about the new place, had made no provisions for it, even in wishes.

"Time for presents!"

Molly loved every gift, the mufflers and long johns for her chilly new homestead, the T-shirt that said, "I am finally ripe," the books, and a very special album put together by her children and Ellen and Nan. It was called "Molly in Wonderland, or How to Become a Basket Case." It began with "Once upon a time, Molly Michaels woke up in a fixer-upper in Santa Monica," and moved through her days in Southern California, ending with blank pages for the photographs Nan's latest lover snapped tonight.

There were more gifts. Stationery with her new address, a subscription to *California* magazine—and then Clay's present, a tiny thimble-size basket tied with a bow. Inside was an antique ring sufficiently old-fashioned to start Molly crying again. The emerald set in a heart-shaped gold frame entwined with vines and delicate flowers spoke all the words she knew Clay wanted to say, and she listened.

Later, after all the boxes had been opened, the wrapping paper cleared away and the cake and ice cream eaten, Molly sat down. From the middle of the stairs she watched the night, memorizing its image and feel. She knew she was going to need it in the months ahead.

"Are you all right?" Clay was suddenly at her side.

"I'm—observing. Still a little in shock."

He took her hand. They both looked at the heart-shaped ring, both saw the claims it made on ties and sentiment.

"It's wonderful," Molly said softly. "It looks like, it feels like —I can't find the right words."

"I'll give you forty more years to find them," he said, and when she looked at him she saw the slyly romantic man with the gorgeous smile. Young Cotton Mather with a fine crazy streak. It had been such a long, long time ago when she'd been on that path and had seen a shock of black hair come through a white V-neck sweater. And then those eyes—so blue their color startled her across the browns and greens of the lawn. So long ago, that first glimpse of something heroic, manly, beautiful, capable of lasting. She could still feel the power and impact he had on her.

She looked at him now, her man, her love, and they were still young, naïve and optimistic. Then slowly she saw the transparent overlays fall across him, each clear sheet a year, a tense night, a season, with tiny etchings that fit beside his mouth, or under his chin, or between his eyes.

They were then, and now, and all in between. How did the time traveling fit together? How could she look out of eyes and a heart that felt unchanged and see that everything had changed? And what was she to make of it?

"Are you sure you feel all right?" Clay asked.

"I was just seeing you back then, back when we met, before we knew what a hell of a trip it all is."

He took her hand and they sat together. "You still look overwhelmed," he said after a while.

"I still am."

"By the party?"

"By that, too."

The next morning, she left her bed and went into the bathroom.

The woman in the mirror yawned. She looked puffy and unappealing. "You didn't ask for enough," she said.

Molly washed her hands.

"I mean with the birthday cake. With the wish."

Molly sighed.

"The point is," the woman said, "given forty candles, you're entitled to something big. Wanting happiness *forever* is big. Asking for twenty-five, thirty years is a good solid amount, but saying, 'Let me hold on to good feelings for a while,' is ridiculous! A while! How long is 'a while'?"

"A while" turned out to be three days and seven hours. For those three days and seven hours, Molly held on to the blissful feelings of that moment when she blew out her birthday candles. And then, on the fourth day, Molly in fact turned forty, Clay flew back East, the vet declared the stray cat pregnant, Janna threatened suicide if the pregnant cat couldn't move with them, the garbage disposal spewed out machine-made vomit and—by far the worst of all—when the children came home from school, they found their grandmother dazed and immobile after a fall.

Very late that night, after she returned from the hospital, Molly brushed her teeth and wondered how she would get through the next few weeks.

"I told you so," the mirror said.

"Hush."

"You can't complain. You got your wish. Ask for a while, get a while is what I say."

"Please stop. I'm already going under. I don't know how I'm supposed to move one dog, one pregnant cat, a bird, three kids and a mother in a full leg cast."

"And me," the middle-aged woman in the mirror said.

Molly looked at her and sighed deeply. "And you," she said. "Where do I fit you into all this, too?"

16

THE HOUSE HAD BECOME A GEOMETRIC NIGHTMARE. Rooms were cardboard warehouses. The upholstered furniture seemed puffy indulgences, lounging between cartons.

Thea and Molly sat in the kitchen. Only they and the animals were left. The children slept at friends'. Molly made tea, using provisions from her emergency rations—the last packed, first unpacked carton containing coffee, tea bags, spoons, knives and sugar. She waited for Clay to call.

A little card sat on the table. It was shaped like an English country cottage. "Happy Move!" the message read. Inside, perky words from Alice Michaels, who was again wont to express her delight with Clay's new title. Every week of her marriage, Molly received letters from Alice, and every week, Molly answered them. They exchanged nothing but pretty lies so that Alice would stay happy. The card on the table had arrived today, a sort of summary and underlining of the message. Clay was a success. His parents were satisfied. No questions asked.

The card was the only unpacked decorative item in the house.

"My," Thea said, "isn't it impressive how much you own?

Although I did see the packers wrap cleanser, a sponge and an empty jar today. I didn't know if I was supposed to say anything about such a stupid waste of time and paper, so I left the room. Does Great Harvest realize what it's paying them to do?"

Molly shrugged. Her attention drifted to the window and the night garden glowing in the moonlight. "I wonder how having winters again will be," she murmured. "I remember some nice things, like sitting in our warm kitchen, having tomato soup and cheese while it was all frosty outside."

"Aunt Sammy's menus."

"Who?"

"Uncle Sam's wife. Spoke on the radio through the Depression with cheap meal ideas from the government. Did you think I'd fished up another relative for you?" Thea shook her head. "You should have been born into royalty, the way you love family trees."

"I like your stories. I like my history. What's wrong with that?"

Thea looked vaguely troubled, but she said nothing.

"Remember how we'd talk?" Molly said. The stories were often prompted by and tailored to fit the seasons. On a bitter night in February, while the wind howled through the alleyway, Thea had told her about a winter in 1930. "The coal miners were organizing," she'd said, "sitting on the city hall steps. Mothers and babies, too. And the mayor had the firemen turn the hoses on them. It was nine degrees out and those mothers froze, trying to shield their children. The water turned to ice on their bodies. Lots of them died later of pneumonia. Happened in Allegheny, Pennsylvania, I think."

Molly sat, her eyes wide, shivering along with the miners.

Other stories were lighter. "Your grandparents went to their graves convinced that the automobile had ruined this country. Rotted out its morals. But the streets sure smelled better with less horse manure on them."

"Thirty-five years ago," she said on a warmer night, "we went out in the spring to change the world. We shouted, 'Come out of the kitchen,' and 'Never darn a sock,' and we thought, aha, now the struggle is complete. And look at you—loving the kitchen and, for all I know, finding socks to darn in private. So much for progress."

Molly loved to hear personal history as well, such as the litany of her mother's family, so sad and exotic with everyone except Thea dying young of flu and TB and diphtheria and two World Wars. "They've cured everything that killed them except war," Thea would say.

But best of all was hearing about Joseph Henry Hawthorne, that Byronesque, English-accented and doomed figure. The repetition and familiarity of the Joseph stories was a comfort, like expected footsteps coming home in the evening. Her father was an endless source of wonder, and the main project of her childhood was gathering detailed information about him.

She loved those long nights when soup simmered and memories percolated. "Wasn't it nice sitting and talking around that horrible old table," she said now.

"Horrible! It just goes to show you. That table was oak. Just not in style again yet. You wanted me to get formica like everybody else's mom. You wanted everything, including me, to be just like everything else. Ordinary."

"I did, didn't I? Only I never would have called it ordinary. It was—spectacular. To live the way I imagined my father lived in England. The way Clay's family lived, in fact."

The first time she'd met the Michaels was in May, a month before she married Clay. Molly had been almost speechless. Harriet Nelson, Joseph Henry Hawthorne's English family, all ideals and speculations were alive and well and living in New Hampshire in a house with an herb garden and a perennial border near the steps and silver napkin rings and recipes great-grandmothers had passed down. With pressed linens and protocol and knowledge of how to arrange flowers.

Molly tried to absorb Alice and Reed Michaels and the good

life, to brush the Thea lint off her shoulders. How lovely to sit down to meals with each major food group in serving dishes the way the home economics textbook had pictured. No more of Thea's slapdash arrangements.

Nobody talked about Korea or Africa, about unions or McCarthy or civil rights. Instead, Alice Clay Michaels softly asked each person about his day. Reed Michaels was a silent, wise and distinguished observer.

Eventually, Molly realized that neither the table nor the house was a haven. Instead, it was a stress-ridden testing ground where each family member had to pass around pleasantries like a dish of chocolates. Reed and Alice had laminated their vision of life and nothing true or painful was allowed to scratch its hard, bright surface.

"Well, I'm not that way anymore," Molly now said. She glanced at her watch. Clay had forgotten to call. It was too late to call the East now.

"Thank God for that. It was a long spell with you caught in fairy tales," Thea said.

"What do you mean, fairy tales? They were about my father, my family."

"I mean—I mean, oh, that TV show you loved—'Ozzie and Harriet.' That Alice and Reed Michaels, to be honest. People trapped in a fairy tale if ever I've seen it. That silly fifties view of men and women and families. Those fairy tales."

"I was thinking, Mom, it'd be nice if you taped your stories for the children."

"No."

"No?"

"I don't feel good telling those stories anymore. I'm tired of them."

"But—the history. Their history. It's so important that they—"

"Let them write their own histories. That's more fun."

Molly didn't know what to say or where the sharpness in her

mother's voice had come from. The fall, the broken leg and its aftermath had changed Thea. First, it meant her stay with Molly was extended. She still insisted she was moving back to Adams Wall, to the apartment on Steeple Street when she was "herself" again, but Molly had faint hope of seeing her mother as "herself" again.

The doctor hadn't been overly optimistic. The dizzy spell that caused the fall might have been a mild stroke, he told Molly. In any case, not a good sign.

She sighed and sipped cool tea now. The house moved many stages beyond silence, as if when free, household objects hummed, filling up the space around them with subtle sounds, but now, muffled and isolated in boxes, there could be no hum, no song, no breath. The house was dying. Molly shivered.

"Do you remember, Mom—" Molly stopped, seeing her mother's frown. Still, she wondered, what else was there to do in a house filled with sealed cartons, except remember?

She sipped more tea and tried not to look at the ominous, bulky shapes all around her.

17

"YOU WAITING FOR THE L.A. PLANE?" THE GIRL asked Clay.

He nodded. It was storming outside.

"Thank God! Thought I'd missed it." She pulled off a wide-brimmed rain hat and shook her pale blond hair.

"They're saying another half hour at least."

"Real shame about the weather, isn't it?" she asked.

"Yes." He saw visions of lightning blazing off the plane's wings, cracking them in two. He looked at her again, instead of the runway. She met his eye and smiled. She wasn't as young as he'd first thought. Just wide-eyed, tiny and curvy, reminding him of some film star of the fifties, a toy woman with saucer eyes. He smiled back at her. Then he looked again at the rain and thought of Molly, and his smile faded.

Last night, he'd called the L.A. Airport Motel, full of love and eager anticipation. So maybe he'd had a few drinks at his business dinner. You'd have thought he was phoning from skid row the way she carried on.

"You're drunk," she snapped. "You know I hate that."

"No," he protested. "Not drunk at *all*. Just had a—"

"We're all squashed into this crummy motel, I just said good-bye to every real friend I have in the world and you—you go out and drink and forget us and don't even call last night and don't understand a single thing I'm going through!"

"That isn't true, Molly, that—"

"That's absolutely true. Why aren't you here with me? Do you know how horrible it is to see that van pull away, to have your kids crying, saying good-bye to their friends, too? Do you know how empty we all feel inside? Why aren't you ever here, Clay?"

"I'm not going to deal with this. It would have been foolish to spend another fare so I could hold your hand. You're a very competent person, Molly."

"You always say my name when you think I'm crazy."

"Molly, that airfare we saved will cover a chair or paint a—"

"Don't patronize me! I know exactly what it costs to redo a house."

"Molly—"

"You're doing it again."

"You're exhausted and you've had a rough spring." But so had he, so had he. "Tomorrow we can talk with no interruptions and no timer. Tomorrow, Moll—tomorrow, we'll be together for keeps."

He'd spent the afternoon planting petunias around the path to the door. He'd cut the lawn and tried to make the empty new house as inviting as possible. "And the motel isn't bad," he said. Good or bad, it accepted pets and they had very few alternatives until the van arrived the following week.

The tiny blonde said something. He asked her to repeat it.

"I said I'm here to pick up a doctor. He's going to speak at Jefferson Hospital. I'm in the public information department there. I get to pick up people at planes."

"He's flying three thousand miles to give a lecture?" Clay was rusty at this. He hadn't talked to a strange woman who had nothing to do with business or his social circle for years. "He must be really special."

"Oh, he is. Gustave Malim. Have you heard of him?"

She had an engaging way of tilting her head while she looked up at him. He wondered if she had frequent neckaches. Molly wasn't tall, but this woman was tiny. Probably shorter than Tony and Ben without her shoes. He could lift her with one arm. She seemed—easy, somehow. "What's his field?" he asked.

"Stress. Stress is really hot these days, you know?"

"Do I ever. Does he have a cure? I'll stop him when he gets off the plane."

She laughed much more appreciatively than the line warranted. "What do you do that causes such stress?" she asked, blue eyes wide with apparent interest.

"I'm with Great Harvest. The food people. In charge of the local division. To be exact, Senior Vice-President for the Mother Lancaster Division." He liked the way it sounded, solid and significant and a fine thing to be. He liked the way suffering from stress sounded as well. Both suggested heavy responsibilities. Status.

She looked impressed.

He'd forgotten how much fun this was.

"I'm sorry," she said, "I should have introduced myself. I'm Didi Simons and you're—?"

"Clay Michaels."

She put out her tiny hand and kept it in his for a few beats longer than a handshake. "Glad to meet you. You know, before I'd see a doctor about that stress, I'd try other approaches."

"Such as?" He could feel himself ease into something familiar yet foreign to him.

"Oh, such as cold martinis in a dark place with soft music. A little grass, maybe. Massages—you know. Relaxing, easy things."

You can do it if you want to, he heard whispered from inside himself. The angry voice on the phone last night wasn't the only voice on earth.

He knew there were lots of Didi Simons. One of the world's few unendangered species. Whenever he was ready, he could put his hand in the stream and lift one out. It felt good knowing that.

She smiled at him again.

His stress was already easing, turning into a pleasant, heavy tension and a sense of anticipation.

"There's a pretty fair dark bar close to this gate," she said. "And we still have lots of waiting to do."

He nodded. Then he burst out laughing.

Her smile wobbled and turned sour. "What's so funny?"

"I am. I'm sorry to laugh, but I thought, for a minute, that I could drink with you, that I was—I forgot I wasn't . . ." He didn't even want to think the word "free."

"I want to be straight with you. I'm waiting for my wife, my daughter, my twin sons, my mother-in-law and her leg cast, my dog, my pregnant cat and my bird. All of them are going to get off that plane angry with me for forcing the trip and the move on them. I'm not exactly—at large."

"No wonder you suffer from stress," she said. "Well, how about it? The dark place is still there and we still have time to kill. And, ah, in case they call the plane and I forget later, here's my card." She penned in her home number. "For whenever you have time and need some attention."

"Because of the stress?" he asked.

Didi smiled and nodded. "Yours and mine."

Molly took another deep breath. Her heart beat a tom-tom of anxiety. "I'll get lost," she told Clay again. "I thought if I could just get through the flight, it'd be easy on this side. But now this! I don't want to drive anywhere. I'll get lost."

"Follow my car. You'll see. It's easy. This isn't L.A."

"You smell like you've been drinking again," she said. "It's only afternoon. What's happening to you?"

"For God's sake! Your plane was late, I met a—I bumped into somebody and we had a drink. What's with you lately? You sound like Carry Nation."

So much for warm welcoming committees, she thought. The man was becoming repulsive, drunk all the time. She sneezed.

"Where's your raincoat? Where the hell is everybody's raincoat?" Clay demanded.

"In the moving van."

"How could you not realize—"

"How? I forgot, that's how! I forgot it rains any old time in the East. You could have reminded me. You've been the one living here. Anyway, you said we were going to rent a van, not a little car. You said a *van*—we'd all fit in a van!"

"I was wrong. The only thing they had were campers and I'm not paying two hundred dollars for a ride to the motel. Molly, what's wrong with you, standing out here in the rain, arguing. You're so—"

"So wet!"

"And—and—"

"At least I'm not drunk! You smell like you've been—"

His shoulders slumped. He shook his head. "Let's get moving," he said.

"That's all I ever do," she snapped.

They stood in the downpour dividing personnel and livestock. Clay got the boys, the dog and almost all the luggage. Molly got Joanna, Thea, the leg cast, the bird in its covered box and the cat in her carryall.

Molly cautiously started her rental car and followed Clay into the flow of traffic. "And this," she said, her jaw tight with tension, "is why they call people like me a trailing spouse."

"Sounds like ground cover," Thea said from the back seat.

"It is. Like dirt."

"You're really getting hard, you know, Mom?" Joanna's voice

was smug and offensive. "All you do is complain, and you're really mean to Daddy."

Molly kept silent. No need to sully the very start of a new life with a mother-daughter free-for-all. There would be world enough and time for lots and lots of fights.

"Why'd you do that?" Joanna said after Molly changed lanes. "Daddy's over there, on the right."

"Damn," Molly said. "I forgot. His new car's maroon, not blue. Damn." She could barely see anything with the rain pouring down in a fierce blur.

"When can we see the new house?" Joanna asked for the fifth time in the last hour.

"Tonight. I told you. After the animals are fed and stashed at the motel."

"Meeowl!"

"Dumples is soooo sad," Joanna said. "She won't see her new house for sooo long."

The baby-girl voice. As obnoxious as the smug voice. Molly tried to ignore it while she was on this alien expressway. She couldn't remember the name of the exit Clay had specified. Her mind squeezed in panic. What if they became separated? How would she ever in her life find him again?

"Dumple's soooo chubby with sooo many itty-bitty babies in there that—"

God that voice was disgusting. But not to think about it now. Just follow the maroon car. Maroon, right? Not blue. That was L.A. New company car's maroon. Is that it pulling over to the right? For a special reason? Is that a ramp coming up? What the hell did he say to watch for?

"Joanna, do you remember the exit Daddy said?"

"Uh-uh, nuffin' but how soft Dumple's fur is."

"Mom? Do you remember?" But Thea was dozing.

"Poor Dumple-Wumple, fwying all awone in that big awful pwane. Was you lonely? Here, baby—"

Molly pulled into the right lane, peering above the car in

front of her. Damn him for letting someone cut in. Was his blinker on? Was it only her imagination? Goddamn windshield wipers were so bad she was blind every time they made their sweep.

"Ittle baby, you wanna stwetch your ittle—"

"Joanna, cut the baby talk! Could you just—*eeeeeeaagh!*"

A round missile leaped wildly from nowhere onto Molly's lap. She screamed and swerved the car.

"Oh! Jesus! Oh, my *God!* I could have killed us all! Oh, my *God!*"

"I'm *sorry.*" Joanna slumped way down in her bucket seat. "She seemed cooped up and unhappy."

"She's a cat! Cats are allowed to be unhappy now and then and—oh, God, Daddy's getting off. I have to—"

Dumpling dug her nails into Molly's legs.

"Don't scream!" Joanna said. "I'll get her off you." She leaned over, obstructing Molly's vision.

"Let her alone until I can see where—just be quiet—watch Daddy, tell me where he's going, I—"

"I was only trying to help." Joanna lapsed into a miffed, open-eyed coma.

"I'll watch, I'll watch," Thea said from the back seat. She meant well, but Molly, with her younger, clearer vision could barely see. The renta-wipers slid over the renta-windshield, switching vision on and off. Clay's car twinkled in and out of sight like the star it contained.

Neither a follower nor a wifey be, she chanted in her head. Oh boy, this is it. I am nothing. His rainy-day shadow. With a cat clawing my thighs. This is it. As low as I can sink.

But she was wrong. Her skirt, at least, was able to sink lower, and it did. She felt it become heavy and warm and clingy. And very, very wet.

"Oh, Dumpling," she wailed. The cat stalked off like a baked potato with legs, leaving behind a three-thousand-mile accumulation of cat urine.

"Mom!" Joanna came out of her trance to pet the cat who now snuggled on her lap. "You're covered with—"

"Yes," Molly said.

"It stinks."

"Yes. I'd like to make it clear that the cat, not I, created the problem. But on the other hand, you have to be kind about pregnancies. I remember when I was having the twins. Sometimes even a good laugh would result in—*what the hell am I saying*? I'm having a nervous breakdown!"

"Mother, what are you going to do about—it?" Joanna's voice was now mature and censorious.

"I was wondering myself. How can I even move, anyway? If I stop watching Daddy, we'll never find him again."

The motel finally appeared, its sign a white blur in the rain. Molly carefully pulled up next to Clay's car. He was already on the curb with his share of the luggage and menagerie. He came to her door, confused by her immobility.

"Give a sniff," Joanna told him. "You'll figure it out."

Clay looked in through the window. Molly's lap had an enormous dark circle that had turned her skirt's bluebells green.

"An amazing amount seems to stay there, like a pond," Thea said, leaning over. "I guess they really are bucket seats, aren't they?"

Molly said nothing. Instead, she slipped off her shoes and stepped out into the rain in her nylons. She let the excess urine run into the puddles on the parking lot and then she held out her skirt, hoping nature would wash out most of the stench. The children, the pets and Thea all went into the motel, but Clay stayed, watching her.

"Why didn't you let her out while we were renting cars?" he asked.

Molly turned her back to him.

"One favor, okay?" His voice was angry and loud in the rain. "Don't overdramatize this the way you do. No talk about bad starts or omens, okay? Let go of it." He turned and went into the motel.

For a while she stood in her puddle, then she retrieved her shoes, muttering all the while. Oh baby, he could have said. What a rotten way to start a new life. Oh darling, what a sterling wife you are, following me through rain and confusion, going wherever I plunk you. Oh love, you don't deserve to be peed on. Dumped on.

Her shoes squished as she walked into the building. She carried the bird's box and hoped she didn't smell as fearsome as she suspected. Through dripping hair she spotted the bell captain and tried to pass him the bird box. He refused it, maintaining his dignity and holding his ground until he had checked her credentials.

She had *bag lady* written all over her.

"You are . . . ?" His nostrils flared with disdain.

She held the bird box out again. The bird, upset and possibly damp, made feeble squawks from inside.

"Madam . . . ?" The bellman remained firm.

"Don't you recognize me?" She stamped one wet shoe. It made a sick and slurpy sound.

He faltered.

She tossed her head. A strand of hair stuck to the middle of her forehead. She stamped her foot again and remembered Dr. K. of Nassau. Assertive! she instructed herself. Assertive!

"My good man," she said, imitating every haughty dowager in every old movie she'd ever seen. "My good man!"

It worked. He'd seen the same movies. He became four inches shorter.

"I am Molly Hawthorne Michaels, the Trailing Spouse!"

While he worked that through his mind, figuring out if it was a new act or a disease, she leaned near to him. "So take my goddamn bird!" she said.

He took it.

18

MOLLY PUT SIX PAPERWEIGHTS ON THE DINING ROOM table. They felt sticky in the August heat. She had cross-filed the air-conditioning man in her empty new Rolodex and had called him twice, once under "A" for air conditioning and again under "V" for Varsi, Louis. But neither call worked. "No time for new accounts, lady," he said.

She stared at the paperweights. On second thought, it was stupid to put them out on shelves she still had to refinish. She would only have to take them off again, so she returned them to their crumpled newspaper nests in the carton, then stacked the carton with the others in the corner of the dining room.

After two months, there were still cartons everywhere. They sat in half-painted rooms, rooms with painted walls but no window coverings, rooms that had been scraped clean and abandoned and rooms where long rolls of wallpaper lay in the corners. Molly wasn't sure why it was so. This had never happened before.

But she couldn't make her brain or muscles work properly anymore. She thought she should find a physician to identify her problem, but she left the search for another, more energetic day.

On cool mornings, she wrote long lists of things she meant to do, but then her hands grew heavy and her eyelids, too, and she felt on the verge of tears or, if not that, then exhausted and weak. There were too many chores, too many children, too many days.

They had been sucked into a gaping vacuum of a summer. Molly tried to give it meaning. Sweating and surly, she, the children and Thea circled Society Hill in a buggy, did the historic homes of Fairmount Park, saw the Liberty Bell and Independence Hall, drove to Lancaster to see the Amish folk, toured the Art Museum, watched the slide show of Philadelphia Past and Present, searched for more and more obscure landmarks—and still the summer continued, as if someone were adding leaves to the back of the calendar as Molly ripped off the front ones.

Clay, of course, *Worked* and Was Too Busy to help fill the void.

In mid-July, Molly began taking naps. First fitfully, then as a planned part of her day, and then as its heart. Sometimes the weight of unattended chores beat in her heart and she lay wide-eyed on the bed in the attic guest room. More often, she listened to old songs on her favorite radio station and, remembering better summers, fell into a thick midday sleep.

Now, Molly stood in the dining room yawning. Her mind roamed the house which bulged with packed and unpacked accumulations, all of which cried for her attention.

Inside those cartons. Inside those cabinets.

Silver candlesticks and cake servers. Copper cooking pots and the firewood caldron. Baskets of dried lavender and Queen Anne's lace.

She paced up and down the room, slowly touching, cataloging the endless objects Clay's labors had brought into her life.

China for the hutch, pottery for the kitchen, crystal wine-glasses and pressed linen tablecloths. Stacks of towels and rows of record albums and liqueurs and cameras and hair blowers and the set of Shakespeare and photo albums, mixing bowls, canned fruit, stamp collections, bath salts, throw pillows, cachepots, paintings and porch furniture. So many things to be protected, preserved, cleaned, inventoried, unpacked, packed up again.

Make it go away, she said silently.

Privileged bitch, she answered herself. Most of the world's starving while you whine about caring for your excesses.

She yawned again. She'd take care of it, of everything, another time. No rush, anyway. And it was too hot. She'd go upstairs instead, to the dormered room at the top of the house. It would be hot there, too, but private. She could listen to the radio, nap, rest before she faced the Burchards that evening. Her whole body pulled toward the staircase, the music at the top of the house.

"You ready then? I'll tell the kids." Thea stood by the stairs. "For the zoo," Thea prompted. "You said you'd—"

"I forgot. I'm sorry, and now it's too late, so—"

"It's eleven A.M., Molly!" Thea moved closer, examining her face. "What's going on with you?"

"Nothing. I—I misread the clock, that's all. I'll wash up and take them." Make it go away, she heard herself say as she dragged herself up the stairs. Thea stood at the bottom of the staircase, looking at her.

Make it all go away.

"I know you don't like her," Clay said.

"Them. I can't stand them."

"That still doesn't justify forgetting about tonight and sleeping until I got home."

"I didn't mean to. I was tired. I had to drag around the zoo today."

"The kids said you were home by two."

Molly looked out the car window into the August twilight.

"All right, no matter. Things will ease up soon. The kids'll be in school next month. Meanwhile, tonight, please remember that Bill is important."

"It isn't as if he's your boss. All he did was screw up Mother Lancaster and be promoted out. And the air conditioning in this car stinks."

"He's the East Coast Division Liaison, whatever that means." Clay ignored her mood as best he could. He slowed the car and peered out the window. "Look for a place called 'Gray Arch,' " he added. "That's all they said."

She wanted to fight. He was driving her mad lately with his nonviolent approach to domesticity. "What kind of stupid name is Gray Arch?" she demanded. "It sounds like a foot disease."

Clay sighed.

"People who name their houses are pretentious. Pompous would-be English gentry."

"There it is."

There was a stone fence around the front of the property and over a plank gate, a gray arch.

"Imaginative," Molly grumbled. "Why didn't they name it Plank Gate? Or Stone Fence? Or Ostentation?"

"We're late. No time for your charming banter." He turned off the ignition. "Please, for me, for yourself, for our mortgage payments, control your observations on life and politics tonight."

"Sure. I'll just listen to Eleanora of Gray Arch sneer at *those* people."

"She's trying to be nice, and her invitation is the first we've gotten since we moved here."

They walked up the carefully landscaped path. "I cannot tell you how happy it makes me to realize that this evening, these people, equal the sum total of our social life." Molly squeezed

the words out of a dazzling, consummate corporate wife class-
A smile which she widened as the door opened.

The Burchards' home was spacious and grand with leaded
windows, slate floors and high ceilings. But this architectural
largess contained a bland filling of nondescript antiques, all
faded to the color of old money.

Most of the evening, Molly did her Helen Keller-as-wife imitation. Blind and deaf women do not irritate East Coast Division Liaisons. She allowed herself smiles and soft noises, rather
like those heard in an aviary. Cheeps complimenting Eleanora's
culinary skills, although the dinner, like the upholstery, was
done in tones of gray. Clucks over the heat wave, the humidity,
the poor season the Phillies were having and coos for the infi-
nite wonders of the Greater Philadelphia area that she and the
children had explored.

"Good to hear you're instilling respect for history in the children," Bill said. "Too many families falling apart today. No
sense of tradition, of belonging. Losing values. What do you
think, Molly?"

Molly smiled. She didn't think. She behaved.

"What's happening to the good old values?" Eleanora asked.

Bill chewed and swallowed some beef. "You know, I spent all
last weekend canvassing the neighborhood, trying to get dona-
tions to save the old guardhouse down the pike. Didn't recognize half the faces and frankly, I don't hope to get to know
them. They didn't give a damn—excuse the French, Molly.
None of them cared. I mean it's their own neighborhood, it's
our heritage!" His face flushed with resentment, patriotism or
indigestion.

"Did you say they were new people?" The words popped out
of Molly's mouth without warning. She felt Clay's sharp glance.

Bill nodded and attacked his gray-green beans.

"Don't you think that might be it?" What the hell, she was
into it. Anyway, she wasn't talking politics and she wasn't agi-
tating. She was bringing the light to these handicapped folk.

"Don't you think that people who move around a great deal have problems investing themselves in any specific area?"

"How's that?" Eleanora frowned.

"It'll be hard, for example, for my children to be nostalgic for any special town or to care much about what's preserved in an area they barely know. We love what we know. But they're becoming portable people with no real ties, don't you see?"

Clay cleared his throat. The Burchards glanced at each other.

"I'm certainly not questioning the system," Molly said. "My goodness, no! Wouldn't do that. Just saying how it is."

"Are you Irish, Molly?" Bill smiled.

She stared at him.

"I see some temper there, a little Irish, and that red hair." He smiled paternally. "Heard about a little outburst in Nassau, too, didn't I?" He chuckled. "Must be the Irish in you."

"Tell me," Eleanora said, "are you interested in civic work?"

"Well, I just signed up to volunteer at the Women's Center. Once the kids are in school, I can—it's really . . ." Eleanora stopped midfeed, holding aloft her fork. "They'll train me to do crisis counseling," Molly said, starting again. Eleanora didn't move. "Is something wrong?" Molly asked.

"Oh! Oh, no. Of course not. Everyone to her own taste. I was going to suggest some groups I belong to, but of course, if you prefer—but honestly, don't you find the types there unsettling? I mean, frankly, all those deviates."

"Deviates? What do you—"

"Molly probably doesn't know about them yet," Bill said. "Nice little thing like Molly wouldn't be involved if she knew."

"And how do you feel about being away from Mother Lancaster?" Clay asked Bill abruptly, flashing chilly eyes at his wife.

You were supposed to become involved, to be a Great Harvest presence in your community. But only on behalf of the establishment, the church, the country club, charities that fought socially acceptable diseases, the PTA of course. It was less than fine to associate your name and your husband's name and therefore the company's name with politicians or causes wishing to change the status quo, or groups that ministered to the unattractive, or who actively fought current problems such as pollution or nuclear proliferation.

Molly didn't know if she had the energy to fight off the pressure Clay would now apply against the Women's Center. Who cared, anyway? Why bother. Just give in.

"Miss her, of course," Bill said of dear Mother Lancaster. "But the new job's a real challenge. First challenge is to find out what the title means."

Molly and Clay knew what it meant. It meant stay on the sidelines where you can't do any more damage to the firm.

Eleanora produced a pink mousse that looked made of polyester and dentifrice. Molly let the talk, all lies and irrelevancies, flow around her.

The mousse entered her system, turned it wobbly, dense and pink. She felt it ooze through her intestinal walls and pulse outward, absorbing her until she melted into a pink, soft puddle and soaked into the timid gray-green petit point chair. Going, going, gone. Down and dissolved. And nobody noticed.

Bill twinkled his smile in her direction.

Molly made more aviary sounds.

After four exhausting hours, everyone was ready for the last round of lies, the repeated exclamations about what splendid food, time, company, fun they'd had. About how they yearned to repeat the evening soon, very soon, this time at Molly's.

"That wasn't so bad," Clay said, once back in their car. He used his new mild voice.

"How bad is 'so bad'?" she said. Then she sighed. She didn't want to fight anymore. She didn't feel close enough to Clay Michaels, who had once loved her but who now was part of some great and hostile conspiracy. Fighting was contact. Fighting was optimistic.

Clay didn't notice her silence. All he ever thought about anymore was his uneasy tenure at Mother L. Or so she supposed. He told her almost nothing. It had been easier when they were literally a continent apart rather than now, when they were just as remote while sharing the same room, or car. Or bed.

Tonight would be no different. She was tired and draggy all day, but once in the king-size bed, her system snapped to red alert and stayed that way for hours. She watched her digital clock, listened to its soft dropping noises as the numbers changed.

"We'll have to have the Burchards over soon," Clay said.

Molly flushed with resentment and considered menus for them.

Ham hocks. Chitlins.

Huevos Rancheros.

Knishes. Stuffed derma.

She depressed herself with her tiny arena, her timid, kitchen-based revenge.

19

MOLLY HAD EXPECTED TO WAVE FLAGS WHEN school started, to push her children out the door. Instead, she drove them the first day, and drove slowly, filled with ambivalence.

"You pamper them," Clay said as she left that morning. "Why drive? There are buses. My mother—"

But what did he know? What did he care? His mother had never left her hometown, nor had he as a child.

He knew it was their first day in a new school. He could have acknowledged their fears and tried to ease them as she was doing. But instead, he made cardboard pronouncements about the fun of making new friends.

Something terrible was happening to him. What was once molten in the man had cooled, and he seemed imprisoned in stone. Even if Molly could find a way to chip through to the core, she was afraid she'd find only an impression of what he had been, like a fossil.

One of the children sighed, loudly. Molly admitted to herself that she was going to miss them. They had given a rough shape to the summer days. What now would?

They had been her companions. Who now would be?

She was lonely. As lonely as she had ever been in her life, and unable to find the energy and spirit to seek out potential friends and cultivate them. She wished, not for the first time, that there was an accepted port of entry for transferred wives. The children had school. Clay had his work. Only Molly had to remake her world and reestablish herself every time.

"We're here," Tony said with no joy.

Molly refused to betray her children with jolly lies the way their father had. "You're probably going to have a rotten day and feel uncomfortable, but grit your teeth and get through it, okay? It gets better. I'll be here at three."

Tony and Ben began their trek to the large brick middle school. They moved cautiously between clusters of children. Alone, alone, they moved among the cliques. Molly thought suddenly of a film she'd seen where orphaned seals crawled around mass colonies of mothers, looking to be adopted. Eventually, friendless, without sustenance, they died.

"Look at that," Joanna said. Her school started later. "Nobody's wearing man-tailored shirts."

Except Tony and Ben.

Molly flushed with empathic pain. There had been no way to intuit the local laws of adolescent garb. Now, her sons were guilty of Obviously Not Belonging, of Standing Out, the worst of thirteen-year-olds' nightmares.

Molly didn't fight her children's lust for conformity. Her kids had too many battles to fight every time they were uprooted to add clothing to the list.

Thea had been less generous on that point. The crucial issue had been the woolly knee socks she insisted upon. In those days, everyone else wore anklets and had chapped legs, both of which Molly envied.

Whenever possible, she had rolled down her socks, hoping a quick glance would let them pass for anklets. It didn't. They passed for deformities, ankle-high goiters. But from such small offenses comes the basis of child-rearing. From woolly knee socks before they were in fashion came, "I'll never do that to my children."

"I'll be late, Mom," Joanna said. "Bet I'm wearing the wrong thing, too." She fiddled with a charm on a chain she'd bought at the end of summer.

Tony and Ben reached the building, but no one was going inside yet. They'd run the gauntlet and now what? Not a single soul turned to say a kind word in their direction.

They seemed tiny and desolate against the enormous brick wall, standing at loose ends, waiting for the bell to signal the next round.

Molly wanted to run to them, grab one under each arm and carry them to the safe place mothers should provide, the place she had once believed in.

Kids adapt, Molly reminded herself. The nursery schools had said so. Clay had said so. School counselors coast to coast had said so.

Nobody ever questioned what adaptation meant. Nobody ever checked to see where the scar tissue formed.

"I don't want to be late the first day," Joanna said.

Molly moved on, leaving her sons in limbo.

20

He did not want to call home. Did not want to tell Molly he had to work late again. Did not want to hear her tight, "Oh. Fine," the tension in her voice negating her words.

But Greg Patrick's wife had gone into labor and all Greg's figures and tables were incomplete. Clay was going to have to finish them, because otherwise, everybody else would be held up.

And Tom Hummel had a herniated disk, so his group was also behind, and Accounting had just called to say the computers were down, and Clay still had a goddamn company to run no matter how much or how fast Campiglia wanted this report.

Clay hated preparing the report even while he admitted its importance and took pride in the thorough and thoughtful job he was doing on it. But it was massive in scope, the bible of Mother Lancaster, equaled only by encyclopedias for the research and committee work it necessitated.

It had taken Clay three months to get a firm hold on the place, to begin evaluating the ambiguous programs Bill Burchard had instituted and to untangle some of the man's more innovative methods of record-keeping. And most tricky of all, to stay politically inoffensive while doing so.

It was taking Clay and his department heads three more months to write the body of the report, explaining the interactions of divisions and philosophies, practices and profitability of each one. There were still projections for the future and suggested changes to write after this. It was eating up his nights, his life.

Clay put his hand on the phone and felt his lunch flame upward. "Oh. Fine," she would say woodenly.

But maybe not. School had started two weeks earlier and the weather was cooling down. Maybe she'd begin to find some interests of her own, some friends. She'd said something about a PTA meeting this morning. Maybe now she'd go out, stop sleeping so much, stop hiding in that room.

God, it was like a Victorian melodrama, like a goddamn version of *Wuthering Heights*. Only Molly wasn't the madwoman in the attic, she was the sadwoman in the attic.

It wasn't funny, and he couldn't handle it. He had to work every day and too many nights. When he had been young, he could handle a schedule like that. Not now. And now, he certainly couldn't handle anything else.

Besides, was he supposed to support all of them not only financially but emotionally as well? Where was the man who could struggle all day with a job that felt as substantial as gelatin and then come home and juggle his family until he shook them into smiles.

He was a man, not a magician, and what was his fair share anyway?

His secretary buzzed. "A Mr. Art Baum? He says you know him."

Clay felt as if someone had just loosened tight bindings. He relaxed into the call, listening to news of Kellogg's, where Art seemed very happy, and giving back, discreetly—but not unbearably so—news of Great Harvest and Mother Lancaster. It was the most comfortable conversation Clay had had since he last talked to Art.

"And Molly?" Art asked. "How's she doing?"

"Ah, she's still—unsettled."

"Bad pun, but listen, my man. It takes them time. I just read a study that said it takes eighteen months to adjust."

"Eighteen months! That's longer than we've lived some places."

"Well, the point is, don't expect miracles overnight. We've been here since March and Joanie still bitches about the lousy markets and the weather and cries for her friends in L.A."

Yes, but does she curl up into a ball and listen to old music and sleep all day? Does your house have cartons all over and not one livable room? But Clay said none of that because he loved Molly profoundly and wanted to protect her and because he'd always been taught to keep bad news to himself. If you kept it to yourself, it became less bad and even less real.

"Kiss her for me," Art said.

And Clay sent regard to all the Baums. Then he sat motionless, his smile fading, because he still had to call Molly about tonight. Finally, he forced himself to dial.

"Molly?" he began, "about tonight. I—"

"I was just going to call you," she said. "About what I should bring."

"Tonight? Molly? What do you mean?"

"Does Peter want us to bring dessert or anything?"

Peter. Tonight. A belated click. "Just ourselves," Clay said. "Nothing else."

"Should I call to check? Do you have their number?"

"No, it's fine. Really."

"Clay? Why did you call?"

"I, ah, I was going to remind you about tonight."

"Did you think I'd forget? I'm really excited about seeing somebody I know again! God, after that stupid meeting today, I—"

"The PTA?"

"Awful. A handful of people, and—I don't want to sound hard, but they were—leftovers, Clay. You know what I mean? Like me, I guess. Anyway, I offered to bake cupcakes and went home." Clay heard her sigh heavily and then, making him believe that perhaps Art Baum was right, that perhaps he hadn't given Molly even the bare minimum of time to adjust, had been unfair, he heard Molly pull her spirits back up. "But there's tonight and old friends, so who needs the PTA!"

She sounded alive. She sounded like Molly.

When Clay hung up, he was so cheered by the resurrection of his wife, he wasn't even concerned with being unable to work on the report that night, with being still one day further behind.

Clay whistled while he changed from his suit into a sports jacket and slacks.

"Do you think my dress is all right?" Molly asked.

"You look fine. It's just a barbecue. Anything's fine."

"I'm putting on weight. This is tight. Are you sure I look all right?"

"What are you so worried about? These are old friends. Don't be so nervous."

She was, though. Years and years had gone by during which they'd lost touch with Peter and Rosemary. However, Molly still had clear memories going all the way back to college when they were so young that all the fifties clichés seemed inspired and sophisticated. Chianti bottles with candle drippings, the spaghetti sauce Peter was so proud of and Rosemary's new bride's delight in his talents.

Molly changed into tailored slacks and a summery cotton-knit top. It was hot for September and besides, the dress was tight at the waist. She wondered how Rosemary, who'd always tended to roundness, would look after all these years.

"You know," Molly said in the car, "I always liked Rosemary. I'm sorry we lost touch."

"Then I'm doubly glad I bumped into Peter. Now you can find touch, or whatever the opposite is."

"I wonder if I'll even recognize her after twenty years. And how many children did they finally have? I wonder if she still paints. She was so talented." Molly felt warmed. The friendship would surely reestablish itself, and having a friend would make all the difference in her life.

Clay parked in the driveway of a two-story house on a pleasant, treelined street. A tan sports car was already in the drive.

"Bet that belongs to Mitchell Miller," Clay said. "Peter said he was going to invite him. Mitch always loved cars."

Molly smiled, looking forward to an evening for the first time since they'd moved.

A young woman opened the door. She wore her blond hair in bunches. She also wore shorts, although the evening was not that warm, and above the shorts a swollen, enormous top that said "Baby"—a needless announcement, because she was either pregnant or exploding. "Hi, I'm Robbie." She took the bouquet from Molly and sniffed the flowers.

Molly smiled, waiting for her to call her parents or otherwise explain herself.

But then Peter appeared and shook hands all around and hugged Robbie and patted her fanny and, slowly, Molly realized that Robbie was not Peter's daughter and that Rosemary didn't live here anymore.

The other wife was of the same green vintage as Robbie. "That's Meredith," Mitchell said. "And Damon."

Meredith waved greetings from where she sat, naked to the waist, nursing an infant. "Be with you in a sec," she said, flashing a smile that belonged over a baton.

Molly, dressed in corporate wife drab, felt musty and prehistoric, something that had persisted beyond its proper time.

They toured the house, admired the nursery, Peter's gym, the hot tub and the bar, and then they settled into heavy spare-ribs and light conversation.

From time to time, Robbie squealed, exclaiming about the ferocity of her baby's kicks. From time to time, Meredith suckled Damon. In between those times, there was a great deal of talk about layettes, La Leche, home deliveries and projectile vomiting.

Molly remembered those conversations. She'd used them up years ago and packed them away, waiting to dust them off when her grandchildren appeared.

She watched Mitchell and Peter grin at their new little wives, their pets. Molly couldn't help but realize these brides hadn't been born when their grooms entered college and Molly first met them.

How was it that men grew older and wives stayed in their twenties? How was it that more and more often, Molly found herself the oldest woman in any gathering of couples?

What had happened to her age group, and specifically, where was Rosemary? Locked in a back bedroom?

"Not a single snort since I'm preggers," Robbie said proudly to Meredith. "I don't care how clean they swear it is."

Where would Molly find a friend?

"So Stevie says, all angry like, 'Did my daddy put that baby in you?' " Robbie leaned toward Molly as if sharing an off-color secret. "Stevie is Peter's by his first marriage."

"First-marriage kids are such a drag," Meredith said and sighed.

"It's a shame he got the name, too," Robbie said. "I wanted my baby to be Steven if it's a boy, but Peter says we can't."

The first Steven. No more than an irritation to Robbie. He sounded young, like the last hope of the first marriage, and where was he now? In the same bin with discarded wives whose shelf life had expired? Wives fraying, withering at the edges, unsuitable for recycling.

Molly shook her head. Women didn't backtrack through time the way Peter and Mitchell had. Women knew that to everything there was a season. Not a repeat season with a new cast. Not an instant replay.

She sat back and said what the hell and let her hair grizzle and gray, her cheeks collapse, her teeth fall out and her skin wither. She was possibly the only old wife in America. The Ancient Marital. Matriarch. Thing.

She listened while the husbands tactfully choreographed information for their baby wives. "There was a TV show years ago," Mitchell said. " 'Your Show of Shows.' Sid Caesar."

"Oh, yeah?" Meredith said, now prepped for the anecdote to follow.

"There was a rule at Penn when we were there," Clay said, falling like a natural into the rhythm of dealing with large-bosomed infants. "Called *in loco parentis*—the university stood in place of your parents and could supervise your moral behavior. Girls weren't allowed in boys' apartments."

"You're kidding!" Robbie beamed at her husband's funny friend.

"No, no, I'm serious. So anyway—"

It was like being with children. Every story required a preface, background notations and footnoting so that the listeners, who had no history, could follow.

They left the beery evening heavy with spareribs and Indian summer warmth. The two couples waved energetic good-byes from the front door. They looked like a wholesome singing group that performs at halftime.

Molly sat in the car shivering.

Maybe the missing first wives had bitched too much about transfers and moving or husbandly indifference. Maybe Clay would soon decide that rather than work anything through, he'd trash her, too. Maybe she'd better stay quiet and smiling, inconspicuous so that Clay didn't notice she was going stale with age. Or had he already?

She couldn't think of a whole lot of long marriages anymore. Partners were lost, blasted away like little ducks in a shooting gallery. But why did she so seldom see the wives pop back up with shiny new husbands?

The evening had saddened her. Not only because she had hoped to renew a friendship, but more because of the mounting evidence that all human contracts were transient. More because of the smiling, casual way lives and connections were severed. Snip, snip, begin again. Throw it away; don't bother mending it. It's old. Get a new one.

Poor little Stevie the first. Poor Rosemary, wherever you are. Poor me.

"Wasn't that fun?" Clay said. "Isn't it great seeing old friends? Boy, did tonight trigger memories. Those parties. Those hangovers!"

"That Rosemary," Molly whispered so that only she heard it.

"See, I told you we'd find people. Just takes time, that's all." He sounded more energetic and enthusiastic than he had in a long time. "Peter said something about going to Atlantic City. See how it's changed with the casinos and all. Sounds like fun, doesn't it?"

She honestly didn't know what to say.

"Ah, Molly, don't be so—so . . ."

So old. So morose. So long of memory and tooth.

So what.

She said nothing. She realized, feeling like a very slow student indeed, that husbands and wives do not share a thing, least of all lives. At best they coexist, sharing a ride to and from temporary stop-offs.

21

"YOUR EYES ARE—BEAUTIFUL," CLAY SAID. THE thought sounding in his mind was that her eyes were the color of his best-remembered summers. But people didn't say such things out loud, or at least he didn't. And certainly not over a first drink with a near-stranger.

"Thanks," Didi Simons said. "Your eyes are beautiful, too. I noticed them right away, and your hair, of course, when I saw you that time at the airport."

There was an awkward pause while they sipped wine, looked around the bar and fiddled with the cocktail napkins.

"Tell me about yourself," he said. "Where did you grow up?"

She launched into a smooth telling of her history. Clay heard echoes of many such starts, many drinking partners listening with interest or ill-disguised impatience to her one good story. She told it with practiced style and phrasing.

Her father and two brothers worked in a bubble gum factory. Her sisters married, her mother prayed. Didi wanted to be different. She rattled off landmarks in high school and after, explained her job at the hospital, which was actually as a gofer, mentioned vague aspirations and hazy plans.

Clay was struck by the shallow way she presented herself, and it caused a thrill to run through him. Being with her would be either terrible or wonderful for its mindlessness.

"No ties," she said, winding up her saga. "That's for sure. I don't want to be tied down."

"What *do* you want?"

She shrugged. "To have fun. What else is there? Why—do you have a better answer?"

He was so full of gangrenous wants that he'd doubled over in pain with them that afternoon. He'd been watching the pale, hopeless sky insist it was winter, no matter what his calendar said. It punched his solar plexus, pinched his desires, pressed on his jugular and said, "Give up. I win."

How could he tell her what he wanted? Would she understand if he said he'd be satisfied to stop staring out his office window, stop fearing that his heart, like the last of the leaves, was brittle, losing its color and its hold.

"I want to be here, having a drink with you," he answered. "That's what I want." He wanted her to look at him with those summery eyes—to look at him the way his friends' young wives looked at them. He wanted to touch her. He knew how she would feel with her milky skin, the bones prominent in her miniaturized body.

He didn't do this kind of thing.

On the other hand, Molly hadn't done her kind of thing until recently, either. In the past, she'd never slept away her life. Now she was addicted to oblivion, overdosing daily on empty time. He was sick and saddened by her attic afternoons and her remote and sullen evenings. She had moved out, leaving an impostor, an automaton. He was tired of going home. Seeing his old friends, men his age, so happy, so energetic, had only made it worse.

"I'm glad you called today," Didi said. "I was really down. It's so gray and cold, and it's only October. Going to ruin Halloween—the kids'll have to wear coats over their costumes. Remember how sad that made you when you were a kid? Anyway, I don't know what made you call after four months, but I'm glad you did."

He tried to believe her smile. Why not be with someone whose eyes flattered and flirted instead of saying "Leave me alone"?

"But what would a Californian like you know about lousy Halloweens or winter?" Didi asked.

"Not true. I grew up in New Hampshire, and besides, we've —I mean I've—lived in lots of cold places since."

"I don't believe it, somehow. Tell me the worst winter story you remember," she said. "And by the way, you can say 'we.' "

Her question reminded him of Tony, who loved statistics and lists. Tell me your five favorite movies, Dad, your least favorite food, the worst dream you ever had.

And Tony reminded him of the worst winter story. "It was a storm that set records, but it was still in progress. I got off the train on a Friday evening, end-of-the-week tired, and instead of my car in the lot, I found an enormous lump of snow. Even if I'd had a shovel, I wouldn't have gotten far because there were stuck cars blocking the exit. So I walked home. It took an hour. A very long hour.

"I had this picture in my mind the whole time—a roaring fire, dry clothes and brandy. You know what home means in the dark, when you're wet and freezing and tired? It was shining in enormous neon letters—HOME! Anyway, it took forever, and my pants were wet with snow, my ears were—I'll spare you the details.

"But there wasn't any fire or brandy. There was just my son, Tony. He was a year and a half old, a real hellion. But not then. He lay in his mother's lap, looking like he'd given up. He was limp, and there was a rash all over him and he was on fire. It was scarlet fever, and the pharmacy truck with the penicillin had broken down."

"So you went out and got the medicine," Didi said.

"Took another three hours. It looks funny in my mind, remembering. Straight out of the silent movies, a melodrama. You know, hunched against the wind and dark, blinded by the blizzard. Anyway, the next day Tony's fever broke and he was himself again. I, on the other hand, was in bed for two solid weeks with the worst cold of my life."

"Ah, but you were a hero."

"Only to the makers of cold remedies." But when Molly had brought him soup and tea, had sat on the edge of the bed and kissed him, saying just that—"You're a hero"—he hadn't made a joke. His throat had been raw, his nose stuffed, his eyes running. But his children were safe and his wife adored him and he'd never felt so fine in all his life.

It wasn't that he believed a man could feel that way forever. But what he wanted now was for Molly to remember such times and to allow for them to happen again. To allow him and home to mean something again.

He suddenly felt as if he might cry.

He looked instead at the girl across from him, waiting with her enormous eyes. She was talking about her worst winter when she'd broken her leg at Aspen.

"But not on the slopes. I tripped on the sidewalk. I was so ashamed—I lied about it for years."

While she spoke, he surreptitiously checked the time. "Would you like another glass of wine?" he asked.

She nodded. "What did you tell her?" she asked.

"Tell who?"

"Your wife. About this. What did you say?"

"That I had a meeting. That I'd be late." He felt acutely uncomfortable, as if now, truly, he was betraying Molly.

Didi studied her fingernails, nodding to herself. "So," she said, "what are you going to be?"

He stared.

She winked and smiled. "At Halloween parties. What did you

think I meant? I'm going as Betty Boop. You know that cartoon?"

He nodded.

"I don't like weird costumes. When everybody else takes off their masks, you're stuck with clown paint or with garbage on your head, you know?"

She was a real pro at cocktail talk, at filling up silence. He felt as if he lumbered behind her, so heavy and slow he couldn't pick up on any of her leads. He was still stuck wondering what the hell he was going to be.

"Why'd you call me?" she asked abruptly.

"Why, to have a drink, to . . ." He shook his head, sighed and silently, honestly, completed the sentence. I thought, I hoped, I'd find answers, or at least oblivion, inside of you.

But now, all he could think of was the brevity and pathetic quality of that solution. Nature had her own trick-or-treat. So much pleasure possible—for such a short time. It could be interesting. It could be diverting. But it, alone, couldn't be enough to fill up his life. What answers would he find in her that he couldn't find in himself?

He angled his wrist on the table so she wouldn't notice, and he checked his watch again.

"Well," Didi said, "you've gotten what you wanted. We've had that drink. Had two, in fact. Now I'll say so long."

"But—but I thought we'd—I thought—"

"I know. I did, too. But look, I was straight with you. My only requirement is fun. I don't want to sound mean, but you're not going to be fun. You're going to be married."

"But you knew that."

"Sure. But I didn't know you'd be the kind of married that keeps checking the watch. Want some advice? Go home. You told her you'd be late, and you are."

He paid the bill and walked outside with her, realizing that he had neither the energy nor the desire to try and change her mind.

After she had driven off, he stood on the sidewalk feeling not angry, or upset, or cheated, or relieved, but a little of each.

Her eyes were like the best days of summer. Then he shrugged and buttoned his coat. It didn't matter. It wouldn't have and couldn't have mattered. Either way, winter would come.

22

It took Thea half an hour to find her little book with the telephone numbers in it. She felt tired, even though it was morning, and annoyed that she needed the book in the first place. Why, suddenly, couldn't she remember Chloe's phone number? Hadn't she dialed it once, twice, three times a week for the last thirty years? She was getting old in rotten ways. Her leg cast was finally off but now her mind was going.

She took the flowered address book downstairs to the kitchen. She turned on the burner to boil water for tea—part of the ritual of talking to Chloe. Molly had a wonderful long cord. You could almost live out your whole life while talking on the phone.

Thea stood for a moment, trying to remember what came next. She shook her head in irritation with her foolishness. She put out a cup and saucer and put the blue-flowered book near the phone, checking the area code.

Six-one-seven. Good. But she still couldn't remember the rest. She picked up the book and read each number, able to push only one before she had to check the book for the next.

She waited while the phone rang in Adams Wall. You had to allow lots of rings at their age. No use pretending they could hurry anywhere or anything these days.

"I know you're home, Chloe," Thea muttered. Chloe had become a night owl, getting up late and never going outside until afternoon. "Come on, I want to talk." There was nobody else to talk to that way except Chloe. Like about their children, now way past anything ever called childhood. Molly was an upsetting mystery lately. She had so much to give the world, but something in her was dying, and what could Thea advise? She'd never dealt with anything as complicated as a long marriage.

It'd be good to talk about it with Chloe who had her own mothering woes. It'd be good to talk with Chloe about anything and good to know she *could* talk about anything.

"Who is this?" Chloe would say in that old schoolmarm voice.

"Who do you think?" Thea would answer, as always.

After seven long rings, each of which echoed deep in Thea's brain so that she shook her head to loosen the sound, Chloe answered. Thea heard the voice, but she still heard ringing as well.

"Hello?" Thea heard, surprised by what an old-lady voice Chloe had. She sounded crackly and far away.

"Hello. Who is this?" Chloe said. Thea smiled, or started to.

Who do you think?

She heard the words start in her mind and thought they were traveling to her lips but at the same time, she realized they were still inside, reverberating with the phone rings, somehow trapped, loose and dangerous.

Who do you think? she started again, feeling it shape in the back of her neck, pushing it up to her mouth. But it stalled, stopped in a great convulsion she could only feel in her head, could only sense. A falling into a blank as parts of her separated, ripped and dangled.

"Hello? Who is this?"

Who do you think? But it fell apart, letters broken in the middle, turning into nonsense syllables, then something even less than that.

Whaaaooouuuiieee . . .

Something made noise far away in the plastic gleaming, the oh what is it with the wire and the buttons—

Who do you thi-thi-thi-

Angry pulses from the shiny, something wrong, don't—

Thea pushed harder toward the squawky, the sounds. There was something, you do a thing, you should—but the words, the hard little pebbles she tried moving out fell into the yawning emptiness before they could reach the outside. Nothing connected. Something cried.

And then there was less, still. The outside remained but unnamed, and there was only surface and nonsurface, inside and out, there and empty. She could see it all and knew it stayed in place, but she spun, became the vortex of a clear white whirlpool cleaning an endless emptiness. Almost magic it was because so free, so almost flying—but wrong, because she flew down and then farther down. Things stayed and Thea spun, looking out through the lines of whirl, mouth open but filled with airiness, the nothing, the white sound.

And then it split to the sides and she felt the hurt of a whistle slice through the center, ear to ear. Then things clamping back together so that she could name the hurt—whistle—scream—kettle. Boil. Stop.

She was dizzy. She was holding the phone and there was a line of saliva on her chin. She felt ashamed, as if she'd soiled herself. She listened to the loud buzz of the receiver. Why was it off the hook?

What had happened to the time between setting the kettle on and the piercing shriek that meant it was boiling? What unplanned, unremembered side trip had she made?

Her heart speeded up although she moved slowly, replacing the receiver, walking to the range to turn off the heat.

Her blue-flowered address book was on the kitchen desk. Open to "D." There—Chloe Denton's name. Must have meant to call her.

And had she?

No. Of course not. She'd remember if she had. Instead, she must have dawdled, lifting the receiver and daydreaming until the water boiled.

That must be it. She was a daydreaming old lady scaring herself half to death over nothing. For shame!

She closed the address book. She didn't feel like calling Chloe just now, and anyway, she knew the number by heart. She felt draggy and frightened, though. Half-memories glinted at the side of her mind, just out of sight. Half-ideas of other lost slivers of time. Well, but probably this was just another part of growing old. No need to create an uproar about it.

Good thing Molly was out. If she'd been home, she'd over-react, make Thea her new baby, her new store, and Thea would rather die than see that happen. Molly already had enough dragging her under.

No need to mention it at all. She'd just stop using the range, or using knives—she'd be careful about where she was and what she was doing, and she'd see what happened next.

And anyway, nothing had really happened today. So absolutely no need to make a fuss about it.

23

THE RINGING SEVERED HER SLEEP. SHE HATED THE shrill alarm, but she didn't want to risk detection, and she didn't want to frighten anyone again.

"Mom!" Ben had shouted a few weeks back. "Mom! Wake up!" He shook her shoulder. "Are you sick? Say something!"

"Didn't mean to fall asleep," she said with difficulty. It was dark in the room. She blinked with confusion.

"I've waited downstairs for you since school. I was—I was—why do you do this, Mom?"

Since then, she had set the alarm every day. Now she blindly pushed at its top. The ringing stopped momentarily, but then it began again. It pulsed over and over until she finally realized it was not the clock, but the telephone one flight down.

Yawning, bleary—she could sink so far down in those dreamless afternoon sleeps—she made her way to the master bedroom.

"Molly? Where were you?"

"Who is this?" She yawned again.

"Clay! Don't you recognize my—You sound funny. Is everything all right there?"

She shook her head and tried to answer, but before she could, he did. "Oh! That's what took so long—you were upstairs, weren't you? Asleep, weren't you? Dammit, I thought you weren't doing that anymore. It's the middle of November, Molly, and—"

"I was tired."

"From *what?*"

"Hold on, would you?" She was now sufficiently awake to realize she needed to be more so. She threw the phone onto the bed and ran into the bathroom, splashing cold water on her face and neck. She shuddered, felt her brain reengage gears, and she returned to the phone. "Now, what's this inquisition?" she demanded.

"No inquisition. Just concern. Molly, you have to do something."

"About what?"

"About your life, your unhappiness. Something, anything. Why not think about going back to school or finding a part-time job. *Something.*"

"I don't believe this," she muttered. "I've gone back to school enough times already. I could have three degrees if we'd stay in one—Oh, who cares? It doesn't matter."

"Then a job of some—"

"I did that already! I have no skills, no résumé, no anything. I've had those little jobs that fit your life. I—Dammit, Clay, did you call me up to do career counseling?"

"No, but—"

"—because there's no point to this. No point unless you swear to me that this is *it*, that this is where I can stay. Can you promise me that?"

He said nothing.

"Then stop playing games," she said. "Stop pretending that anything matters except you. Who cares what I want to do? I want to sleep—and you're ruining even that." She started to cry loudly.

"Don't do that," he said.

"I *liked* what I was doing in L.A.," she said, sobbing.

"Don't do that!" he said. "It's time to grow up, anyway. Adjust to reality. You can do whatever you want to do. Nobody can stop a woman anymore. Nobody would dare. The revolution was won years ago. Just say what you want and stop whining—and stop sleeping!"

She felt herself grow icy. He knew nothing about her life, or he didn't want to see. The revolution may have been won in a distant country, but not where she lived.

He cleared his throat. "Listen, I didn't call for any of this. I'm sorry. I called because I have to go to Washington tonight. I have to leave for the airport now. I'll try and call later."

She stared at the telephone after he clicked off. Had she really been blasted out of her cocoon upstairs, her wonderfully silent and safe center—for this? Or was she still asleep and had this been a nightmare?

Slowly, she walked back up the attic stairs, muttering indignantly. Who did he think he was with his questions. And anyway, she knew what she wanted, even if she couldn't make him understand.

She wanted him—the way he used to be. She wanted her children and her marriage and all the currents of love that sustained and enriched her.

But she wanted work, too. Tangible, coherent work that grew and changed over time. She wanted challenges, other adults, the need to prove her best. She wanted to earn her own money. Wanted to test her capabilities.

She knew all that. What she didn't know was how she could possibly hold on to love and connections and marriage, and have the rest as well.

She looked at the little brass alarm clock. There was an hour before school let out, and Thea was still at her Gray Panthers meeting. Molly yawned and pulled the comforter over her.

*　　　*　　　*

"Darth?" Molly waited for a correction, but none came. "Like in the movie?" she asked.

Darth Faber nodded. Slowly, as if his head were very heavy.

Tony held his new friend beside him like a trophy. Look, Ma, I caught me one. He had been bringing home peculiar finds. Molly didn't know if it was the age, the stage, or whether new kids were only allowed to approach the droppings.

"Nickname," Darth grunted. He had a strange, hoarse undertow in his voice, speaking the way a verbal frog might.

"Oh, Darth's a nickname?"

Again he nodded with his heavy head. He was sweaty and looked as if a fever had just broken.

"Where's Ben?" Molly asked Tony.

"Computer Club."

Tony attracted mutants and Ben attracted machines. Molly tried to believe that computers were valid companions and Ben's electronic generation would inherit the earth.

How they would reproduce remained a question.

Joanna walked in, her face flushed by the chilly winds of November. "Can I use the phone in your room, Mom?"

"Hello, and there's a phone right here," Molly answered.

Joanna sighed. "I'd like a little *privacy*. It's *personal*." She rolled her eyes at the male duo and fiddled with the charm she always wore around her neck.

Privacy for what? Personal with whom? "Fine," Molly said. She didn't have the energy to probe her children's lives anymore.

"Darth plays with green phlegm," Tony said.

Molly gagged.

"That's a band," Tony said. "Green Phlegm. Darth plays drums for them."

Molly tried to remember what made children leave. "There's some leftover Halloween candy in the big jar in the family room," she said. She felt inspired.

They left immediately in search of sugar. "Darth of Green

Phlegm," she said. "Oh, God, I'm so tired. So tired all the time . . ."

It was noisy, with winter banging and shuddering against the house. Loose bits of earth and debris slammed around the night and Molly sat in the family room, rereading Ellen's last letter. The television played as background.

"I haven't written," Ellen said, "because I've been wallowing in misery. Seems that long before he checked out, John-the-Bastard removed whatever would be mine in a fair settlement. He sold our assets and put the money overseas, we think. His new job pays less (he *says*—my lawyer's sure he's getting cash under the table) and we have no community property left to split except the house—which J.-the-B. refinanced last year. *Says* he invested—and lost—that money, too.

"Thank God for Sinfully Good, which prospers. Our catering business is booming, and we owe it to your party! Did you realize what you were starting? Anyway, with my nonsettlement, I'm not going to be able to buy you out. I'm looking for a third party. Sam Collins (who always sends his love to you—he says that when he's in Philadelphia he'll give you a call) thinks he knows somebody . . ."

Molly put the letter down on her lap. She didn't know how to answer it. The cool ruthlessness of John's retreat, his treacherous moves against his wife of fifteen years, suggested ideas and possible truths Molly didn't feel strong enough to confront.

Instead, she stared at sordid news stories on television. She didn't know how it profited her to learn of the crash of a small private plane, the unknown whereabouts of a retarded child or the death by fire of a family of five, but she sipped brandy and kept her eyes on the screen.

Lately, when she tried to read, she found herself listening and waiting for something fearful. She couldn't concentrate on the lives of the people in the book, finding them protected and smug in their false self-knowledge. They wouldn't share enough with her. They wouldn't turn themselves inside out and show her what it was she should do next.

So she put aside books and tried to keep her mind from flickering on and off or wandering. Her mother was no help and certainly not an alternate form of entertainment. Talking with Thea had become steadily more difficult.

This very night, Molly had again broached the subject of Thea's apartment in Adams Wall. For most of a year now, Thea had continued paying rent on her flat, insisting she would soon return to it. Now the charade had to end because the flat and the hardware store below it were coming down, to be replaced with an office building.

"Mother," Molly had said, "what do you want to do?"

"Do? Do? Oh, cure cancer, save the world, write a symphony. How about you?"

"About the letter, Mom. About your apartment."

"Oh." She shrugged. "What choice do I have? I'm more interested in what you're going to do. You have lots of choices."

"Mother, the letter came four weeks ago. We don't have much more time, so let's discuss your future and not mine."

Thea looked uncomfortable. "Let's wait until after Thanksgiving. That's only two weeks away. What's the rush? We're just going to abandon ship, haul the works to the Salvation Army."

Molly wouldn't lie and insist that her mother could live alone again. Thea was thinning at a cellular level, her ectoplasm becoming transparent, her smile more distant, her ideas less clear. She sometimes seemed to be calling from a distance.

"But I want you to understand something," Thea said. "I won't live with you if you make me your life's work, if you substitute me for something you should be doing in the world. I'm worried about you. You seem run-down. Your energy's been sitting still so long it's stagnated. It's not enough for a person like you to paint half a room or attend a few PTA meetings, or carpool. You aren't involved in a single thing outside of your family and frankly, Molly, most of the time you don't seem much involved with the family, either."

"Give me some time, all right? I'll find something. It isn't the way it was for you—you had big issues to fight, reasons to activate with wars and depression and whatever. I don't."

"Nobody can be as sad as you are and claim there's nothing left to fight."

"I'll be fine. I'm adjusting. Little by little, I'm—"

"I have a little-by-little story," Thea said. "They claim that frogs, if put in boiling water, will leap out to save their lives. But if instead you put a frog into tepid water, then slowly raise the temperature degree by degree, it will acclimate and stay until it boils to death." And with that, Thea had pushed herself up on her cane and gone to bed.

Molly, feeling more alone than ever, turned off the TV, turned down the thermostat and went upstairs. In a ritual so old she didn't think about it, she checked her children to be certain they were safe.

Tony lay sprawled on his back, mouth slightly ajar. On the floor next to his bed was a wand and a magician's hat. He and Darth planned to have Tony the Punk Magician as the lead act for Green Phlegm.

Joanna, woman of secrets and mystery, slept clutching a worn teddy bear.

Last stop was Ben, usually so buried under the covers, pillow over his head, that looking in on him was an abstract gesture. He was never visible.

Except tonight. His open eyes met hers. His expression was calm but mournful, his body flat, his arms by his side as if he were a corpse.

"Ben? What's the matter, darling? It's nearly midnight!" Molly went in and sat on the side of his bed, automatically stroking his dark blond hair.

He didn't move.

"Want me to sit here a while?" When he was small and unsharable fears wracked him, Molly would sit in his doorway where he could see her guarding against night devils until finally he relaxed and slept. That had been years ago, but he reminded her now of that tiny boy in his footed sleeper pajamas.

"Ben? What's wrong?" She whispered, making the words soft, but they still felt dangerous. Ben could gather up all the hard edges of wrongness and forge them into something true and sharp that would pierce her. She couldn't bear to know how wrong things might be with someone she loved this much.

Ben shuddered. "I hate it here." His voice was rough. "I hate it."

Oh, no, she thought. Don't tell me. I need to pretend you're happy. I was so scared for you, but now I'm so tired, so scared for me and so useless, and I cannot bear for bad things to be true for my children. I thought you were happy with the computers. I thought—

"I'm not popular." Ben's whisper was so harsh she could feel in her own throat how much it pained him to say those words and believe them true. To be thirteen and short and not a good athlete and shy and a stranger.

"I'm not popular," he repeated, and she knew he'd been saying it to himself the last several hours. "Nobody likes me."

She felt mortally injured. Her own cells were there on the bed in pain. She remembered the wounds of her own adolescence, remembered their virulence. But even so, they'd been contained inside her own skin, given to her in her own time. Nobody had ever warned her that her flesh would again submit through the bodies of her children.

And that it was worse the second time.

Someday, she knew, Ben would learn to protect himself. He'd stop admitting things like this out loud. He'd keep silent, hold his shoulders more defensively, convince himself it didn't matter and that everyone else was a fool.

But not tonight. Tonight he was a skinny undersized boy

who couldn't understand why he was being put through this pain. Tonight he still trusted his mother enough to let her see it, to hand it over for her ministrations.

Her muscles tensed and her rage exploded. How *dare* they! Her gorgeous, sensitive, talented Benjamin. The sweet spot in the family. The unique one, unlike any other soul on earth. How *dare* they make him feel bad and not love him!

She wanted to maim the world, smash it for hurting him this way. But she was only an adult.

Not all her love for him, not all her dreams or hopes could spare him a moment of his allotted pain. She couldn't shield him, wrap him up, kiss away the hurt.

Instead, she stroked his hair and murmured things that didn't help, because being loved by your mother doesn't make up for a moment's indifference by your peers. She crooned until his exhaustion won out and sleep took him over.

And then, her hands clenched, her heart pounding, she sat in his doorway until dawn.

24

"BUT YOU KNOW I'M DRIVING MOTHER UP TO ADAMS Wall tomorrow," Molly said. "I thought I'd see you tonight, before—" She listened, nodded, and hung up the phone. "Daddy won't be home until late. Unexpected business dinner."

"Then do we still have to eat leftover turkey?" Ben asked. Molly wondered if the dinner menu was Clay's only relevance to his children.

"Can we have pizza?" Tony asked.

"It's miserable out. I don't want to dr—"

"I'll drive!" Joanna's brand-new license was a source of terror to Molly.

"It's icy and it's going to snow and you said you had a lot of homework."

"Anyway, what would you do with Duffy?" Tony asked.

Joanna's class was conducting an experiment in parenting. For two weeks, each eleventh grader had studied the expenses of child care—diapers and food and equipment—and had cared for one hard-boiled egg in lieu of a baby. Someone had to "sit" for the egg if its parent wasn't with it.

Two weeks ago, in the initial flush of enthusiasm, Joanna had named her egg Duffy and lined a jeweler's box with cotton batting and painted yellow curls and bright blue long-lashed eyes on her charge.

Thanksgiving eve, less enchanted, she broke the rules and put Duffy in her pocket and sat on him at the movies. Now Duffy had a hairline fracture and visible albumen in his painted curls.

"Grandma, would you watch Duffy while I go get pizza?"

"You can't drive tonight," Molly said. "It's going to snow. We'll have tomato soup and cheese and crackers. I used to love that on winter nights."

"I have to drive in snow sooner or later."

"Later."

"I don't want to babysit," Thea said. "I'm playing solitaire. Anyway, don't rely on my generation. Old people are liabilities and burdens, not helpers. Ask anybody."

Joanna glared. "I thought that when I drove, things would be different."

"Ah." Thea slapped a black ten on a red jack. "We all think everything will be different than it is. We think so many wrong things, make up so many stories."

"Watching an *egg* isn't work," Joanna muttered.

"I don't like tomato soup," Ben said. "It's too red."

"A king!" Thea exclaimed. "Goodie. Speaking of red, Ben, do you know what the Mongols ate when they traveled?"

Ben shook his head. He outlined leaves on a family tree he was drawing for school.

"Horse's blood," Thea said. "They took extra horses along, and every night they'd slit open a vein and drink some blood."

"I can't believe how *gross* that is," Joanna said.

"It was the first fast-food take-out," Thea said.

"Maybe you should do that next, Mom," Tony said. "Open a place called Bloody Good!"

"You're disgusting," Joanna said. "You're making me sick."

"Order of the Colonel's blood to go. Clots in a bucket."

"Stop it or I'll rip up your book report, Tony!" Joanna grabbed across the table.

"Watch it!" he shouted.

The cat, finding its dish empty, yowled.

The bird began his nightly hysterical wing-flapping. "Yawk!" he screamed. "Yawk! Yawk!"

"A McBloody Burger!" Tony shouted.

There is nothing happening in my life, Molly thought, but all the same, there's so much noise and clutter and confusion.

"A Big MacBloody!"

"That does it!" Joanna's shriek was not unlike the bird's. "I can't stand this! I'll never have kids! Never! They're gross and disgusting and they keep you from ever having fun!" She grabbed her egg and hurled it to the floor.

"You killed it!" Tony looked at Joanna with horror. "Duffy's dead, you murderer!"

"It's an egg," Joanna said. "It's not a Duffy! I hate it and everything else. I hate Valley Forge and school and this house and this kitchen and what happens here. This isn't the way it's supposed to be!"

She's right, Molly thought.

"May I ask how it *is* supposed to be?" Thea sounded annoyed.

"Not like this." Joanna folded her arms across her chest.

"When I was Joanna's age, when I'd think about how it was going to be, I thought there'd be a shape to it." Molly felt as if her voice were coming out of a dream, all the words smoky. "I thought it would make better sense, have a visible pattern. I thought it would move slowly, show its skeleton. I planned for something very different."

"Different? How? In violation of the laws of the universe? Molly, what are you talking about?"

Molly shook her head.

"However it is, is precisely the way it's supposed to be," Thea snapped. "It's only those stories of yours that keep mixing everybody up. Make-believe. Probably my fault, too."

Molly looked at Joanna. A companionable, understanding smile was on her daughter's face. There was hope for them, if only in shared disillusionment.

Joanna cleaned up Duffy's remains. "Do you think it's too stale for the cat to eat?" Thea asked.

The boys looked at her as if she'd suggested boiling and eating them.

"See?" Thea said. "More make-believe. Gets so you can't see the hungry cat and the egg for the baby story. That's it, then. Not one more story from me."

"But I love your stories," Molly said. "They were the best part of my childhood."

"That's the problem," Thea said. "I started you in never-never land. Maybe you got stuck there."

Molly didn't understand her mother, but that was nothing new. "Clear the table," she said. "Let's eat in here."

"Wait," Ben said. "I have to fill in my great-grandparents' names. Then I'm done."

"Rebecca and Thomas Mueller," Thea said. "My mother was born in 1872, my father in 1865."

"And my other grandparents?"

It was Molly's turn. "Uh, Alice Morgan and I think it's Wesley Clay. And Reed Michaels, Sr., but I can't remember his wife's name. Daddy will."

"When will he be home?"

"I don't know." Molly felt a momentary sourness.

"What about the other set? The Hawthornes?"

"Millicent and—"

"No," Thea said, interrupting Molly. "No."

"No what?"

"No Millicent and no Dennis. Lies."

"You mean phonies? Pretentious? I thought you never met them."

"Couldn't, because they were stories. Lies. Just like their son, Joseph Henry Hawthorne."

Molly took time to process the words. "My father was a lie?" she finally asked.

Thea nodded.

"How can a man be a lie?"

"I made him up," Thea said. "I made the lot of them up, the Hawthornes, their cousins and cottages, their deaths, the blitz, the pony when Joseph was small. I'm sorry, but it seemed the right idea when I started, and making him English seemed even better. Harder to check after the war."

Molly sat down heavily. "Who's my father, then?" She felt like a fool. She knew the answer from forty years of winter evening stories, from tomato soup and frosty windows, from fuzzy photographs, the few books with his name in front, the color of her hair, her birth certificate, Thea's memories.

"I don't know who your father is," Thea said.

"Then who was Joseph Henry Hawthorne?"

"A story I made up."

"But the photos, the books, the—"

"Oh, Molly, who *knows* whose photo that is, and it's easy enough to put a name on a birth certificate. Or to write in a different hand in some old books." She looked disappointed with her slow-witted child.

"Grandma," Joanna said, speaking with exaggerated calm. "Do you mean you had a—a—lover?"

"Then?" Thea shook her head. "Nothing so serious as that. Never did catch his name, even. A one-night fling!"

Joanna looked panic-stricken. "But you're my *grandmother!*"

"Well I wasn't, then," Thea said, "and I wouldn't have been, without it. And what of it, anyway? Oh, I know I just dropped it on you all, but why does it upset you so much, Joanna? Don't tell me that in this day and age, I'm *shocking* you!"

Joanna looked glazed and distant. She shook her head, although as if in answer to her own questions, not Thea's.

"You're illegitimate, Mom," Ben said.

"A bastard," Tony said. "Well, that's the real word."

"Mother," Molly said slowly, "why'd you tell me now?"

"I just said, no more lies. Too much make-believe and you get Joanna giving up on real life and her mother agreeing. I don't want any part of it."

"Then why not from the start?"

"Because people—people can be cruel to a little girl with no father."

"But why not sooner?"

Thea sighed. "I certainly meant to. But you turned into such a prig—all that fifties good-girl, bad-girl stuff. How could I say I was what your fool friends would have called a bad girl? You wanted absolutes. You wanted to be so ordinary. And then I was going to tell you when you were getting married, but once I met that proper Alice Michaels, I knew I couldn't tell the truth."

It had started to snow. The dog scratched to come in. He settled under the table, smelling like wet wool. The soup simmered, steaming the windows. It was just the way it had always been. Soon they'd listen to "Ozzie and Harriet" and then they'd talk about how Joseph Hawthorne had wooed and won Thea Mueller. And Molly would have a vision of how the rest of her life would be.

"Molly," Thea said gently. "You're forty years old. Isn't that old enough to make do with the truth?"

"It feels peculiar. As if part of me—a favorite part—was amputated. Without anesthesia. It hurts. It's hard to believe my father was made up."

"Oh, twaddle. Most fathers are made up. Mothers' myths. Look at yourself tonight. Where's Daddy? And you answer. You take a million factors and pick the ones you want for your children's story. You decide where Daddy is and why Daddy's there and what a daddy is. How many kids in this country really know their fathers? How many are just told stories about a good man or a lousy man who is sometimes or never there? So it doesn't seem so different to make him up from whole cloth. I wanted you to have the best, and you did. Now I think it's time for soup."

Molly ladled out portions, then she stopped. "Why Hawthorne, then?"

"Why not? It has such a solid, elegant sound. Besides, it was my joke, after *The Scarlet Letter*. My letter. It wasn't easy, Molly. I was forty years old and I was afraid. But I tried to make it safe for you. You needed the labels that keep a kid from being pushed around. It was hard. I had to leave New York, find work that fit mothering, think everything out all the way through. I had a few private jokes to lighten things up. Hawthorne was one, and your middle name, Pearl, was another one from the book. Remember Pearl, the child of sin?"

Molly sat at the familiar table like an amnesiac trying on a past a stranger insists is true. "Feels weird," she said several times.

"Perhaps," Thea grudgingly agreed. "But nobody has a real past. We make it up and get on with it, choosing whatever we like as the truth. Write your own history, Molly. Start now."

"Yes," Ben said. "Okay. But then what do I write on my family tree?"

Thea smiled. "Oh—Joseph Henry Hawthorne, son of Millicent and Dennis of Kent, England. That's the truth, too—as long as you understand it's a fiction."

"This is very strange," Ben said.

"Then it's very true," Thea answered. "Now let's drop all talk of truth and illusion or of how things are supposed to be, and let's do some serious eating."

Nobody disagreed.

25

"*GELATO*, GENTLEMEN. THE SPECIAL TONIGHT." THE waiter smiled solicitously.

Clay shook his head. "Coffee, please."

Across the table, Dom Campiglia's L.A.-tanned face studied the menu. "One second please," he said. "One single second here."

The meal had been a studied, slow-motion affair, and Clay became more impatient with each bite, slice and forkful.

"What flavor *gelato*, my good man?" Campiglia asked after due consideration of the other dessert offerings.

"We have tonight vanilla with a kiwi sauce, or we have tonight a mango with a lemon sauce, or we have tonight strawberry with a Cointreau sauce."

All day long Clay had watched the steely sky pregnant with snow and had felt that tonight he and Molly would turn things around. Tonight they would come close in a warm house in the first snowstorm of the year. It was important, before she drove her mother up to take care of the apartment. Her departure made him anxious for reasons he didn't understand.

"Vanilla, mango or strawberry, eh? Vanilla, mango or straw-berry."

But Campiglia had walked into the office, unannounced. Bill Burchard, grinning and stupid, accompanied him. "Look who's in town! The new Senior Vice-President for Marketing. Ta-da!" Clay again congratulated Campiglia on the promotion. He'd already written a note saying the same thing.

"Thanks," Campiglia said. "And how are you? Don't let me interrupt. I was in New York and I thought hell, why not jump on the train and see an old friend, right?"

"Could I have vanilla *and* strawberry?" Campiglia now asked.

"Of course, sir. Would you like a sauce, also?"

Clay waited another few beats to hear the momentous choice. Campiglia was always fearful of the simplest decisions, dawdling until change or circumstance pushed him along. Yet that unpromising trait got itself promoted. Nothing made sense.

Campiglia chose to have kiwi sauce, ordered coffee and fi-nally sat back and relaxed. "I appreciate your taking the time, Michaels," he said.

"My pleasure," Clay lied. Not a second had been plea-sure. He had guided Campiglia on a tour of the plant, de-scribed each division's work, talked for an hour and a half in his office about plans and estimates. And every word he had spoken was underlined by the bitter knowledge of the report, the report over which he'd sweated, the report that Campiglia had wanted, the report that said all these things— the report that had been sitting on Campiglia's desk for weeks now.

"Good meal," Campiglia said. "Veal was perfect and the fet-tuccine reminded me of my mother's. L.A. doesn't have it when it comes to Italian food."

Clay was having trouble focusing. Surely the point of this visit would be touched upon now since it had been avoided for the last four hours.

"I'd like brandy," Campiglia said. "Always like brandy to cap a perfect meal. You don't have other appointments, do you?"

Family appointments didn't count. "I'll have a brandy, too," Clay told the waiter.

"Well, then," Campiglia said. "Let's run over that new marketing strategy of yours."

Clay wanted to grab the man's tie and demand an explanation of why he hadn't read the damn report. Weeks of working late, pushing his staff, ignoring his family, had gone into those proposals, budgets, ideas. However, he answered the question instead. "All our studies show that our prime prospective buyer is the isolated, insecure shopper who doesn't know what's right, doesn't feel competent about domestic duties, the—"

Campiglia brushed away the words with his hands. "No news there. No news there."

Clay sipped brandy, controlling his anger. "The point is, we aren't fully exploiting that market. Mother Lancaster is a passive, grandmotherly symbol of wholesome natural ingredients. I think we have to update the package and move into the eighties. Sexist or not, men sell. We need a male expert on the TV screens. Make them a team, but include him, the teacher, the technician, the guide. I see him as a scientist—but when he takes off the lab coat, he doesn't want chemicals anymore. You know, not everything should come out of a test tube. Also, we haven't tapped the second-buy customer. The divorced man who doesn't know a can opener from a quiche. The suddenly kitchened, for want of a better term. If we give him an expert he can identify with, something that's going to replace the wifely cook he's lost, then—"

Campiglia shook his head. Slowly, reluctantly, with great sorrow forcing his jowls down farther. "Nice, Clay, but you can stop there. Let me level with you. I think you deserve the truth."

Clay's back muscles tightened.

Campiglia leaned his elbows into the table, man to man. "Clay, Mother Lancaster's one sick broad."

"But I've only had nine months to—"

"On the critical list."

"But—"

"Not that we don't already see your improvements. She's trimmed down, lost fat, looks perkier."

Clay waited for the "but" like a fish with its mouth around the hook.

"But off the record, she doesn't look good enough. Not that we blame you."

Blame me? Me? It's your jackass buddy Burchard who let everything slide. I was sent to fight fires when everything was already charred. Blame me? "What do you mean, 'doesn't look good enough'?"

"Hell of it is, the demographics are against us. Half the population's worried about finding enough to eat, not about its purity. And even the rest don't care enough to pay upscale prices. Pesticides and additives don't scare them that much when they're worried about nuclear bombs. She's an old idea, Clay. Hippies and health food. Not eighties."

"I think you're wrong," Clay said softly. "All our market research shows that people care more now about—"

"But not enough," Campiglia said. "Not enough for us. And if they do, they make it themselves or go into those smarmy little gourmet shops, the kind your wife had, am I right?" He waited until Clay nodded, then continued. "I'm not blaming the economy on Molly, but facts are, that's where those shoppers go. Not to us."

"Then why don't we distribute to those little shops?" Clay asked. "We have to see what happens with more efficiency, better distribution, a new campaign. We have to think in new directions. We have to—"

"No we don't. No. We don't have to. Maybe we will, but we do not have to."

Clay's heart pounded insanely, erratically. He was sure Campiglia could hear it across the table.

"Ready for some hush-hush?" Campiglia asked.

"I'm—I'm—Yes, of course." Clay's mind tried to decipher what Campiglia had and had not said already. Were they closing Mother Lancaster? Easing him out? Giving him warning? Not giving warning at all? Was he paranoid?

"My new game plan," Campiglia said, "is to consolidate and strengthen the small marginal divisions under one new banner —the Golden Great Harvest label."

The words took some time to creep across the table and stand at attention in front of Clay to be comprehended. Then Clay stared at Dominic Campiglia with undisguised incredulity. A single label? Hadn't he and Art Baum suggested it, worked out a master plan for it? Hadn't they been told their ideas were impractical and told so by the man now claiming the idea as his own?

Clay used the last of his brandy to busy his mouth. He was numb with belated understanding. Campiglia had stolen the idea, had fired Art, packed off Clay and then climbed the corporate ladder using the one-label idea as a step stool.

"Interesting," Clay said in a low voice, refusing to go down for the count without a murmur. "I prepared a report with Art Baum on that idea. A single corporate label."

"Really?" Campiglia wrinkled his brow. "I'd forgotten. Obviously, it's an idea whose time has come. But as for your man in the lab coat, well, just between us, who knows if he'd fit the new unified image?" He lit a cigar. It surprised Clay by being fragrant, but the ritual of clipping its end, lighting it and gazing at the initial cloud of smoke heightened Clay's anxiety. "These are hard times," Campiglia said, rolling his cigar in his fingers. "Cutbacks, belt-tightening, rough times." He sighed and drew on his cigar.

Clay was fast becoming numb. What did any of this mean

except that he'd been outsmarted, outplayed, outmaneuvered and hadn't known it at all. He was stupid and clumsy, not the person he thought he was at all.

"And now," Campiglia said, "if you meant it about the ride to the hotel, I'd be mightily obliged." He had a girl, a hooker, waiting. Clay had heard that about him, and Bill Burchard made it clear he could provide whatever comforts visitors might desire.

They went out into a serious-looking snowfall. The ground was covered with a thin white throw and more fell in large, resolute flakes.

"Kind of pretty," Campiglia said.

They drove in silence. When Clay finally reached the hotel, a bellman moved out from the canopy and opened the car door. Campiglia shook Clay's hand. "Good seeing you," he said. "My best to your beautiful wife." And he left.

Clay felt like a tourist who'd seen a play performed in a foreign language. Only a scattering of the words made sense, and none of the idioms or underlying meaning.

"Sir?" the doorman said. "There's another car behind you, so if you'd please . . ."

He moved on. Made room for someone else. Was pushed out. Everywhere. He rolled down his window because he didn't feel certain he could stay alert otherwise. Icy flakes blew onto his temple. Nothing really happened, he told himself. Hints, old statistics, nothing real.

Chunkablunk went the wipers. Chunkablunk.

His heart denied what his mind kept insisting. He felt that something had, indeed, happened. The horizon had moved farther away from the quicksand in which he was mired.

How had it happened? He'd started out with such a blaze. He was going to be important. President of something big. He heard a low, injured wail deep inside himself.

He was a loser. Maybe it wouldn't become official for a while, but the label already hung heavily on chains from his neck.

Chunkablunk went the wipers. Loser, loser.

There was a summer he remembered when his parents still had the house at the lake. A summer dark with green leaves when Clay, scrawny and shadowed by his older brother, spent every minute building strength and speed into his crawl. Back and forth across the lake like a water insect he went.

"I'm going to win the Festival Swim," he confided in a rush one day. "I want to win the way Reed did."

His father looked amused. "That's admirable," he said. "And I'll tell you what. If you do, I'll reward you."

"Reward?" His father was never this companionable. He felt warm in his skinny chest at being noticed, and maybe even approved of.

"Have anything special in mind?" his father asked.

"Yes!" Clay said immediately. "An overnight—could we camp out at the North Point?"

"Like your buddy Tom and his father did? Well, I hadn't meant—well, let me think."

Clay tried not to breathe.

"Oh, why not," his father finally said.

Clay increased his practices, whipping through the lake like a shark. At night he dreamed of that camp-out with his dad. They'd roast marshmallows and his father would call him "pal" and they'd have secrets nobody else knew.

Which might have happened, had not neighbors had a house-guest who was interschool swim-team captain in his home state of Georgia. The lake was already a closed and privileged community. There were no rules about term of residence or status as far as entering the race was concerned. If you were at the lake and hadn't already won a Festival Swim the way Reed Michaels III had, then you could enter. And win, if you were the inter-school swim-team captain from Georgia.

Clay waited for a sympathetic word. None came. Finally, he approached his father. "I know I didn't win," he said, "but I was second best, so could we still . . . ?"

"I'm really disappointed in you." His father used his most remote voice. "Rules are rules. You lost."

"Yes, sir."

"Nobody's interested in runners-up and there's no such thing as second best. There are winners and there are losers. Remember that."

Remember that. Remember that. Not a day of his life had he forgotten it. Or that there was always a kid from Georgia waiting. And always a loser.

Chunkablunk. Loser. Chunkablunk. He felt so old, so tired, so unfamiliar in his own skin.

Chunkablunk, chunkablunk. Loser, loser. Nobody's interested in runners-up, loser. Remember that. Chunkablunk.

26

MOLLY LAY IN THE TELEVISION'S BLUE-WHITE GLARE,
waiting, listening.

He was late. She had finished in the kitchen, gotten into bed
and blindly watched two sitcoms. Now, previews of the late
news hurtled from the set, but Molly could only focus on her
own news bulletins.

"Dow Jones tumbles!"

Where was Clay?

"Truckload of anchovies missing. Foul play suspected."

How could two men with nothing in common but an employer dawdle so long over dinner?

"Teens blame fear of nuclear bomb for increase in sexual
activity. More at eleven."

What did her revised history mean? The amputation of her
father was having peculiar aftereffects. Molly was suddenly
anonymous to herself, mysterious as well. She wanted to use
her newness as a way of touching Clay. It could be their crutch
or excuse or whatever, but for sure, they needed something.

She yawned. The new show began with a chase. She pushed
the remote control and found—Daniel! It was that Daniel from

the airport. He was only on for a moment, but in that flash, she relived the excitement she had felt more than half a year earlier. Then she sighed. It had ended in humiliation, and anyway, the fully alive Molly of the airport seemed a character in a yellowing history book.

She waited in vain for Daniel to reappear. After fifteen minutes, she switched channels again.

The screen filled with men who looked mildly uncomfortable. They held mikes and wandered around in front of a bank of people talking on telephones.

She thought about her non-father, about her mother's real life. She wondered how much of her own life had been spent in search of the man she'd thought herself cheated of and of the life she thought she'd missed.

She drained her glass of wine. Onscreen, a man asked her to support public television. He didn't look like an actor. He looked awkward and appealing and sincere. "And now," he said, "we return to *A Doll's House*."

Molly perked up. One of her favorites, repeating through her life like a motif in a tapestry. She'd read it first in high school and had been annoyed by Helmer's stupid terms of endearment, his patronizing. "My little squanderbird, my squirrel," he called his wife. Molly had snorted with derision.

Onscreen, Nora tried to save herself and Helmer from the bank clerk. Damn. It was the second act. Molly tapped impatiently on the comforter, then decided to find more wine and her copy of the play.

She walked through the silent house. It felt cavernous at night with the glow of the entryway lamp blurring the dark rooms. But a nice house all the same. Good house.

Doll's house. She found her battered paperback on one of the shelves she'd begun refinishing, and she carried the book and a bottle of wine upstairs.

She'd read the play again at Penn, but academically, as an

interesting example of realistic drama. Then she'd moved on to interesting examples of symbolist drama.

In Boise, trying to complete her dangling degree, Molly found *A Doll's House* required reading once more. This time, the play burned through her system like acid. Yes, she said as the twins banged pot lids and she cooked with the play propped next to the range. Yes, while Janna whined. Yes, while she fed them and bathed them and put them to bed, freshening her makeup and keeping Clay's dinner and herself warm for his late arrival home. Yes.

"I have another duty which is equally sacred . . . my duty toward myself," Nora said, and Molly read, the words crackling as if a live wire ran through every one of them. Yes.

But slam the door? No. And if no door slams, then what happens?

Still later, her reading group in Atlanta spent a winter on significant women's literature. Again Nora entered Molly's living room. But by then, Nora seemed familiar. It was 1975 and everybody was slamming doors. Except Molly. She closed the door on Nora.

Molly wondered if Clay and all his sex didn't yearn for the first-act Nora, the pre-door-slamming Nora. A cutie who put on party clothes and entertained and adored her husband. A party doll, like the one in that old song that had been playing when she saw Clay at that fraternity party. A party doll—everybody wanted one. . . .

Wasn't that what she'd become? Mrs. Clay dressed up, smiled and entertained. Mrs. Clay whipped and basted and broiled for business, coming out of the wallpaper only to amuse, to flatter and to feed. To Nora.

Yes, men wanted and got their party dolls. Only thing was, dolls wore out. So they discarded them and bought new ones.

Maybe Clay was with the next doll now. Someone firm and beautiful with every winning trait Molly lacked or had lost. Someone dimpled and lovable and young.

Someone not like Molly. Molly's thighs were her most dimpled part and all the rest of her was falling down. Chin, cheeks,
breasts, belly, rear, sliding, slipping, giving in to the siren call
of gravity. So why wouldn't he want a fresh new Nora doll
who'd idolize him the way Molly once had?

Was it thoughts like these that made Clay put on silence the
way other men put on weight? That kept him out late tonight?

It had been different for so long, through so many cycles of
joy and laughter. She suddenly remembered one particular
day, several months after they were married. She'd been standing on a corner in Chicago, the wind making her eyes tear. But
she was warm, wrapped in a moment of clarity and bliss, a
perfection of self and life that approached religious intensity.

Clay was her husband. She was his wife. They had made
promises they would keep and there would be more and more
of them, of this, of the joy that washed through her veins and
warmed her.

They would last. The whole street corner—the whole city—
gleamed with the force of her revelation. The joy would last.
She had been shaken by the gift of that knowledge.

Now she sighed. What was she to do with such memories in
this dry season?

Onscreen, Nora was being a prig. Dr. Rank confessed his
love. Nora objected.

"That I have loved you as deeply as anyone else has? Was
that horrid of me?" Rank asked.

"No—but that you should go and tell me. That was quite
unnecessary."

Fool girl. Tell *me*, Rank. Somebody, tell me. Clay won't. Not
Clay, the taciturn Yankee, fearful of a surfeit of words, a be-
liever in deeds.

Well, deeds were fine and he was a good man, but Molly
needed words. Validation. Praise. Declarations. Love words.
Molly words.

Unsaid words were clogging their system, damming feelings that might otherwise flow freely. Unexpressed concepts festered.

Molly was able to go full turns of the moon without a fix of words. But then something—a romantic novel, a scent of lost springs, a dream remembered, old songs on the radio—made her crave, insatiably, the words that could give her the rush, the hot fullness, the sense of life that would reshape her out of the lumpish creature she was becoming.

She was going to die. That was the daily message of the lady in the mirror. She could not control the fate of her flesh or the meaning of time. That's what the uninvited sags and lines and pouches announced. A few well-chosen words wouldn't change the facts, but they'd make them less bleak and meaningless.

Onscreen, Nora was replaced by the man asking for money. Words danced from his lips with no sign of stopping, like a bubbling spring of water. Molly felt a rush of affection for him.

"We need you." He stared directly at her.

A pulse in her throat ticked. She could feel his voice enter her in the dark. She could imagine him here, in the room, next to her, that smooth and comforting voice telling her all about herself.

She envisioned her body as containing caverns and cathedrals, pink-walled and mysterious with secret passages, jeweled treasures and hidden naves. She heard the rich music of her heart flood that deep crimson world.

And she knew that soon, too soon, the music would stop, the cavern walls collapse, the jewels twinkle a last time and the sky go black.

"Come home, Clay," she said. "Come home and tell me it's all right I'm not young anymore. Come home and let's make things better."

A branch scraped the window and the wind howled. And suddenly, she knew that Clay wasn't coming home. He wasn't with another woman. He was dead. Frozen by the side of the road, his car overturned, his open, unseeing eyes collecting snowflakes.

It was too late to undo any of what had come between them.

She cried quietly, tensely waiting for the phone call, the knock on the door. She remembered Clay and their life, seeing all of it in sunshine now. Seeing him, that blue-eyed hero, that man who had, from the start, stood out from all the boys around him on campus. Her man, for whatever. Despite whatever.

She clicked off the TV and sat in the dark.

27

CLAY DROVE ALONGSIDE THE RIVER. HIS DINNER churned in his stomach as if Campiglia's words had turned it into a witch's brew.

The wind whipped snow against the car. He leaned forward to help visibility. Damn. There was something, a crippled Ford ahead. He pulled into the left lane, then accelerated to pass, all the while hearing Campiglia, trying to understand what the man had really meant. He felt so tired, so weighted, with everything giving way, his homelife, his work . . .

He passed the Ford, cut back into the right lane and straightened the wheel. But the car kept moving to the right, toward the river and the dead brambly banks below. The wheels skated, the car spun, skidding on ice in a river-bound whirl. He held his breath, his chest as frozen as the ground that propelled him into the river.

And then he pulled his hands off the wheel.

Let it happen, then. Let me smash on the riverbed. Let it end.

But his hands ignored him. Through reflex, they reclaimed the wheel and cajoled it out of its rebellion.

He exhaled loudly and began to shake. A film of sweat slicked his face.

As soon as it was safe, he pulled over and sat in his car, his head resting on the steering wheel.

He'd been ready to surrender without a fight, to give his life over like something he'd outworn.

How had it come to that? Was he that fragile, then? He'd always thought himself stronger and more complex.

That morning, he'd cut himself shaving and had watched the bubble of blood with some awe. Until then, he'd never let himself realize how thin skin really was, how tenuously we hold our vital organs safe. A razor, a nick, and the contents tumble, the system bleeds.

Now he knew that words could do it, too. Words, threats, broken promises; the feeling that very soon you'd no longer be who you were. Who you had to be.

He waited until he could breathe normally again, then he started the car and moved slowly toward home, hunched over the wheel like an old man. His senses felt muffled by the whiteness, the unnatural silence.

He crept along the river road, carefully feeling his way, and he suddenly remembered the river in Oakmont and winters when he was the age of Tony and Ben. He could feel again the stinging wind, could hear himself laugh around its pinpricks. But most of all, he felt the smooth slide of his skates on the frozen river. He flew faster than anyone else, frightening warnings out of adults, but he never slowed down.

Sometimes now, Clay awoke from dreams in which he, a grown man, flew above his childhood park with the frozen river winding below. And even though in his dreams he carried the weight of a man, his heart sang its immortality the way it had in youth. He held a force too strong to ever die. He could sustain the world, outrace time and physics and the puny evidence of science. This was it and it was his.

And on he'd fly, holding his arms toward forever, laughing.

He shivered in his cold and solitary car and knew he'd never have that dream again.

He yearned for Molly and home, his warm harbors. But he wanted the old Molly, not the angry one of the past six months who thought herself his victim, who shared his life as if it were a grudge debt.

Dear God, if she even suspected his new fears, if she had to consider their future vague again, contemplate relocation another time, she'd pull so far inside herself she'd disappear altogether. He couldn't tell her. He wouldn't. He'd keep this to himself. Handle it like a man.

He reached his street and the untouched snow of his driveway. The house was dark except for the light in the entry. All asleep and just as well.

He paced through the first floor, measuring his life in the size of the rooms and their count. He stepped on the first riser of the staircase, then changed his mind. He needed a drink. Needed lots of drinks. He couldn't figure any of this out, but maybe he could blur it.

He sat in the dark family room, working on a drunk that refused to come. Outside, a white world shrugged and rearranged itself. Clay felt as if he were in a pit. Around him the wind whispered terrifying syllables that said he was not the man he'd thought he was, and that he'd never become him.

He drank as if administering medication.

Loser. Runner-up. He'd forgotten again that there were slick surprises in the race. He'd taken things for granted, like his competence, his family, his marriage, his strength and his sanity.

Loser. He heard his father's voice in his brain. Loser. His mother's never-uttered refutation of that verdict. Her silence still roared in his ears.

What if his worst fears were valid? What if Mother Lancaster shut down? How could he move his family again? *If* it were true, and *if* Campiglia didn't somehow block Clay's reentry into the mainstream and *if* . . .

The unemployment rate this month rose to—and your hair is gray, you aren't young, you . . .

His thoughts rumbled down in an avalanche, bouncing against each other, leaving nothing but rubble.

There must be a mistake. I'm not understanding something clearly. Whatever it is, it isn't my fault, I—

Nobody's interested, son. Nobody's interested in losers.

I can't tell her. That's the one thing I know. She's already on the edge; why make it worse? This is all speculation and innuendo anyway. And even if I knew for sure—I still wouldn't. Not until I solve it myself. She can't call me a loser, a weakling. She can't . . .

Molly heard the car approach and ran to the window as he drove in. Thank God. Oh, thank God.

She went to the stairs, began to rush down to greet him, but then she reconsidered. This couldn't be just another night, not after all that emotion. This couldn't turn into another of their stiffly polite greetings where his reserved manner shriveled whatever excitement she felt.

She would greet him instead in the dark, waiting until he was in bed, then touching and beginning without words, the way he liked best. And then, later, they'd talk through the night, letting their words fall back on them like a sweet warm blanket.

She waited, willing her body to relax and move past the anxiety of the night and the anger of so many months.

Then she waited some more. She heard him walk around, even heard his foot on the stairs, but then she heard nothing more, as if he'd disappeared. She watched the numbers change on the digital clock.

They changed many times. The snow subsided, drifting against the house and sighing in the wind. Only Molly and Clay stayed in place, far apart, like ceremonial lions guarding the extremities of a wide and dangerous place.

"No." She got out of bed. She changed into a daffodil peignoir set Clay had given her a year and a half earlier. "No," she said again. "I'm not going to lie here and let this happen." She brushed her hair and put on a little lipgloss. "No," she said one more time.

"Hi." She stood in the family room doorway.

"I woke you. I'm sorry."

"No problem, I was up anyway." She rubbed her arms. "Is everything all right?"

"Sure. Sometimes it's hard to unwind."

"Ummm. Was Campiglia okay?"

"You know how he is. Eats slowly, too."

"Uh, the driving, was it bad?"

"Not good. You still planning to leave tomorrow?"

"Unless it's really bad. But it's stopped, so they'll plow and—yes, I probably will." She shifted weight from one bare foot to the other. "Clay? You sure everything's all right? Do you want to talk? I mean I'd love to, if you would."

"Just tired, Moll. Why don't you get your sleep? That's a long hard drive tomorrow. You have chains, don't you?"

"But, uh, I keep thinking we could—I mean, surely you've noticed we barely, we don't, I mean couldn't we . . . ?" She was having difficulty breathing. She felt cold and embarrassingly revealed in her gauzy yellow wrappings. She picked up the afghan from the couch and pulled it around her.

"Molly," Clay said, "just let me unwind. Been a long day. How about you? Everything okay here?"

"Oh, sure. I stocked up the freezer for while I'm gone. We might stay up there a few days."

He nodded.

"I, ah . . ." She waited. "Good night, then," she said.

"Good night."

28

THEA AND MOLLY STOOD IN THE DUSTY LIVING
room in Adams Wall. "Ah," Thea said softly, touching furniture, remembering through her fingertips. Molly, too, heard
deep sounds of recognition and relief inside herself. Nothing
in the room had changed.

Thea continued her tour. She touched framed photographs,
ran her fingers over books, lifted a Spanish mantilla and put it
back over the sofa's worn spot, picked up a lumpy clay sculp-
ture Molly had fashioned in grade school.

"There's so much," Thea murmured, putting the statue next
to a large piece of fan coral.

Molly's home lacked this layering of memories. Odd items
didn't travel well and each time she relocated, she minimized
their baggage. She wasn't ruthless or without sentiment. She
carted her offspring's clumsy clay statues, but only a few, carefully selected as best of breed.

The Michaels had no junk drawers, overstuffed basements,
uncataloged attics or cluttered garages. But, Molly knew, in
carrying less of a past, they impoverished their futures.

*   *   *

The next morning, they sorted out the bedroom. In the white winter light, they considered Thea's rough filing system. She had filled what was once Molly's half of the closet with stacks of labeled shoeboxes. Unfortunately, her favorite filing category was "Misc." Together, Molly and Thea examined yellowed manuscripts, unidentified photographs of peculiar gentlemen in old-fashioned swimsuits, sheets of rolled music, letters from friends, forms rejecting manuscripts or saying there were no jobs, and notes from the children of Emerson School in whose office Thea had been a fixture. During Molly's infancy, Thea had worked downstairs in the hardware store and taught herself typing and shorthand. She graduated into the public schools the same time her daughter did. And then, from what Molly could see, she saved every scrap of paper that crossed her desk.

There was a box of loose clippings, the peculiar news items Thea loved, and there were seven shoeboxes dated and labeled "Molly." "Your letters," Thea said, "starting with the first Mother's Day card you made. I've reread them all several times. They're like a book about you."

The idea chilled Molly. She'd written her mother at least once a week for the last twenty years. Hundreds, maybe a thousand, letters. An unconsidered, unwanted journal of two decades. The idea was frightening, as if someone had wrung a confession out of her by torture.

"You should read them," Thea said.

It was the last thing Molly wanted to do.

"I really mean it." Thea's voice was less gentle. "You'd see where you've been, what you're becoming. Or were becoming. Of course, they stopped nearly a year ago, so God alone knows what's been happening to you since then."

Molly turned her back. "Let's not be dramatic," she said. "Toss out the letters."

"No! They're your story. It's time for you to pay attention to it."

Neither had anything more to say for a while. They passed the awkward moment by circling it, both turning to other projects. Thea made a stack of skirts and shawls, most of which were ancient and all of which she wanted to save.

The clothing stayed. The letters stayed and of course, the photographs stayed. Molly took a break and thumbed through the oversized album she remembered from her childhood. There were her grandparents, her mother as a young woman, herself.

"Molly," Thea said, "I never once was sorry about you. I was nearly forty. I'd been told I could never have children. And then, there you were. Magic. I was never sorry I had you or kept you or that you got yourself created."

Molly kissed her.

"Even if you won't read your letters," Thea added.

They both looked at photographs of Molly growing up.

"And there's another thing," Thea said. "Yesterday I was pretty flip about your father, or your non-father, but I want you to understand how it was. I was turning forty and feeling that nothing—not a piece of my dreams—would happen. Everything had gone flat. The world hadn't become better; instead, there was another war. My plays weren't really good; my job was boring. And then a girl I worked with got married, and I went to the wedding. She looked so beautiful, so purposeful walking down the aisle. I envied her so much for having dreams and someplace forward to go. I burst into tears. Not nice tears, not the kind you should cry at a wedding. But I couldn't stop.

"That's how—well, he was fine-featured and he listened. He seemed to care. He was her cousin, from Michigan. We went to his hotel. I kept crying on and off the whole night. I never saw him again, but I know at least that he was kind and he listened well." She sighed heavily. "And that's that."

At the back of the album was a photograph Molly remembered. It was on heavy stock and not tacked down as the others were with little black corners. When a child, Molly had hoped the man in the portrait was her father. But her mother said he was not.

Still, he was so appealing, with a look around his eyes that made his whole face seem to laugh.

"That was the one man I truly loved in my life," Thea now said. "That was Joseph."

"Joseph? But that's my—I mean you told me he was—wasn't —is this man, then— What do you mean?"

"He died the summer of 1929. Twelve years before you were born. Two months before we were going to be married. Infantile paralysis. Isn't that a childish name for something so deadly? And then, by autumn, the whole country seemed dead, too. We were saving our money to move out West and break into the film industry. He was a wonderful photographer. Anyway, it was all lost. Joseph, the dream, our savings, maybe the country."

She stared at the picture, then reached down and touched it. "I think it would have lasted," she said. "I gave your make-believe father his name so I could say it out loud sometimes. And also—please don't laugh—also because you have Joseph's silky copper hair and nobody else I ever knew had anything like his hair. I can't explain it except for how much I had wanted him and his babies, except for the wanting that never stopped with his death."

"Why don't I know anything about you?" Molly asked.

"Because you're my child. That's how it is."

"Isn't it odd how painful this is?" Thea said a few hours later. She blew her nose and wiped at her eyes. "I mean this stuff is junk! Possessions! Material goods." She patted the back of the sofa. "Only it's been part of me for so long that leaving it feels —fatal." She sat down on her soft and shapeless favorite chair.

She looked small, like Alice after she'd shrunk. She clutched each arm, holding on as if she'd slip otherwise.

Molly suddenly remembered Tony, aged four, pulling a broken child-size chair out of the trash and sitting on it, there on the sidewalk, his hands on its arms the way Thea now clasped her chair.

"No, no, darling," Molly had said. "That chair's broken. The seat's falling through. When we get to our new house, we'll find you a nice, new—"

Tony's face turned dark, his hands pulled into fists and he stared in a way that made her ashamed of her size and power. "I don't want new! I want mine!" he'd shouted.

Children and old people were allowed very little baggage, Molly realized. She looked at the tension in Thea's hands as they gripped the homely old chair. She looked at the stack of magazines on the side table, at the nicked shelf where her mother always sat her teacup.

"Mother," she said, "you aren't giving away that chair, are you? Or the end table? You couldn't."

"But they're worn out and your house is already furnished with beautiful things, and I thought—"

"The things in your room were put there temporarily. I really want them upstairs, in the guest room." She was an amazingly glib liar. She rather enjoyed it.

"Really?" Thea's grip on the chair relaxed. "You mean that?" Molly nodded.

"Then—is there room for the bookcase and some books, too?" Her voice sounded younger and fuller.

"Sure. We'll rent a big U-Haul." The bookcase was homemade and clumsy, a gift from one of the unshaven unemployed in exchange for many dinners.

"And that lamp," Molly said. "It always reminded me of Ali Baba. I used to rub it and wish for selfish things. Oh, and don't you want the rug the crazy man gave you?"

"Oh, yes, Misha's rug." Thea considered. "We're not making much headway, are we? I thought the object was to travel light."

"Why? We're not escaping from anyone."

"Good. Then I'll bring my scrapbooks, that hassock there, the painting the school gave me when I retired, the rocker, the . . ."

By midmorning of the following day, they had sorted the apartment into "keep" and "let go" piles and Molly had made arrangements for the removal of bulky giveaways and for help loading a U-Haul the next day. But nothing had yet been moved and the apartment, chaotic and disheveled as it was, still felt familiar and comforting.

Thea was out, visiting her friend Chloe for the rest of the day. Molly had been invited to join them, but she was sure they'd prefer saying good-bye without her along. She opted instead to wallow in nostalgia, which she did wonderfully well, sitting and reabsorbing the past. She made tea and sipped it slowly, setting her cup and saucer on the pull-out leaf of the table.

The room was filled with an amber light that belonged only to this apartment, built as it was of Massachusetts winter sun, Thea's yellowing curtains, the ancient brown velvet couch and the old wood of the table. Molly had bathed in the tea-tinted light—during other Christmas seasons when, on vacation and loose with her time, she could let the golden hours warm her.

She could almost feel her old clothing, hear the music she listened to day and night. She felt completely at home, pulling idle questions through the topaz light.

Then she stood up. She went to splash water on her face before taking a walk.

The woman in the bathroom mirror said nothing about how much time had passed since those other winters. She didn't need to.

Molly saw herself with shock. She had half expected the old Molly to have survived here, along with the other mementos.

She put on her coat. Walking would do her good. She buttoned up and saw the seven boxes of letters arrogantly waiting on her mother's dresser. She viewed them cautiously, trying to define what made them frightening.

Carefully, she extracted a sampler, two letters from each of the seven boxes. She put them in her pocket and left.

She walked for over an hour, up and back from the church that gave Steeple Street its name, and in and out of the side streets of her childhood.

Her feet began to hurt. She'd forgotten her gloves; her hands, jammed into her coat pockets, ached. Her nose was icy. She retraced her steps and again approached her mother's apartment. Then she remembered the letters, and she went instead into the Steeple Pub, a more neutral setting for their reading.

The wood-paneled room smelled of stale cigarettes. Molly seated herself at a small table, ordered wine and arranged the stack of letters chronologically.

The Case of Molly Michaels, Chapter One. She lit a cigarette and examined the evidence.

First, she read the details of Psych. I, Soc. I and Eng. Lit. 100. The young writer seemed overfond of exclamation points, but attractive and alive.

The next letter, full of newlywed prattle, brought smiles. Molly remembered the act of will it had taken to shape her overweening joy into a coherent letter, to let her mother understand that Molly and Clay had invented love. And of course, as reassurance for Thea, so disappointed about the forsaken scholarship, Molly mentioned academic pursuits and goals. "I'm taking two courses at U. of Chicago," she had written. "They won't transfer most of my credits from Penn, but so be it."

Molly remembered the girl, the courses, the glow of those days. What she couldn't remember were the urgent emotions that had made it impossible to wait two years and finish college before she started marriage. What she really couldn't remember was being young.

"Everybody loves him," she read in another letter. "He has a brilliant future. Everybody says so." She constantly brought in outside opinions that way. "Everybody" was her favorite source. Also "they." She hadn't stayed in college long enough to learn proper research techniques. "They say he'll be president of something big—a Fortune 500 company." She never mentioned her own future. What had she anticipated? Fortune 500 companies didn't have First Ladies.

Molly put the letter down. The president of something big. She'd forgotten those early assumptions. She wondered if Clay had. "Poor Clay," she murmured, answering her own question.

There were three letters devoted to pregnancy and newborns. Molly read of healthy milestones—first smiles and propped sittings, and the hallowed moment when words joined and the idea of sentences—the idea of ideas—was born.

Still, the longer she read, the less Molly she found. The earliest letter had been about her mind and her own activities. Then gradually, those that followed turned into cheering sections for Clay's adventures and chronicles of their babies' growth.

Now and then she glimpsed Molly in a shifting, optimistic series of schools, plans and goals. But there was mostly news of paint and wallpaper and remodeling and entertaining. Some letters read like menus or newspaper society columns. Who had been to the house for dinner and what Molly had served.

She picked up the most recent letter. It was postmarked Atlanta, and she had just been offered a full-time position with the hospital where she worked as a volunteer. "Imagine," she wrote, having grown more temperate with exclamation points, "they're ignoring my lack of credentials because of the work

I've been doing gratis. I can hardly believe my luck. Yesterday, a volunteer who wrote press releases; today, Director of Public Information and a paycheck."

And tomorrow, tomorrow news from Clay that they had to move again, this time to Los Angeles, that media-rich city where her month-long résumé didn't razzle-dazzle anyone.

And so it went, little peeks from Molly looking up above the domestic routines and then ducking down again. She suddenly felt her long months of anger congeal and grow hard, like a palpable—and disposable—object. "No more," she murmured to herself. "No more." She wasn't sure what it meant, but she was sure she meant it.

"Pardon me." A man stood beside her table, holding a drink. "Am I interrupting you?"

She shook her head and folded the letter.

"Then may I join you?"

She couldn't think of how to explain to a stranger that she wasn't really there, that she'd fallen between the lines of old letters, the disguises of old roles, other people's ideas of her. She was an old party doll. Nora stuck in a revolving door.

But *no more,* she reminded herself.

"You seem to be catching up on your mail," he said.

She became interested in the moment. The Molly of the letters and the past was invisible, but someone was surely sitting here, attracting this man.

She felt changed, on her first solo flight. She was suddenly an anonymous, mysterious woman in a bar with the power to pull a distant man into her orbit.

"You must have been away for a long time," he said.

"I still am." She delighted in his puzzlement, especially as it became a look of enjoyment, as if he'd just joined a game. "I don't live here," she added.

"Neither do I." He smiled. "And I know you aren't going to ask where I'm from or what I'm doing in this little town. I like that about you."

Now she smiled. She was passing all manner of surprising tests.

He looked like a sketch for something special. His features were ordinary and without character, but she liked his hands, and besides, nobody had looked at her that way for a long time.

Oh-Molly-you-aren't-thinking-of-*that*-are-you?

Why not? she told the voice. Everybody does.

Because - you - never—you - said - no - more - but - you - didn't - mean—this - is - silly - you - wouldn't - think - of - that - think - of - your - family—

That's all I've ever thought about! But now—no more!

"You know what?" the man said. "Don't laugh, please, but I saw you and I had to talk to you. I've had a fantasy for years and you've always been in it."

Oh - no - you - don't - wise - guy - close - your - ears - Molly - don't - listen - of - course - he's - done - this - a - thousand - times - don't - listen - don't—

His words trickled inside her like honey. "Tell me about it," she said.

"I'd see it this way. I'd be in the most unlikely place. A place like this, a day like today. I'd be there by chance, as I am, a stranger stranded between towns, resting and expecting nothing. And then I'd see her—I'd see you." He paused, allowing her to object or pull back. But she had to find out what he saw.

"Something about the coloring, the shape of the head—I honestly don't know what makes you so beautiful. That's what's wonderful about it. Your mystery, your slightly sad, closed-in look, as if you were missing something sweet you'd once known."

Don't - listen - no - no - fancy - talker - all - words - don't - listen - danger - danger - all - women - look - sad - miss - something - he's - a - fake - he's - a —

Hush! His words sifted over her skin like powdered sugar. She liked his rhythm, the confident way he proceeded, the way he was determined to make her participate in his dream.

"Shall I go on? Is this all right?" His voice was low and intimate, and when she nodded, she felt she had given him permission to do anything he liked.

"The rest is like a dream because there is great silence, that sensual, bottomless silence women like you contain."

Ahhh, God, I have a sensual bottomless silence and I never knew. What else don't I know?

"We don't say much. We don't have to. Instead, we leave, together, to bring the dream to reality."

The - dream - into - reality? — Yuk! — Molly - he - isn't - your - kind - he's - a —

He took her hand and held it with both of his and she felt herself slip into him. "It's up to you," he said.

The room enlarged, the walls pushed back and noise receded. She remembered other times when the blood had raced hard and all the surfaces around her were outlined with light and time pulsed in a strange soft beat, pausing to hang on her choices. Those other times had been long, long ago.

Then she sighed deeply and shook her head.

"No?" he said with surprise. "No? Are you afraid?"

"It isn't that, really." Her throat felt raw and constricted. "It's that I'm trying very hard to grow up now. To stop being anybody else's fantasy."

"Interesting," he said. "But what a pity all the same." He picked up his coat, smiled at her once again, shook his head and left the bar.

29

YOU MADE A MISTAKE.

The words taunted Molly through December.

She had come home from Adams Wall determined to reclaim her energy. She would stop hiding from reality and would begin shaping what she'd been given to more pleasing dimensions.

But still, while Christmas carols piped through the shopping malls, she heard it.

You made a mistake.

And the man from Adams Wall broke through her screen of busyness. She'd hear him instead of the holiday crowds. She'd see his smile instead of the wrapping paper she taped around a gift. She'd feel his hands instead of the cookie dough she shaped and decorated.

Mistake. You made a mistake.

Like a yeasty mix, it rose and even though she punched it down, over and over, it expanded and rose again.

You made a mistake.

What had it gained her to refuse momentarily to be someone's fantasy? What else had she been all her adult life? What else was she now if not the idealized mother/wife fantasy readying her tiny world for another holiday extravaganza?

Christmas came.

In Adams Wall, a man had wanted to be her lover.

In Valley Forge, her lover, Clay Michaels, gifted her with the year's most popular cookbook, a warm woolly bathrobe and a four-record album featuring the songs she climbed upstairs to hear every afternoon. She felt very matronly and mournful.

You made a mistake.

Christmas went.

Clay requested a quiet family New Year's Eve. The image of her family toasting each other by firelight pleased Molly, but she was once again confusing fantasy with her life.

Joanna refused to be part of the picture. She had her own plans.

Nor had Molly pictured Darth Faber in her blissful tableau. However, she was so glad to welcome a friend for Ben, a shy, freckled boy named Lawrence, that she smiled as well on Darth.

At nine that night, she sat in the family room being part of her intimate family evening. Nobody noticed her. Ben and Tony debated with Clay about bedtime on such a night. They stopped the harangue only when it was their turn to play video games. For his part, Clay seemed hypnotized by the games, no matter who played them.

Molly supplied bowls of popcorn and cans of soda and went into the living room where her mother was reading *Gone With the Wind* in large type. "I like to start the year with something untrue," Thea said.

Joanna waltzed in wearing the periwinkle sweater and tiny gold earrings she'd received for Christmas. She looked shockingly sophisticated. Molly stared openly, unable to imagine when the change had taken place.

Joanna smiled, obviously proud of how she looked. Then her expression abruptly drooped. "Guy's father's in Cherry Hill," she announced.

"And *our* Father art in heaven," Molly answered.

Joanna sighed. "Guy Robertson, Mother. My friend, remember? His father was going to let him use the car tonight."

"Wait—you mean 'guy' was somebody's name? Not just 'a guy'?"

"You *knew* that!"

Had she? Had her fog cover made her miss everything since they'd moved? Half a year lost? Good Lord, she was paying as little attention to her daughter's social life as her own mother, infuriating her, had paid to hers.

"But his father's staying in New Jersey, so—"

"You need a ride."

"And since you and Daddy aren't going anywhere—"

"All right. I hadn't planned to carpool on New Year's, but—"

"Mother! I didn't mean— Can't I have the car?"

"It's been stalling. Has to go into the shop."

"Then Daddy's?"

"Anyway, I don't like the idea of your driving tonight. There are drunks all over the—"

"You treat me like a baby! The state, the government gave me permission to drive! I can't believe—"

"I know you don't understand, but it's New Year's Eve. Teenagers aren't nervous enough about it, aren't serious enough about cars. Do you realize how many adolescents are killed or crippled every year because of—"

"If I were a *boy* you wouldn't be this way. This is sexist prejudice!"

"How many?" Thea's eyes twinkled with interest. "How many adolescents killed or crippled every year?"

Happy New Year, Molly said to herself.

Clay sat in the family room attempting male camaraderie. The boys ignored him, commenting on and hooting at each other's performance on the video games. Zings and whirs filled the room. Clay sat on the plaid sofa trying to see the future, but his mind was trapped in a web of a thousand "what ifs." He ached for the release of knowing something for sure, no matter what it was. He was slowly going mad with uncertainty, locked tight around a churning sickness.

The video game pinged and he thought about having to pawn it. And the couch and the house and the dog and the boys.

He went into the living room where he could hear a human voice. "Daddy!" Joanna said immediately. He was stunned by her. She was suddenly a beautiful adult.

"Daddy," she repeated. "I have a problem."

Indeed she did. Her father, the breadwinner, wasn't sure where or how he was going to win the bread anymore. But he didn't think she meant that.

"The car my friend Guy was going to use is in New Jersey."

"Two thousand, do you think?" Thea said.

"What are you talking about, Mother?" Molly sounded worried. Clay didn't blame her. Thea's mind seemed a little patchy lately.

"Adolescents killed or crippled every year," Thea said. "Or do you think more than two thousand?"

This family talked entirely too much and made no sense, Clay decided. He'd grown up pretty damn well without this blathering, this debating of every point. He handed Joanna his car keys. "Be home by one," he said.

After she left, Clay settled in his chair and went back to tending the murky caldron in which his "what ifs" simmered.

"What's wrong?" Molly asked Clay after a half hour of silence. He shook his head.

She tried to remember how many times she'd asked him that question lately. Probably the same number as there were adolescents crippled and killed every year. She watched him pick up the history of Philadelphia that Thea had given him for Christmas. He read and sipped champagne.

Happy New Year! she told herself again, draining her own champagne glass. This wasn't a party. There weren't any more parties, only more nights.

"Let's go watch that special, that one about the movies," she said after an hour of silence.

"In a minute," Clay murmured.

Bitterness seeped through her system. Some intimate evening this was. She took a new bottle of champagne into the family room.

"Want some? Will your parents mind?" she asked Lawrence. He reminded her of a character out of Dickens, the small boy who never got his fair share.

"They gave me some once," he whispered. "At the hockey championship party."

"I'm gonna join, Mom," Ben said. "Hockey." He grinned, signaling a clear "all's well," and Molly felt the first real joy of the evening. Ben had survived the transplant. He might even thrive.

"Will your parents object, Darth?" she asked, although she doubted that he had parents. There was instead a scientist in a basement somewhere.

"Is it all right if I watch TV?" Molly asked. The boys, feeling adult and tolerant with their champagne, released their hold on the video games.

Fred Astaire glided onto the screen looking like the spirit of New Year's. Beautiful people in gowns and black ties swayed and moved gracefully through mansions as the music asked them to change partners. It had been Sinatra, not Astaire, asking that years ago. Sinatra, and then Clay Michaels. Time glided in reverse until Molly, dancing in a frayed fraternity, changed partners for the most beautiful, most heroic, most solid man she'd ever seen. The man with the blue eyes, the black hair, the cleft chin, the man she'd seen on the path in autumn and had later thought a hallucination when she couldn't find him again. The memory went through her like a blade.

Darth belched. The other boys laughed.

You made a mistake.

Thea entered, still holding *Gone With the Wind*. "Did I ever tell you," she said, "how women in Scarlett O'Hara's time wore corsets that put at least twenty pounds of pressure on their internal organs? They had shortness of breath and fractured ribs from it and sometimes, the pressure of the corset was so terrible that their uterus would be forced right down and out of their—"

"Gross! What kind of gross book is that?" Tony made retching noises.

"Nothing like that's in this book. This is a romance. Scarlett just holds her breath and laces up, but what I said is the real truth. And they fainted and had violent indigestion and constipation, too. Isn't that interesting?"

Molly tried doubly hard to focus on Fred Astaire, to believe that people lived his way, somewhere.

She realized that Clay was standing in the room now, watching the television as the music swelled toward its end. He must remember that song, that night. She looked at him, a smile ready for sharing on her lips, all their memories written on her face. Clay stared at the screen impassively. Not a flicker of recognition or sentiment.

The program switched to another Astaire musical. This time he was in a green bower, standing in a rowboat with Audrey Hepburn who wore a wedding dress and veil. And they floated, glided onto the most beautiful river ever, cathedralled with leafy trees, the sunlight filtering through. The music and the current, both elemental and strong, carried them.

"Yo, looka dese tits, Tony," Darth said, holding up a magazine. "Oh. *Sorry,* Mrs. Michaels."

Ah well. This was no riverbed. She wasn't Audrey Hepburn, young and dewy in a white veil. She was Molly Michaels, former bride turned forty. Pretty much used up.

Still, if Clay would only care about her again. Would love her again. If he'd look at her, old as she was, the way Astaire looked at Audrey, just now and then. Just now?

Midnight approached and all seven of them watched the screen and the crowds at Times Square as if something real were about to happen.

"Ten-nine-eight-seven-six—" the boys shouted.

Shortly after the general kissing, Thea went to bed and Clay prodded the four boys toward theirs. Then Clay started another year by picking up his history book, and Molly hugged her knees and looked to the colored shadows of the TV for company.

She tried not to feel cheated. She was so lucky. So privileged. People were dying elsewhere, mourning, ill, homeless, enduring wars and revolutions. She told herself this several times. She actively counted her blessings. Then she returned to her ugly thoughts.

"She's late," Clay said at 1:25.

Molly poured herself a brandy. "Want one?" she asked.

He shook his head. "No, thanks." He sank back into his book.

This is next year, Molly told herself. This is the first day of forever.

She remembered a New Year's Eve thirteen years earlier when the twins were tiny and Joanna a chubby toddler. Molly had nursed her newborns and come downstairs to the living room, quiet except for music—Liszt, she thought it was—and the pop of a champagne cork.

At midnight, her babies slept and Molly lay naked in front of the fireplace with champagne beside her and her husband inside her. A soft snowfall had begun, lacing them into their warm and complete world.

How had they slid from that sensual peace to this silent numbness? How could she bring feeling back?

"Clay?" she tried. "Do you remember St. Louis? When the boys were infants and we spent New Year's Eve alone in front of the fire?" She watched him, waiting for the soft easing around the eyes that memory would supply.

He put his book down, his finger marking his place. He smiled, waiting. He was trying to be sociable. It made her even sadder. "What about it?" he said.

"Oh. Just wondered if you—remember."

"Of course," he said. He yawned and covered his mouth.

"What do you remember? What do you think about when you think about us?"

"I remember everything." He stifled another yawn.

"No, I mean concrete images, things that imprinted themselves."

"Oh, Molly, how can I sit here and reel off—"

"Then just one? One thing you remember about us?"

"I don't want to. I'm really tired. I can barely keep my eyes—"

"Never mind. I'm sorry." Nothing sorrier than a baggy old flirt, was there?

"I remember how much you used to laugh." He stood up. "My back's bothering me—mind if I wait for her upstairs?"

She shook her head.

"You coming up?"

She shook her head again.

He came over and kissed her forehead, held her face in his hands for a moment, then kissed her lips. "Happy New Year," he said. "I'm sorry I'm such lousy company. I'm sorry for not being able to make things better."

She sat on the sofa letting the private sounds of her house cover her vigil for Joanna.

By 1:55, Molly was breathing rapidly. By 2:17, she had tried and abandoned every relaxation technique she knew. When she closed her eyes, she saw terrifying images. Cars crumpled, crushed, flaming, and in them, Joanna, her impossible, querulous, annoying, mysterious, precious, irreplaceable Joanna.

"God," she said, "I'm sorry for complaining. My life is *fine. Perfect.* I'm happy. Just don't let Joanna be hurt or dead or even scared."

At 2:30, Molly's terror clamped her throat tight; only that kept her from screaming out loud. "I *knew*," she whispered. "I knew she shouldn't drive. I *knew!*" She stood up. Clay had to share this, bad back and tired or not.

Then she heard the key in the lock, and her knees sagged with relief. She felt hysterical laughter, tears and anger instantly surface and combine. She had wanted to stop feeling numb—wanted the power of love to make her feel intensely again, and it certainly had. "I didn't mean that kind of feeling, God!" she said as the key turned and the door opened.

"Oh, Joanna," Molly cried out. "I was so—" She stopped and faced her changeling daughter. Joanna looked moist, plumped up beneath the skin as if tiny porous spots had been filled. She looked contented and glossy.

"Where—why are you so . . ." She couldn't stop staring. She knew that look. She'd seen it in her own mirrors over the years. It was the triumphant smile of the discoverer, the face of the word *Eureka!* Joanna had found out what all the fuss and love songs were about.

And Molly had been worrying about simple things like car wrecks.

"I drove Guy home and we talked and talked and he's so nice, Mom, and Dad's car clock doesn't work, and I guess we forgot the time."

Light poured from Joanna. She flooded the entry with radiance.

"You really like him, don't you?" Molly asked softly.

Joanna bit at her upper lip and smiled. And blazed.

Molly felt her daughter's brightness settle on her, highlighting the lines on her face and the veins in her hands. She'd been a mother for sixteen years, but tonight she was officially, finally The Mother. The torch had been passed.

Joanna floated up the stairs, turning once to smile beatifically. She could have been on that green shadowed river, on that boat moving to the rhythms of a love song, a strong male paddling and singing to her. And Molly was far back on the shore, a well-wisher in the shadows.

The music swelled with Joanna's song and the little boat disappeared around a curve. Molly sighed. Then behind her, the man from Adams Wall whispered. "You are my fantasy. You are a woman of mystery and depth. Come into my boat with me. I sing, too." She turned to him, her hand outstretched, ready now for her ride. But he was long gone.

You made a mistake. You made a mistake. You made a mistake.

30

"WHAT'S HAPPENING?" THE LADY IN THE MIRROR asked as Molly, naked, turned left and right and scowled.

"That's a roll of fat," Molly said. "But no more. New year, new me. I'm getting into condition, finding a way to feel good again. I want to explore new worlds, have my own adventure."

"You're going to climb the Himalayas?"

Molly brushed her teeth.

"Molly, you aren't talking sex, are you? The wide world of adultery? This isn't your strike for individuality, is it? That's so trite!"

Molly flossed and flashed a wide smile so she could admire the straightness of her teeth. "Forget individuality. How can I be special? There's nothing left for me to be except what I was groomed for—someone to make nice to a man. What has my marriage been training for if not that? So I'm going to find one who will at least make nice back. I'm going to find me a fantasy."

"The Himalayas are a smarter bet."

For the first six weeks of the new year, Molly had skimmed the want ads, determined to find a manageable part-time job that would suit both her and her family's needs. She'd found none. Instead, she found the personal columns with their explicit job descriptions and she realized she was better qualified for and more interested in them than in part-time shoe or heavy machinery sales, or jobs that required degrees or mobility or experience she lacked. The personals were the Yellow Pages of desire, and she let her fingers walk all over them.

"What has four legs and fun?" one asked. "We do," it answered. "Interested in joining us, call . . ." But no, she decided over morning coffee. Her life was already one long group activity. She wanted attention. No sharing allowed.

"Attention, ladies! Your daydreams and loneliness are over. Now you can have your very own 19-year-old stud to fulfill your every fantasy."

She sat, after Clay and the children had left for the day, and she read her ads, feeling her excitement rise at the possibilities in the little square blocks of print.

"Cosmopolitan successful w/m welcomes discreet sedate affair with civilized, slender w/f."

"Adventurous couple seeks bi-lady for weekends in our mountain hideaway."

She sat in her kitchen with flank steaks defrosting and a pile of clothes waiting to be ironed. She read her paper, smiling.

"W/m, bright, affluent, witty—lover of mountains, music and massage . . ."

And she saw Clay, strong jaw jutting, silence settling on him until their bed frosted over and the sheets hurt with the cold.

"Friendly stranger desires friendly stranger for daytime and discreet fun . . ."

"Winter's here—how about hibernating together?"

"Spirited sinful man seeks shapely seductive salacious she for safe salutary sensual satiation . . ."

She evaluated their vocabularies, humor, imaginations. She envisioned them out there—an army of playful, spirited, sensual males waiting, hoping for a note from Molly, who could bring them joy and discreet sex.

She eliminated the dimwits, those who were too enamored of fuzzy or sloppy imagery. ("Do you love puppies, sea mist and laughter?" She hated him.)

"Incarcerated Taurus, well put together, wants to correspond with open-minded female." She eliminated those that were futile or frightening or both, as this one was.

"Gentleman of good taste seeks lady who tastes good." She didn't feel ready for him.

"Desire lady into healing, God, crafts, meditation and country living." She wished him good luck.

"I'm looking for the child in me." She wasn't looking for children anywhere, least of all in a lover.

She eliminated those seeking willowy twenty-year-olds and those wanting long-term permanent commitments. She looked for something more manageable. That's what her family had suggested. "Mom," Joanna had said. "I think you're bored. Why don't you find some cute part-time job?"

"Moll," Clay had said, "there must be some pleasant part-time work around, don't you think?"

Yes. She thought so. She was hot on its trail.

"Attr. married man has lots of TLC for married lady . . ."

Her days became more exciting. She smiled. Her family noticed. She spent less time in the attic. Her family applauded. She joined an exercise salon. Kinkiness was acceptable, but only perverts tolerated middle-aged spread.

"Prof. man w/boat and lots of love wants slender lady . . ."

She acquired a post office box under a different name. Gillian, she called herself. "I've come out of the pages of novels you've read in bed to find you and love you deeply. Slender nonsmokers only . . ."

She stopped smoking and started running. Her family congratulated themselves on how successfully they had turned their moping wife and mother around.

"Exciting housewife for a good time or a long time . . ."

"My liberated wife travels a lot. Want to fool around?"

Her cooking improved. She papered the guest bath. She sewed curtains for the boys' bedrooms. By mid-February, the house looked permanent and lived in. The Burchards came for dinner again, and Molly was radiant and cordial.

"You're terrific," Clay said, kissing her and going to bed while she finished the dishes.

"Single professional in 40's seeks attr. Fm. who needs discreet, sensitive attention . . ."

Yes, yes. She was one attr. Fm. A needy attr. Fm. For once, she was qualified to answer the ads.

"I'm looking for something," she told Clay, who beamed as if she were a clever, house-trained puppy. "Something in—public relations."

She narrowed the contestants to a few finalists.

"Celebrate the ephemeral nature of earthly pleasures by letting me dance into your heart or your bed. I'll leave you smiling when the dance is over." Ah, but would he be fun, or just silly?

"Somewhere, a married lady is missing the attention she deserves, but she only dreams of an affair. Sensitive w/m in similar situation is looking for her if she's not too scared to stop dreaming and reply." And would he be marvelous, or somber?

Then she declared a winner and champion. "Handsome man seeks to fill Monday afternoons with attr. w/f who needs a slow hand and an easy touch after weekends with her family. I'm safe, eager to meet your needs and very discreet."

To the point, specific, without ties—and safe.

Molly wrote eight drafts of her answer. With each new version, she felt as if she were refashioning herself. She was becoming Gillian, a sophisticated, sensual, direct woman of the world.

"Weekends are hard," she finally wrote him. "And so are weekdays. I'd like to meet you."

She had her hair cut into a new and more becoming style. She bought designer stockings, not her supermarket regulars, and invested in lavish underwear. She checked the post office daily, and her hands shook when she received his answer and an official assignation date. His name was Alexander.

She worried about her wardrobe. It was not heavy on sophisticated, sensual and direct garments. She finally decided that she would wear a silk blouse with a high collar and billowing sleeves. She told herself that its faintly Cossack overtones gave it a racy, exotic air.

And one Monday afternoon, she found herself entering the recesses of a midtown bar, where she saw a man sitting alone, wearing a white carnation.

"Hello, Alexander," she said with a smile. She sat down across from him, the heroine of a thousand films.

"Gillian," he answered.

She flushed, loving her *nom d'affaire.*

"What a surprise," he said. "I was sure a plain woman would walk into the room. Not that it would matter so much, but still, I never expected . . ."

She, too, was surprised. The man had advertised his handsomeness honestly. She could envision him on slick magazine paper, smiling behind a snifter of expensive brandy, wearing a tuxedo, even in the morning.

"Why don't we go right to the apartment," he said. "It seems foolish to talk about what we expected instead of appreciating what we found."

Actually, she wanted to sit and talk. She enjoyed the first acts of plays, the buildup. She wanted to dawdle, speculate, find out why he had advertised, who he was, what he did the other six days of the week, why he had Mondays off. She wanted to find out if he had a sense of humor, or interesting ideas.

But obviously that wasn't the protocol of dating-by-the-classifieds.

The apartment was spartan and impersonal. "This isn't my

place," he said. "My company maintains it for out-of-town guests. Or today, for me. For fun." He poured them wine and sat beside her on a long couch.

"What I like best," he said, "is how different we all are, how different each face, each neck, each shoulder is." He put his wine on the coffee table and stroked her face with both his hands.

She tensed. A stranger's hands were on her, the feel of his fingers unfamiliar and their route foreign. She willed Gillian to take over.

"And I love how beautifully we're designed," Alexander continued, "so that whatever the need, whoever and from wherever, we can pleasure each other. We can come here with no past, with nothing but now, and make this time ours and fulfilling."

His words brushed her neck along with his lips. Yes, but, she heard herself think. I'm not sure I completely agree, I— His hands moved over her and she had a strong sense of events speeding too quickly, of missed stages.

Oh, what do you want? A two-year courtship? she asked herself in an annoyed voice.

She tried to pay more attention to him. Tried harder to relax. Tried to stop trying so much.

His hands moved over her blouse, under her hair at the base of her neck, over the silk on her shoulders. Her cheeks flushed.

He unbuttoned her blouse, touched her skin lightly and smiled. "I want to massage you," he whispered. "Let's go to the bedroom."

She felt stupid and uninformed. What were the rules, the timing, the etiquette of sex with a stranger? She wanted to do this thing the right way.

She lay on the bed. Alexander's hands had a sprinkling of dark hair on the top of each finger. Clay's didn't.

The tendons at the back of her neck tightened.

My breasts, she thought. Those hands are touching my

breasts. What was his name again? Pay attention, Molly! He has a very good technique, don't you think? Relax. Look at that. Didn't you want to feel good? He's certainly trying. Look—that's different. Clay never—no! Censored! Don't think about Clay *now*!

If only she could stop thinking altogether! But she split in two, and her more enthusiastic self, an on-the-spot reporter, leaped up and stood beside the bed. "Hi! This is your nightly newscast. We're right here, covering Molly-Gillian's first fling, folks. Look there, the fellow's working now on her midriff. Boy, is she nervous, but he isn't. He's—"

Maybe they could take a break and drink more wine. Lots more wine. Get past this. Maybe it's just first-time jitters.

Alexander didn't seem to want to stop right now. Molly closed her eyes and tried to simply experience, to feel good and nothing more.

It was pleasant. She took a deep breath and felt his hand gentle its way onto her stomach, lifting the pantyhose, sliding it softly, gently, down . . .

"All *right*, folks. Now we have Molly-Gillian nearly starkers on a stranger's bed. Isn't this interesting? If you'll just move that camera in for a close-up, we'll—"

Molly closed her eyes still more tightly.

"You're beautiful," Alexander murmured.

"You hear that, folks? He's saying the right things on cue!"

"I love to make love," Alexander said. "I love to watch women react. Women are endless, insatiable. I love them." He stroked and kissed and—

Who was he? What was he doing? What was she doing?

This is nothing, she told herself. Nothing. Just get through it and you can go home. This is the training session.

For what?

Stop magnifying its significance, okay? The whole process is nothing more than a lot of nerve ends and synapses. Very mechanical. You push a few buttons, rub a little, move a little and big deal, some vasomotor constrictions, right? You wanted to feel good, right? So stop acting like a—

But look, now he's—and I still don't know who he is, and—

This wasn't fun. It was her fault, completely. She was retarded, old-fashioned, a perpetual clod. She didn't want this, after all. She wanted to feel special, not just good. She wanted a lover—shouldn't it have something to do with love?

"*I'm sorry!*" she said, loudly.

He popped up. "What?"

"I'm sorry." She sat up and grabbed her pantyhose and held it against her. "I can't do this."

"What do you mean, 'can't'? You *are* doing it."

"No, I, oh God, you see, this isn't *me*. I honestly wanted it to be me, but I was wrong. I can't. This isn't what I want."

He relaxed and smiled. "Oh, okay. Then tell me what you do want. I'm always interested in new—"

"I want to talk."

"Talk? You mean say dirty things, tell you what I—"

"I mean *talk*. About us. I don't *know* you."

"Jesus! That's the whole idea."

She felt a dangerous mix of hysteria and guilt. Was she a middle-aged version of the high school tease? Would he become furious? Hurt her? He was still dressed, barely rumpled at all. Did that mean she was allowed to stop now or did that mean he'd feel doubly cheated? Did she have to worry about any of this?

"Drink more wine." He sounded grim. "Relax, Gillian."

"Listen, Alexander, this is important. *I'm not Gillian.*"

He shrugged. "I'm not Alexander."

"But—but—I mean I'm really not—I—" She burst into tears.

"I don't believe this," he said. He frowned. He cleared his throat. He looked around as if an answer to this impasse might be found on the walls.

She stood up and shuffled to the side of the bed, reclaiming her bra and slip. "I've been married such a long time," she whispered.

He stood up and stared out the window while she scurried around, retrieving her things.

"So sorry," she said. "Ruined your Monday."

"There'll be other Mondays. You weren't the only one to answer my ad, you know." His voice was a hammer, hard and steely. "Want to know how many others wrote?" He turned and faced her.

She shook her head. She did not want to know. Her campaign had been a private quest. She didn't want more proof that nothing she did was original. She put on her shoes and found her coat and said nothing.

"Forty-five," he shouted. "You hear? Forty-five wives and mothers who can't stand their lives! Forty-five women who need *me*! I'm going to see every damn one of them, lady, and I'll bet you, whoever you are, you'll be the only one to act this way. You're *sick*, you know?"

She ran out, then rode down the elevator, her heart beating rapidly. She did, indeed, feel sick. Cowardly, confused, stupid woman, Molly cursed herself. You fail at everything. Now you've even failed at cheating.

31

ONCE HOME, MOLLY SHOWERED AND SCRUBBED with a vengeance worthy of Lady Macbeth. After that, she didn't know what to do or in which direction to point her feet. She wasn't Gillian and she no longer knew who Molly was. She was nothing now and she had nothing to look forward to.

The idea of an Alexander had kept her alive for weeks. She had shaped her days into arrows pointing toward this afternoon. Without the hope of redemption through similar afternoons, Molly had no bearings.

She walked downstairs unsteadily, groping her way.

"Daddy called," Joanna said. "He'll be late."

Molly felt relieved. She needed time to collect herself. She stood at the sink, pulling apart semifrozen chicken pieces. She was sure she could break off brittle pieces of herself as easily. It took her a while to realize Joanna was talking. "What?" she said. "I'm sorry, I—"

"I said I have a bad problem."

Molly felt nauseous and weak. A problem. A bad problem. She put down the chicken and went to sit at the table with Joanna. For two and a half months, ever since New Year's Eve,

Joanna had been rosy and secretive. She had deflected every move Molly made to understand her, although in truth, Molly had been too absorbed in her own quest to really pay attention. A wave of guilt added itself to the nausea and fear.

"Want me to leave the room?" Thea asked.

"Stay," Joanna said. She twirled the little charm on a chain around her neck. "I—" Her face was flushed against her rich auburn hair. "I did something stupid, and now I'm really messed up, I . . ." She twirled the heart-shaped charm again.

"Now look," Thea said firmly. "You can't shock me. I was once unmarried and pregnant myself."

Molly waited for Joanna to react to the word "pregnant," but Joanna seemed in a private daze. "Don't laugh, please," Joanna said softly. "First of all, you have to understand, I'm in love. I didn't know it for a long time. When school started, Guy was going with Cathleen." Her voice was dreamy.

Molly felt her intestines twist into a knot. This was going to be one long recital, with a detailed history of the grand passion before it reached consummation. While her daughter chronicled each progression toward the coupling, Molly thought about the results of said coupling and of possible courses of action. There were no good ones. The world, already stale after Alexander, seemed rancid when Molly thought about abortion clinics and her daughter.

"I became so close to him, you know? My best friend. But then, around New Year's Eve, well, he started looking different. I felt different, you know?"

New Year's Eve. Ten weeks ago. Long enough. And all those times Molly had tried to talk to her about sex and Joanna had reared up and galloped away like an angry horse. That time Joanna read that horrible poem about abortions and Molly tried so hard to have a heart-to-heart about contraception while Joanna practically screamed at her to stay quiet. Now look. Molly was an enlightened mother, for God's sake, but Joanna refused to be an enlightened daughter.

"Guy's beautiful, don't you think?"

Personally, Molly thought he looked half completed, but obviously, the completed parts were in working order.

"And did you notice his eyes?"

What if Joanna wanted to keep her baby the way her grandmother had? Could Molly, a kept baby, logically refuse? Molly felt overwhelmingly defeated, felt as if on this day, both she and her child had reached dead ends.

"His eyes are definitely nice," Thea said, "but what is the problem?"

Joanna sighed. "I did this stupid thing. I lied. When we moved here, I told everybody I was going with a guy in L.A. I bought this charm and said it was from him. I did it so that I wouldn't have to, you know, *be* that way. I wouldn't have to kiss, or be touched, or—you know."

"But then?" Molly prompted. Oh, then. Then, wow, then . . . She felt bitterly disappointed in the ways life worked out.

"No then." Joanna swallowed with embarrassment. "That's my problem."

Wait. Molly reined in her thoughts.

"I mean a lot of guys make you feel not real," Joanna said. "Like you're something that was invented for them, not a person. It made me think I didn't like anything, you see? But that's because I didn't know Guy. He listens, he cares. He makes me feel like a special, a real person. But I'm stuck with my imaginary steady, and I want Guy and I want to, well, be able to have a whole thing. You know? Friends *and*—you know?"

"I know," Molly whispered. Her throat hurt. "I know."

"Tell him the truth," Thea said.

"I can't tell him I lied. He admires me because I'm different, trustworthy, loyal. I can't tell him I've lied for six months!"

"Then tell him how you feel, then break up with Mr. Imaginary." Thea drummed on the table.

"I can't. It'd be fickle."

"Okay, then." Thea stood up. "Lucky you have me around.

I'm an expert at killing off imaginary men. But of course, I used a world war for Joseph Hawthorne. There aren't any wars now, are there? Imagine that, just when one would come in handy, we go and have peace."

Joanna looked offended.

"I'm sorry. I know this is serious. Okay, honey, he's going to dump you. He'll write you a letter and break your heart. From then on, it's up to Guy and fate. Just don't be a copycat and make up any more imaginary lovers."

"I didn't know about yours when I created mine." Joanna smiled. "Maybe it's a family trait." She jumped up and ran to Thea and kissed her. "You're so smart! You saved my life! We can mail the letter to Ellen and she'll mail it back from California. Thank you!"

"Saving lives is tiring," Thea said. "I'm going to take a quick nap before dinner."

Joanna hummed while she set the table. "One thing," Molly said. "I hope you never again feel you need a cover story. You don't need excuses for what you want to do or don't want to do. Understand me, Jo?" Understand me, Molly? she silently added.

Her daughter nodded, then seemed in doubt again. "What if you think you want something and then, when you get it, you realize that wasn't what you wanted at all? Or don't grown-ups worry about things like that?"

Molly busied herself with the defrosting chicken. "I'll answer that one when I'm a grown-up," she said, hoping Joanna thought she was joking.

She did a lot of sitting and waiting for people to come home. Now it was for Clay, late at his meeting, his dinner, his report preparation, his whatever.

The night wore on. Thea went to bed. Molly turned off the lamp and sat in the dark. I have botched my life, let it zoom by as if I were a sightseer on a train, she thought. What now?

She tried to move away from her thoughts. She walked from room to room, passing the countless Michaels possessions, the fruits of Clay's success, the care of which gave Molly something to do.

She picked up Tony's magician's hat from the floor and found a school notice she should have seen the week before. She checked the kitchen burners and wiped crumbs off the counter. Her arms felt heavy and defeated. All she could ever remember doing was wiping crumbs away.

She noticed that Mr. Cheeps' cage was still uncovered. Poor bird, ignored while people switched lights on and off, making days and nights, dawns and sunsets, over and over for him.

"Poor Mr. Cheeps," she said, going to the cage. "And you're so good and quiet about it."

He was beyond quiet. He lay on the bottom of the cage, feet up, all life gone.

Like a cartoon character, but with no laughs.

"Dead," Molly whispered with horror, opening the cage door and touching his yellow feathers, watching them ruffle as she whispered.

"Dead." But why? When? With what struggle, what fears? Dead, alone, unnoticed, still locked in his little cage.

She started to cry, holding his inconsequential body. "I'm so sorry," she said. He was soft and weightless. She had betrayed his trust, his simple requests. She had failed him. And then she thought of all the houses she had left behind, all the tiny animal cemeteries, the last resting places of the Michaels' animal victims.

So many small things entrusted to me. Abused. Used up.

She cried for turtles with softening shells and chameleons lost in the dying grass of autumn. She cried for baby chicks who never saw henhood, for goldfish dying soundlessly in brackish water. For lizards starving in the corner of a bookcase. For hamsters fondled to death. For her brutal disregard of all their souls and of what they wanted and needed of life.

"Oh God," she cried, stroking Mr. Cheeps' tiny head. "I can't take care of anything. Everything is dead. Everything."

Clay came home twenty minutes later. He found Molly sitting on the kitchen floor. She cried and made no sense. Over and over she explained the bird's death, the bird's life, and said, "Don't you understand? Don't you understand?"

He didn't understand anything anymore.

32

"I DON'T KNOW," MOLLY SAID. "I'D RATHER HAVE A female therapist, and not one your company suggests."

Clay closed his eyes with exasperation. "I can't do anything right, can I? Norman Vernon's supposed to be excellent. Don't throw up roadblocks all the time. You have to stop crying, don't you?"

His words brought fresh tears to her eyes. She blew her nose, dried her eyes and nodded.

"Then talk to the man."

She talked. Chronologically, as Dr. Vernon suggested. She talked about Adams Wall, the hardware store, being poor, her mother's revolutionary friends. She seldom cried, because they didn't talk about the issues that pained her.

"And your father?" Norman Vernon prompted.

"Well, it's peculiar. He was made up. I mean I have a biological father somewhere, but not the one I thought. I found out a few months ago."

"Ah." It was a deeply satisfied sound. "And was that before or after the crying started?"

"During. That's irrelevant. Kind of sad, yes, because those

stories kept me warm in my childhood. And disorienting, I guess. But actually, I think it was lovely of my mother to provide such a fine father. And I can keep the stories. What difference does it make? Anyway, that has nothing to do with my problem."

He pretended to believe her, but he constantly returned to the topic of the imaginary father, prodding her conversational march whenever it listed to one or the other side of the road.

"He's not doing me a bit of good," she said to Clay after four sessions with Vernon. "It's kind of a joke, in fact. Why should I go?"

"Be patient. The company's paying for it. Enjoy yourself. You always say I don't listen enough, so here's a guy who will."

It was an interesting idea. A busy executive buys a shrink to listen to his wife in much the same manner his wife hires help for her onerous domestic duties.

"I will not discuss my father anymore," she said the following week. "He is a figment. If we're going to talk about fathers, we'll have to talk about yours."

Dr. Vernon filled his pipe and nodded. "Let's talk about now instead of the past. How are relations between you and your husband?"

"Not good. I cry a lot and can't seem to do anything, and he's tense and abstracted and doesn't talk, and my kids are obnoxious and needy at the same time, and my mother's health is failing, and I feel lonely and isolated, caught in the middle and, at the same time, all adrift, and I guess that's about it."

"Well, ah, relations of a more intimate nature?"

She glared at him. "How do you think they are if the days and the evenings are horrible? Don't you know anything about *people*?"

"You would characterize it as less than satisfactory?"

She slumped down farther in her chair. "I wouldn't write songs about it."

He nodded.

"But that isn't my problem! If the days got better, so would the nights. I'm here because I can't stand my *life*. I'm not a disturbed person, not a neurotic. I used to be really happy. Oh, I worried about the normal things—about how to handle a family and a job, about my kids, about getting old. But I was happy in L.A. I had everything." She sniffled. "See?" She grabbed a tissue. "It's always like this. If I think about how h-h-happy I was, then th-this happens." She blew her nose. "I'm too old to go through this over and over."

"You perceive yourself as old?"

"Too old. For this."

"Do you want to discuss your feelings about aging?"

"No." She blew her nose again, and suddenly wondered what she was doing there, why she was expending so much energy trying to explain herself to this muddleheaded doctor. "No, I don't," she said, and she stood up. She felt a little light-headed. "In fact, I don't want to discuss anything anymore. I don't want you to 'cure' me, to make me adjust to how it is. You don't even understand me. But you know what? I do. I've understood my problem all along.

"It's simple. Every time I get my act together, somebody changes the scenery. I'm a sane person, but the system is crazy, bumping us around, destroying everything stable for the greater glory of their products!"

The doctor's voice was exceedingly mild. "Don't you think you're overly dramatic about relocating? A bit hostile?"

"Hostile? Me? For God's sake, look how the Palestinians have carried on for forty years about one single relocation! And me —I've moved eight times! You don't see me racing around with a machine gun, do you? If only you'd tell those Arabs that it was a company move, there'd be peace in the Middle East." She paced the room.

"That is hardly relevant to the real issues of your life," he said. "Your difficulties in personal relationships with your husband and—"

"Don't give me Freud! Freud wasn't transferred every few years. Look, analysis takes longer than I've ever lived in one city, so don't give me a man who thought people had endless time to work things out."

Norman Vernon shook his head and said nothing. Molly cleared her throat, sat back down and spoke quietly.

"I'm being strident, aren't I? I used to be a nicer person. More likable. Ladylike. Look what's happened. Did you know that corporations prefer divorced men so that nobody gets the way I am—uppity and hard to handle? Oh, it's so hard, though, so *hard* to be nice and good and loving and keep things together and not be angry all the time. Love shouldn't do this to people. Love shouldn't narrow down the world to a sliver, to only my husband and my children and my house. Love should free you so you can reach farther out. I want to be part of the whole world, the—I want—I—"

"Yes?" he said. "What do you want?"

"Freud again? What does a woman want? Oh—I want it all. I want to be more than Mrs. Clay. Mrs. America. I want my marriage, but I want my work, too. I want more than minding the children, smoothing the moves, caring for the house and providing sex. I'm not a geisha or a cute little consort! I'm a forty-year-old woman and I want to grow up before I die!"

Dr. Vernon did a peculiar thing with his lips, pushing the bottom one out in a quasi-thoughtful manner, beginning to nod. "Indeed," he said, removing his glasses and carefully wiping them.

"How can I have that?" she asked. "It feels as if everything's rigged against me. The system— What should I do?"

His eyes, exposed without their glass shields, veered in her direction. She was sure he saw only a blur. He shook his head, put on his glasses and said, "Only you can answer that question, and only after you work harder, longer. Stop sidestepping important issues, stop refusing to really work on this. Every time we touch on a central relationship, you—"

"That's it, then." She stood up. "Everything I've said is about central relationships. People don't marry only people, except in songs. People marry roles, too. Why don't you know that? I'm married to a chunk of a corporation, and that's what I've been talking about."

"That isn't at all what I—"

"Oh, I know what you mean. You want to know if I can only achieve orgasm hanging from a light fixture or with a light fixture. But lives are twenty-four hours a day, spent mostly out of bed, and I'm going under from the dead weight of the middle hours. I'm sure those questions are important, but right now, I don't have time for them. I'm not going to ask any more questions or wait any longer. I'm the expert on me. I'm not asking anybody how to do it—I'm just going to *do* it. I'm not going to adapt, dammit! I'm not going to change myself, either! I'm going to change my life!"

"Mrs. Michaels, I—"

"No! I'm going to find a job and save money and figure out how to start my own business again. I'm going to feel good and complete and occupied again. I'm not crazy—the only crazy thing is what took me so long to realize any of this!"

"Mrs.—"

But she ran out of his office, into the elevator and through the lobby, stopping to catch her breath only when she was outside on the pavement. She half expected a posse to break through the doors and grab her. It was probably illegal to shout at your psychiatrist or to leave before your hour was up.

She took a deep breath and looked around her. She was back out in the world.

She smiled and hurried on. She had *work* to do.

33

MOLLY PUT AWAY GROCERIES WITH THE PLEASANT sensation of having made progress. In half a day, her world had redirected itself and she was again at its helm. Dr. Norman Vernon seemed years, not a few hours, away.

She had walked and looked and planned. Either Ellen would be able to sell Molly's share or she would not. There began to be ways to handle either contingency. The thing was to find a site, think it through. She was enormously optimistic and could feel her skills itch at her fingertips.

She stacked soup cans in the pantry, enjoying the fine way things could be made to balance.

Thea opened the back door. "Terrible out," she said, "like being slapped with a cold, wet sheet. Did you have a good time with the doctor?" She pulled off her red cap and mittens.

"Wonderful. I quit. I'm healing myself. See? No more weeping. I've made about a zillion decisions since nine A.M. How was the Gray Panthers meeting?"

"Interesting. What kind of decisions?" Thea peered into the pantry, her head cocked to the side, finally choosing a box of crackers.

"I'm going to find a way to finance a new store. I'm going to have my own work and my own business. Want to be a sales-girl?"

"Saleswoman, for God's sake." Thea kissed her cheek. "Congratulations. What I'm going to like best is how happy you're going to be. Every day. Even when you won't know you're happy. But I'll remind you. Now, how are you going to do it?"

Molly shook her head. "Small Business Administration—I have a track record now. Second mortgage, find investors, I'm not sure yet, except that I'm going to do it. I'm good at it and I like it. I don't feel as if I have to justify it anymore. I don't have to think I'm crazy because I want it."

Thea smiled and nodded. "Good for you. Good for you. Did the mail come yet?"

Molly felt a small chill. "It never comes this early, Mom. You know that."

"Oh. Of course. I guess I'm so eager for that danged letter to get back here. I wrote it two weeks ago—maybe longer. Yes, longer. What's taking so long?"

Molly put away the produce. "I think Ellen went on a vacation. Her mail probably piled up and she couldn't forward the letter right away."

"I can't wait to see Janna's reaction. I made it very fancy. I hope that Ricky person was supposed to be the thoughtful type. It was my first creative writing since—what did I used to write?"

"Your plays?" Molly busied herself with apples so her mother wouldn't notice her expression. Little bits of Thea's memory seemed to simply go, leaving dots of space. And it was happening more and more often.

"Yes. Plays. That's right." She looked worried herself. "One was produced, called—"

"*Courage House.* Is that the one you mean?"

"Was that it?"

"Mom? Are you—how do you feel?"

"Yes. The meeting maybe. Well . . ." Thea put the box of crackers on the table, or dropped it there. Then she walked out of the room.

"Mother?"

Thea waved her hand, low, near her hip, a signal to stay back. She wanted to be alone.

It felt strange. Like a window opening inside her head. Something familiar in the feel. Something scary.

She left the kitchen so Molly couldn't see, but she wasn't sure what it was Molly shouldn't see. She should know, though, because it felt remembered. It felt—again.

She went up the stairs slowly. Maybe a nap, she thought. She sat down on her bed and took off her scarf, then unbuttoned her winter coat. Top button, then the next, then—and her hands froze on the fourth button, all messages lost in pulled wires and space. Her head grew small, smaller, until it was gone, but spinning at the same time, burning into white wordlessness that her flesh remembered and recoiled from. Red sparks streaked and circled, connections severed and energy snapped idly.

And she sat, paralyzed, all she had been, all memory and meaning losing its place and falling into a central pit and then, finally, the container collapsing, toppling onto the floor with hands still tight on the fourth button.

Molly put away the pancake syrup and the cornstarch and considered ways of helping Clay understand her new decisions.

It would be difficult now, with the tension higher than ever while he waited for his performance review. Maybe she'd wait until tomorrow, until it was over. He'd never been this peculiar about being evaluated before. Now he was acting like a bad student facing finals.

Still, by tomorrow night the review would be over and she

would tell him. She'd make him understand that it was her route not only into the world, but also back into the heart of their marriage.

She heard a muffled thump and she looked to see what she had dropped. The floor was empty. She looked at the back door, went to peer through its panes to see if the dog was scratching for entry. She looked around, vaguely interested, then felt forever had passed before she came out of her absorption and realized the thud had come from upstairs.

"Mother!" she shouted, taking the stairs two at a time. "Mother!"

Thea was crumpled on the floor like the empty shopping bags downstairs. Her hands were on the front of her coat; her eyes stared at nothing. Her mouth was half open, as if surprised.

"Please, no," Molly said, all the while cradling her mother, easing her hands off the buttons, opening her coat, putting her head to her heart.

Not like this. Not now. Please, give us more time. She needs more time, God. Not *now*. I need more time!

She felt as if the wall of the world had blown away and a cold wind sucked them both into the void.

She heard a furious pounding and realized it was her own pulse banging in her ears. She pulled away and saw Thea blink. Her mother's eyes stared at nothing, but they blinked.

She kissed Thea's forehead and, still holding her, reached for the phone by the bed and dialed the emergency number written in large letters for Thea's poor eyes and for Molly's, now half blinded with tears.

"Please," she said, waiting for the ambulance to arrive. "Please give us time for good-byes, for all the things we forgot to say. Please?"

Molly stood in the hospital corridor in front of the phone booth trying to remember what made a phone work. She knew it had to do with the slot, with the dime, with numbers. As if she, not her mother, had had the stroke.

Stroke. What a fool word. Thea had been mauled, bashed around malevolently. She'd been raped by an unseen force that went for the core. Not stroked.

Massive, the doctor said. Coma. Maybe—with a miracle.

Molly was so tired. Something had gone wrong with her muscles and bones so that each step and movement required enormous commitment.

Her fingers finally unlocked and she pressed buttons. She had to connect with Clay. She couldn't remember ever needing him this desperately. The little house she'd thought to rebuild had crashed, and both Thea and Molly were going to be casualties unless Clay pulled Molly out of the rubble.

She shook her head, nay-saying to invisible voices. This couldn't be how time moved on, in lurches and staggers, knocking down bystanders, clearing a belligerent path. There was supposed to be a pattern. For every thing a season, a grace to the progress. Her season now was for reawakening. Exploring. Growing. Not for death and abrupt severings.

She had taken for granted advance warnings and final chances, deathbed scenes that lasted as long as there were words and emotions to fill them.

Clay. She needed Clay to put the planet back on its axis. Her hands shook.

"Mr. Michaels' office." Molly felt a wave of relief so sudden and complete, she almost cried out.

"Oh, Clay," she said when he was on the line. "Thank God you're in. Clay, I'm—Mother's had a massive stroke. She's—they don't know if she'll live. She's in a coma. It happened—like that. She was talking to me and then she—Clay?" Her voice became higher and thinner until she had to stop. It hurt too much to let it pass through her throat.

"Molly, I'm so sorry. My God." His voice was hushed with pain. "For all of us. I love her too. The kids—do they know?"

"I left a note. I don't know when I'll be home. There's nothing I can—they said leave, but I can't. They said maybe in a few hours they'd know more, but I'm so upset, so on the edge of—I feel all alone, Clay. At the end. I'm so glad you weren't out somewhere. I'm so glad I reached you. I'll wait right here in the intensive-care waiting room. Or should I go to the main lobby? I'm at Jefferson, and—"

"Molly." His voice stopped her like a hand clapped on her mouth. "God knows I wish I could be there now—wish I had been there all along. I feel awful about this. And worse about being completely unable to be there until tonight. Probably around seven. If you could see what's going on here—anyway, that's irrelevant. I know you're going through hell, and in any fair world I'd be there with you, but I can't be there today."

She had never once considered his not coming, his not standing close and holding her so that she didn't fall down, so that she didn't feel so exposed. "You won't come?"

"Not 'won't.' Can't. Not until evening. You remember, Moll. I have that Douglas thing, the man from the coast. The performance review."

"That's tomorrow," she whispered.

"Starts later today. Anyway, that's irrelevant to what you're going through, but trust me, it's important."

"Of course," she said.

"You remember, don't you? I told you about it."

"Yes." But they'd talked about it before her mother was smacked down and time and sense were pummeled out of shape. Surely old entries in date books no longer applied.

"Tell you what," he said. He always said that. Always did that. Told her what. "I'll get home as soon as I can leave here. I'll check the kids and then meet you there by—oh, seven-thirty, all right?"

"Yes," she said, even more softly. The clear plastic phone booth had sealed and become her coffin. She stood in it, mummified, the last of her kind.

"Maybe make it eight," he said. "I don't know how long Douglas will want to take going over the data."

"Clay," she managed, her voice thick. "Clay, I don't think I can hold out. I *need* you. I haven't ever said that. Haven't ever felt this way in all our marriage, all my life. But right now, I'm so—I'm so s-scared."

"Molly, I know you can do it. Hang in there. I'll be there by eight."

Hang in there. She felt as if she were hanging *on* there, holding on to a generational cliff, waiting for her fingers to be pried off the rock.

The nurse told her to go home, told her that nothing was likely to happen for some time, that they would phone. But she couldn't go home where everything had happened. Home, where the upward pull of the attic room would lead her to curl into her own past and will herself gone again.

No. She couldn't ever do that again. Not in the name and honor of Thea Hawthorne who had so wanted her to wake up and act alive.

"Now get out there and change the world," Thea would say, clipping a barrette on a long braid of Molly's hair. Those words, a kiss, lunch in a brown bag, and the day was officially begun.

She had always meant to ask Thea how she was supposed to do that, and she had always thought the world would give her enough time in which to ask the question. She'd been wrong. And now, unspoken, the secret, all secrets and solutions, were dying.

34

MOLLY HUNCHED AGAINST THE WET MARCH WIND, fighting it as the only tangible enemy she could combat. She walked in large city loops, circling the hospital again and again as if she were stalking it.

I'm not a child, she thought. I must stop behaving like one. This very morning I shouted that I wanted to grow up.

But the feelings of a child resurfaced until she accepted the sorry truth that on this day she was indeed a child, perhaps for the last time. She walked around the hospital again, letting the wind take blame for her smarting eyes and the nose that reddened and filled.

She loved the brave woman in there. It was wrong for Thea to be struck this way in an unbalanced battle, a sneak attack. Wrong to be robbed of an exit line, a final news clip that would make all the knowledge fit together. Unfair to be so special and be given no reward. Molly would miss her forever.

Forever. The enormous word inflated and howled down the windy streets. Molly circled the massive buildings, pressing against forever.

She remembered Thea, not long before, being peeved by something Molly had called "sad." "Sad is for when it can't be expected," Thea said. This wasn't unexpected. This was inevitable, natural, an inescapable part of the process. This was the price of being born. But dear God, that made it much worse than sad.

She thought of Thea, fingers locked on the coat button, eyes and mouth wide in shock. It was wrong and ignoble and it made no sense.

She hurried, rushing her circles, pulling her coat tight, breathing deeply, crying, then stopping, then crying some more.

Her stomach growled. She heard it above the wind, above a car honking. She looked down at her midriff, feeling no relationship with it, and she walked on.

Her cheeks felt whipped and the back of her neck hurt with cold. Her stomach growled again. She felt dizzy and nauseous. She couldn't remember when she'd last eaten, but she knew it hadn't been that day.

She suddenly saw herself from a distance, racing around the hospital. She was a rat in an experiment, scuttling around blocks of brick. She broke from the hold of the hospital and walked down a side street.

She had no real friend in this city, no friendship strong enough for the weight of this. And she didn't have Clay anymore.

But she needed warmth, human shapes and smiles even if they had to be impersonal. She craved smells that would give the lie to death. She wouldn't give in, wouldn't believe in it. She'd find a place for life and sustenance.

She chose a route through streets of stores, but found nothing. She passed a cluster of Colonial shops with gas lamps and multipaned windows, but they displayed clothing or shoes or FOR RENT signs.

Her stomach churned. Her feet hurt. She finally saw a doorway with an awning. There was something male and sedate about the place, something that said it was for business lunches, not for middle-aged children in pain. But it was the only available refuge and it was too late to keep looking further.

The restaurant was almost deserted, but the waiter still took his time. She read the menu and realized she could stomach nothing. Still, to justify taking up space, she ordered soup and salad and wine.

The wine eased the knots in her muscles. She tried the soup, but even the soft carrot chunks felt impossible to master. She sat with her head in her hands.

"Excuse me, but aren't you—"

She blew her nose and wiped at tears that continued to fall as if they'd decided to do so forever.

"—aren't you Molly Michaels? Didn't you live in L.A.?"

She saw only a watery blur. She wiped her eyes again.

"It's Sam," he said. "Sam Collins. Collins Imports? Your teapot man."

She nodded, and fumbled for another tissue. He passed her his handkerchief.

"I thought it was you when you walked in," he said. "But it felt like too much of a coincidence—I was going to call you. I was in New York for the gift show. Thought I'd come down here and do some business, and—but why am I going on like this? Molly, forgive me for asking, but what's wrong?" He sat down across from her.

She looked at him, finally able to see clearly. There he was, kind Sam who always had time for a cup of coffee and talk along with business. Now, he looked at her with real concern.

How good it was to have someone look at her that way, to acknowledge her existence and her pain. She had paid Vernon to do it and he had ignored it. And Clay—she mourned him as painfully, as intensely as she mourned her mother. He had abandoned her, had turned his back and dried up into nothingness. Only Thea had cared. Molly started to cry again. "I'm so sorry, I can't seem to—" She pressed the handkerchief against her eyes.

"I'm really glad to see you," he said. "I mean, not to see you like this, so upset, but I'm—Molly, wouldn't it make you feel better to talk about it?"

She shook her head. "I couldn't do that to you."

"Ah," he said, "what are friends for?" He waited a moment, then he continued. "Anyway, I have an appointment with a department store buyer this evening, and nothing before then. Could we spend the time together? You can be absolutely silent, if you want to. But if you don't want to, I'm a good listener."

He felt comfortable, familiar, yet not overly so. There was an easiness between them, but no old history that might present impediments. She relaxed.

He waved over the waiter to order more wine, and then he waited, peacefully, with no pressure. He was, in an astounding, incomprehensible and comforting way, simply there. Available. Caring.

"It's my mother," she finally said. "She's had a stroke and she's unconscious and they don't expect . . ." She shook her head and wiped the corners of her eyes.

"That's rough," he said. "I've been there. We think we're all grown up and then a parent dies and the truth comes out. I remember I felt so old and so young at the same time, and neither one felt bearable." He pushed her soup in front of her. "You ought to eat, you know."

"I don't have anybody else. No father, no brothers or sisters or cousins. There was always only the two of us and I can't bear —I simply cannot bear—"

He took her hand. "Shhh," he said. "Look there. You're still wearing that wedding band, so there's more than just your mother and you. And children? I remember there were children."

"But they seem—irrelevant. They were once so central, but now they're barely there. Everybody's leaving."

"Everybody?" He looked at her hand, at the wedding band.

She nodded.

"You want to talk about that part?"

She shook her head.

And he waited again. Clay was never this way. Clay pushed for solutions, argued logic or ended the discussion. Sam was simply there, a shelter against unanswerable questions.

"I feel ashamed," she said. "Crying in a restaurant. Feeling stunned. Abandoned. She's eighty and I'm forty. Nothing is premature or shocking or tragic. And that makes it worse."

"I know," he said.

A part of her brain registered amazement that she was saying things to him she wouldn't say to Clay—not to the Clay she'd lived with this past year. Certainly not to the Clay on the phone today. But this man she barely knew took her words and cradled them, respecting them and letting them alone.

"They said I should pray for a miracle." She sipped wine and sighed.

"For my sake a miracle," he said.

"Excuse me?" She tried the soup, but it was cold and filming over. She chewed a small piece of bread.

"The one poem I know. The poet says that sooner or later, lousy things happen to us. It's the basic condition of life. And he asks how he can possibly separate himself from all the rest of humanity and ask that for his sake alone 'there should a miracle be wrought.' "

"What does he suggest in place of miracles? Despair?"

"No, he says he'll adjust to reality. He'll make his strengths, he says, 'here in my bosome and at home.' It's by Ben Jonson and it's four hundred years old. Nothing much changes."

She pulled off more bread and ate it.

"Tell me about your mother," he said.

Molly thought a while. "She pleased herself. She didn't make a large mark on the world, but she tried to make things better. She lived as she chose and she was brave and adventurous. I didn't inherit any of her good traits.

"She was convinced she could learn everything. She read whatever she found, but she focused on weird stories. She'd clip them out and paste them in scrapbooks, believing that someday they'd all fit together and make some grand pattern she'd missed."

"Like what kind of stories?"

"Like . . ." Molly's mind went blank. Her life was full of her mother's stories, but they had blown away in today's wind. "Oh," she finally remembered, "there was one about hamsters eating through the walls of an apartment building."

He smiled.

"And one of my favorites, the Great Molasses Flood." A tear dribbled out of her left eye as if, no matter what her other organs chose to do, that eye would continue grieving. "Fifteen-foot-high tidal wave of hot molasses. Killed twenty Bostonians and injured one hundred and fifty more."

"Come on. I thought you meant real news stories."

"It's true. Happened in 1919. Ask my mother." She bit her lip. "God, I'm going to miss her. She had grit. She tried for everything and made do with what she wound up with, and she survived and triumphed. While she was here, she was really here. She lived."

She stopped. She had put Thea into the past tense and had written an epitaph. She felt comforted. Sam had been right. It did make her feel better to talk about it. Which meant Molly had been right, asking Clay to come talk with her. But she didn't want to think about him yet.

The waiter stood next to the table, clearing his throat. "I'm sorry, sir." He ignored Molly. "We're actually closed now. We're only open for lunch. If you wish to continue eating, the Damask Room across the lobby is open now."

Lobby? Molly could make no sense of what he said. Then she

looked to the back of the restaurant and saw etched doors and realized this was part of a hotel.

"I don't think I'd want to be anyplace called the Damask Room," Sam said.

They walked out and then stood awkwardly in the lobby. Molly looked at Sam, a plain, almost homely man made handsome by the kindness, patience and goodness in his face.

"Don't you have some kind of appointment I'm keeping you from?" she asked.

"No. That Wanamaker buyer's not for a while."

"I want to thank you. You'll never know what a lifesaver you've been, how much I needed somebody to listen, to talk."

"I'm still available," he said. "I mean that."

"I should probably . . ." She looked out the lobby doors and saw people braced against the wind. She didn't want to go back out there, didn't want to wander and fight death all alone in the wind.

"They don't make lobbies the way they used to," Sam said. "At least not businessmen's hotel lobbies." This one was cramped and functional, designed for quick handshakes and little more. There were no soft spots for lounging.

She didn't want to risk solitude. Soon she would come to terms with this, but not yet. This man had magically materialized, a miracle for her sake. She needed more time with him.

"I'm going to make a suggestion," he said. "I have a suite upstairs, complete with sitting room. My company is famous for extravagance, especially with me, since I own it. Anyway, we could take off our shoes and talk as long as you like."

His hotel room? Only a few weeks had passed since Alexander. She reminded herself that Sam was advertising nothing more—and nothing less—than friendship.

"Are you still married?" she asked him, surprising herself.

"Very." He grinned. "And happily. And I still have all those kids, too. Two by my first wife, one by my second and a step-

daughter who's my second wife's by her first husband. My credentials are the same."

"Because you understand I'm not—I wouldn't—"

"Of course not."

"It's just that I'm afraid to be alone."

"I know. That's why I made the suggestion."

Upstairs, he ordered wine from room service. Then, sitting
on opposite ends of a blue silk sofa, they talked about nothing
in particular and everything that was important, avoiding all
specifics of families and lives. They talked about Capital-L Life,
as Clay would have said with a disparaging curl of his elegant
lips. She felt as if Sam had been her confidant forever. He had
no unfamiliar edges.

It turned dark outside. They sat in circles of lamplight and
continued to talk. Molly suddenly saw Sam as if for the first
time; saw how good he was and how much of a difference it
made to be near such goodness. This was what she wanted, as
close to her as possible. She heard echoes of Thea. "I was so
lonely," she had said of the night when Molly was conceived.
"And he was kind. And he listened. Can you understand?" And
of Janna, loving Guy because he listened, he made her feel real.

One thing about this family of women—sooner or later, they
knew what to value.

She felt her cheeks flush. "Sam, I—you're—I—" She leaned
toward him. She wanted to touch, to join.

And then she straightened. She wanted miracles, not one
evening's illusion of communion. Sam was a gift, but for only a
few hours. When his woman grieved, he'd be with her. When
his woman was joyful, he'd share her laughter. That was what
Molly wanted for herself, forever, not a dusky winter evening's
approximation. She wanted a Sam of her own.

Nothing could stop the turn of the seasons or suspend death.
But having a friend made the inevitable less painful. She
wanted her best friend back, along with the completeness they

had vowed to try for, years and years ago. She didn't want bits of one man, bits of another, bed here, talk there, like ingredients in a stew. She wanted continuity, permanence and trust. Not only the act that symbolized and completed joining, but joining itself. For keeps. Molly wanted Clay.

Ah, but he was gone, lost down some corporate rabbit hole.

She mourned him again with new grief.

Sam looked at his watch. "I have to meet that buyer," he said softly. "I'm sorry. I'm running late."

"You have nothing to be sorry about," she answered. "Thank you for everything."

They rode down the elevator together. "I have to go toward Chestnut Street. The far doors," Sam said.

She was going in the opposite direction. They stepped off the elevator and said good-bye. Sam took her hands in his. "You'll be all right, then?" he said softly.

She nodded, wishing she could keep holding on. "Thank you," she whispered. "I'll never forget . . ."

"I'm glad I was there," he said. He looked at her intently, and she was sure he also wondered what more there could have been between them. She wondered if the question hurt him as much as it did her at that moment, because at that moment, and for that moment, she loved this man. "Good-bye," he said, kissing her lightly on the forehead.

She sighed heavily, said good-bye to that and to Sam, took a deep breath and turned. And saw her husband, standing across the lobby, near the desk, staring at her. He looked like a man who'd been immobilized for some time. Like a man who'd seen his wife leave a hotel elevator with a strange man.

It took hours, years, to cross the lobby and approach him. His expression barely changed in all that time. She pulled on her coat while she walked. She could feel her cheeks, her arms, her back, her chest flush and flame.

"Clay," she said, "Clay—it isn't—I wasn't—"

"I came to drop off some material." He rushed his words as

if he felt guilty, a voyeur, as if their roles had been reversed. "Douglas is staying here, I—"

"Clay, I know you saw me, but—"

"No. Please. Please don't. I don't think I could—" He shook his head.

He's afraid, she realized. Afraid of what I might say. But what would I tell him, anyway? That Sam meant so little? I suppose he did, but he also meant so much. How do I explain that honestly?

"I canceled my meeting," Clay said. "After I talked to you I felt so ashamed. I called Douglas and explained and he suggested I drop off the data so he could look at it tonight. And then I took care of the kids and then—I feel like a fool. About everything. About how I'm living my life. I felt sick after we hung up. I felt like somebody else, somebody I never meant to be. I felt like I'd betrayed you and myself and—"

She shook her head. "Clay, it's okay, I—"

"No. It isn't okay. It's the worst feeling I've ever had, feeling like somebody else. I hope I haven't—the way I've been for so long—I hope I haven't destroyed anything. Ruined anything." He looked at her intently.

"No. Nothing's ruined. No matter what you think, I wasn't—"

"I love you, Molly. More than anything. I haven't said it enough, but I mean it. I'll always mean it."

They walked together to the hospital. They were silent and cold but they were side by side. She hoped that meant something.

35

ALL NIGHT LONG, CLAY SAW ELEVATOR DOORS BUMP open and split his life apart. To have Molly step out of that elevator with that man, so obviously coming from—For how long had she spent her afternoons that way? And why?

He didn't really ask why, because he knew the answer. She'd been trying to tell him why all those nights when reflexes and fears made him twitch away from human contact.

For a year, they'd incubated a disease that fed on his coldness and her apathy. He didn't know how that had happened or why they were antagonists. They were supposed to be on the same side. Partners.

Maybe he should have told her more. But wasn't it cowardly —unmanly—to spread the anxiety around? To ask her to share it? She couldn't do anything about speculations except worry over them. More honestly, he couldn't bear seeing his fears mirrored in her eyes, of having to guide somebody else over the quicksand. They'd both go under. And finally, he needed one familiar landmark—Molly's faith in him—to remain on his horizon.

He'd meant well. But the day before, hanging up on her call, he understood how completely he'd locked her out. He was filled with revulsion for the single-minded, blind creature he had become. He quickly changed plans with Douglas, cleared his desk, tended to his children and headed for Molly, driven by an urgent need to thaw and undo the damage he'd done. To come back into his marriage.

And then there was Molly, stepping off the elevator, holding hands, making a last farewell. Every time the scene replayed in his mind, nausea surged through his body and he realized he was an old man.

He had trouble listening attentively the next morning and he couldn't eat the cheese omelet in front of him. His eyes felt gritty, tired of seeing elevator doors part like curtains at a bad play.

Usually he preferred the efficiency of breakfast meetings. You didn't have to cope with the drinkers who stretched lunch over the whole afternoon. But today, breakfast felt premature and painfully early. Ted Douglas, a decent-seeming man, looked well rested and scrubbed. Clay felt like hell and was sure he looked it.

God, when he thought—There'd been opportunities for him. Lots more than just that tiny blonde from the airport. Others. But he hadn't wound up in a hotel room.

"You probably expected Campiglia for your review," Douglas said, buttering whole wheat toast. "But he's swamped with Project I.D."

"I.D.?" He had to pay attention. Had to.

"I thought you knew. It's the new corporate identity. A way to make our image less diffuse. All the local brands are now going to have a—"

"Of course. The single label. I didn't recognize its new name. I—I worked on that before I—right before this assignment." The clamp on his temples grew tighter, the buzz in his brain louder. Missed signals everywhere. Stupid. *Loser.* That elevator.

"Really?" Douglas said. "You've been here a year, so that must have been when Campiglia was first developing it."

"More or less. It doesn't matter now." The elevator doesn't matter either. Nothing matters with her except today and tomorrow. Don't mix up what's important.

The waitress brought fresh coffee. Clay's head pulled in on itself so tightly he could hear the sides clash.

Molly. Campiglia. Thea. Clay. All fall down. He was deaf. The world was gone. His brain convulsed.

"—dreams," he heard.

"What's that? I'm sorry."

"I said these are bad times and nobody's risking experiments or unprofitable dreams. Too many firms going belly up." Douglas shook his head. His voice became less crisp and businesslike. "Look, Michaels, I'm trying to ease into this, but there isn't a good way to say it and I wish like hell I didn't have to at all."

The roar returned, louder, as if someone had twisted his ears and turned up the volume. He drowned in sound. *No!* His head filled, pressure pounding on his eyes and ears. *Don't say it. No!*

"We're cutting Mother Lancaster from the roster," Douglas said quietly.

How had that soft voice breached the barricade of sound?

"But I'm turning it around," Clay said. "Did you read the figures I dropped off? The division is—aside from a few— Did you read it? Did you?" He tried to catch his breath so he could speak in full sentences.

Douglas smiled and gave half a shrug. "Listen, I know this is going to cause a great deal of pain. You have how many people here?"

"Four hundred and three." Clay was amazed he could speak. "Are there any plans for—anybody?"

Douglas shrugged again. "Unfortunately not. But Great Harvest has a good reputation for being decent. The layoffs will be gradual. We know this is difficult. We want to be fair."

"And—as for my position, am I—where am I . . ." He couldn't finish the sentence. He couldn't beg. He fought off the urge to let blackness surge through his head, make him topple over and stay down for the count. Was he going to have to tell Molly they were moving again? Was he going back to L.A. and furious Campiglia? Out to the boonies? Demoted? What?

"Clay, I have the terms of a very generous package. Half a year's salary, in fact. Feel free to use your office and secretarial staff while you investigate your options, and trust that we'll provide excellent recommendations. It's a real shame this had to happen."

"I'm *fired.*" Clay was incredulous. "Fired!" Not transferred, or sent someplace rotten. Not anything. Fired. After twelve years. Because he wants me out. Afraid of me. *Fired.* Like that. He thought of the slaughter of seals. A quick head bash, belly slit, blood on the snow and out.

"It isn't personal, Michaels. These are rough times. There are cutbacks all through the system. Lots of adjustments."

"Not personal? It's my life, Douglas. How much more personal can you get?" He kept his voice low. Damn clever bastard axes me in a restaurant. Campiglia probably suggested it. Said WASPs like Michaels don't make scenes in public. Want to punch him out. Somebody. Want to cry.

"Your record is excellent," Douglas said. "It's a pity there's no other slot, and that you relocated here to a division on the slide. Somebody really goofed. They knew this place wasn't—but I suppose there was good reason for wanting you here."

"Yes. A very good reason. It's out of the way. Listen, I know it's too late to make a difference, but I want you to know that

Art Baum and I developed the label idea a year ago. Then Art was canned and I was transferred here because my old job was done away with in some kind of reorganization. And then Campiglia was promoted, using my ideas."

"Ah." Douglas looked down at his hands. He shook his head.

"Didn't you wonder at that generous settlement? Just understand that it's a payoff. Guilt money."

"I wish there were something I could do, but you understand that it's out of my—"

"I know. I just wanted it in the open. Maybe there was a point when I could have caught it, stopped it, understood it faster. I don't know . . ."

Douglas appeared uncomfortable. He cleared his throat. "We can work out the details of pension fund and stock options and any other accumulated benefits. If you want use of an outplacement firm, we'll work with you on that, certainly link in with an executive search. Look, I know this has been a blow. It can't be pleasant, but the company wants to make it as easy as it can be."

Clay could barely think. He stared at the man across the table. A mild-seeming man. Not a slaughterer. Nice human touch, Great Harvest had, sending the bearer of bad tidings 3,000 miles. All firings done by hand. The Great Harvest Humanitarian Program. My God, my God. *Fired.* And forty-five. So old, my hair so white. Should I dye it? Should I die?

"We'd like the reorganization—"

"You mean shutdown, don't you?"

"Well, yes. We'd like it to begin as soon as possible. Why don't you take some time off meanwhile to think this through, make some plans. You'll handle the rest better once you have your own perspective straight."

Clay waved away any more talk. The only truth was that Clay Michaels was forty-five years old and out of work. Like a bum. On the streets.

He'd never been out of work in his life. He hadn't included the possibility in the underpinnings of anything he lived by.

What will you be? his parents had asked. What are you?

Nothing. I am, I will be, nothing now.

He no longer existed as part of the working, functioning real planet. He lived in a subterranean netherworld of failures, also-ran's and losers. He was gone. A dead man.

36

MOLLY DRIED HER HANDS ON THE HARSH HOSPITAL towel. Her nose was still deep pink from her last walk around the city. She had taken four such walks since morning, and had canvassed at least half of downtown Philadelphia.

Neither sitting and keeping vigil nor walking made her feel any less agitated or any less doomed.

"Don't you want to say something?" she asked her reflection. They both looked gray and fuzzed around the edges, out of keeping with the crispness of the hospital. Molly looked like every would-be mourner, the visitors who arrived with bodies sloped and defeated, waiting for word on long benches.

"You've become mute, is that it?" she asked the mirror. "Time was you were a regular chatterbox."

"Time was," the mirror woman said, "I was more optimistic. A lot of it feels like a waste of breath now."

"I don't know what to do," Molly said. "How to convince Clay I didn't—I really didn't—"

"Oh, who *cares* about the technical details of yesterday? Or are you talking about something else? Something serious, like murder?"

"Are you saying what I did or didn't do means nothing?"

The mirror woman shrugged. "I'm saying that precisely where two sets of sexual organs were at a given moment is not the problem. Anyway, *I* told you to climb some mountains, remember? But all I'm saying is that yesterday was about real things—loneliness, fear of death, feeling betrayed, abandoned —lots of serious stuff. That's what you have to take care of. Those are problems."

"Too much is happening. I can't handle it all."

"You could live under glass, the way I do. Nothing much happens in here."

"You don't understand."

"Molly," the mirror woman said. "Clean up your act. Stop looking for daddies, even if they're nice guys like Sam. They can't save you and they never could."

Molly closed her eyes, trying to stop a sharp pain that whipped trails of light behind her eyes.

"Stand up straight and listen," the mirror woman said. "You know those puppies with enormous paws? We say, 'Oh, look, he's going to grow into them.' You know?"

Molly nodded.

"Then open your eyes. Come on, look at me. You certainly gape other times, moaning and groaning about how I'm doing. Now look at me."

Molly did as directed.

"What do you see?"

Molly shrugged. "Me. Nothing much. A middle-aged lady."

"Molly! That's a grown-up's face. Do you understand? It's been ready for you for a while. Now grow into it."

"Mom?"

Molly whirled around. Joanna stood at the door, smiling shyly. "The nurse said you might be in here. I can only stay a minute. Promised the boys I'd take them to dinner. How's Grandma? Any change?"

Molly shook her head. "They aren't optimistic, love." She leaned against the sink. "What's up? Is everything okay?"

"I wanted to show you this." Joanna pulled an envelope out of her bag and handed it to her mother. "I can't believe it—it feels so weird." She swallowed hard and shook her head.

Molly read the letter.

> Dear Joanna,
>
> This is difficult to write, because I love you very very much. I love you enough to say that it's time to go our separate ways. Some things die a natural death sooner than we expect them to or want them to, but we can't curse nature.
>
> I wish I could share your life forever, but you must have realized that it's impossible. I'd like to think, though, that some part of me will always stay in your memory and in your heart.

"As if she knew," Joanna said. "As if two weeks ago, or whenever, she just knew how it would be when we were reading it."

Molly blew her nose. "Listen, could you read that last line to me? My eyes—the line's dancing like one long wiggle."

"I think you'll have to read it yourself." Joanna's sudden giggle amazed Molly, who blinked hard and finally read:

> In closing, Jo, remember what the Indians of Massachusetts said: Cargoggagoggmanchauggagoggchaubunagunamaugg. Which means: You fish on your side, I fish on my side, nobody fish in the middle.
>
> I'll think of you while I fish on my side.
>
> Love,
> Ricky

"I'll bet she's been saving that word for years, looking for a way to work it into a conversation." Molly's eyes filmed over again.

"I never knew her to worry about how to work something in. She just bombed it on us." Joanna carefully refolded the letter. "I'm going to miss her."

They both blew their noses. "Maybe we'd better freshen up," Molly suggested.

"Guy's waiting for me."

They splashed water and patted and for a moment, stopped and regarded their images. For a second, Joanna's reflection looked so familiar to Molly that she locked herself into it. She felt at home under the long cap of hair, with the clean line of jaw, the smooth cheeks, the lovely newness.

And then, suddenly, she didn't want to be plain that way anymore. She didn't want to be unmarked, waiting for life to engrave her. Poor Joanna, she heard herself think. So much living to get through before you earn your stripes. Takes years and years and it sure as hell ain't easy.

"Good for you," the mirror said.

"Thanks," Molly answered.

"You say something, Mom?"

"Thanks for coming," Molly said. "I'm glad you wanted to show me the letter. I—sometimes I was afraid that we—"

Joanna kissed her. "I think maybe we're both going through phases."

Guy, looking extraordinarily tall, leaned on the wall across from the ladies' room.

"Did it work?" Molly suddenly whispered. "The letter, did it work?"

Joanna winked. "Mom, is it wrong to be this happy while Grandma's . . . ?"

"Absolutely not. And isn't it nice she helped make it happen?"

Joanna kissed her again and left with Guy. He walked atilt,

leaning in her direction as if to protect her. The air wrapped their bodies with a tight bow.

Molly went in to visit her mother. Time dripped as slowly as the IV in Thea's arm. Molly sat by the bed, feeling already orphaned. The rest was formality. Her mother was gone, and in her place, a creature of tubes, pumps, tapes and needles. Eight decades of action and talk ended on white sheets.

Could Thea still remember? Did she lie filled with sorrow because she hadn't saved the world after all? Did she see again the dreams that had evaporated into silence? The real Joseph of the coppery hair, the writing career in Hollywood or on Broadway, the bank account, the radical world plans?

Or was having held the dreams and fought for them enough? "What you do will probably be insignificant," Gandhi and Thea had said, "but it's important that you do it."

By her own lights, Thea had done it. Molly stroked her mother's hand, hoping Thea knew she was there, loving her. She felt peaceful, a part of a whole. There was Joanna, blazing and new, there was Thea, ebbing, and there was Molly. They merged into one, and Molly felt the continuity between her daughter's discovery of love and her mother's quiet exit. And where Molly sat, in the middle of life, in the heart of its processes and chaos, felt comfortable and dangerous all at once.

"I'm catching on at last," she said to her mother. "Slow learner, but not without promise. I love you. I hope you can hear and remember that." She left the room and nearly bumped into Clay.

Molly was as startled as if her mother had stretched and stood up. More so, because Thea was apt to do the unexpected and Clay was not. "I thought you'd be with that man until late tonight, I . . ." He looked ill. "I didn't expect you today."

"I'm full of surprises," he answered flatly. He sounded like a bad actor reading a script.

She took his hand and held it for dear life. "You seem very upset."

"I am. I have a lot to be upset about." His voice was harsh and scratchy.

A nurse frowned at him.

"We have to talk," he said. He seemed to be trying to whisper, but his voice was loud.

The nurse scowled and cleared her throat.

"I love you," Clay said. "I love you, Molly."

The nurse stood up and moved toward them.

"Outside," Molly whispered.

"I trust you," Clay said as she guided him outside. "Yesterday has to become yesterday forever as far as we're concerned."

"Clay, if you'll only believe that I—"

"I do. I believe you. But there's no way for you to believe that I was anything except what I was, a jackass, a fool. But that was then. I swear I want to get past it, Molly. I love you and I'm afraid my stupidity has wrecked—"

"No." They walked hand in hand. "Nothing is broken." She smiled and believed she was speaking the truth. "How could it be? Maybe bruised, but we both want it to be better, so it will be. We'll make it wonderful again. It's ours to remake."

They walked close to each other in silence for a while. The evening was milder than the day that had preceded it. It was possible to believe in spring and summer; faint scents of future growth permeated even the city street.

"I hate to be mundane," Clay said, "but is there someplace we can eat? I couldn't eat breakfast and I missed lunch and I'm hungry."

"I don't think there is," she said. She knew there wasn't. The knowledge had directed her walks all day as she circled and checked, then returned to inspect the empty Colonial gift shop and to call the number on the FOR RENT sign. She was full of ideas because of the very absence of nearby restaurants, but this wasn't the time to deal with her plans. It was the time to avoid the only comfortable dining room nearby, the one at the hotel, with its unpleasant memories.

"How'd the review go, Clay?"

He hunched his shoulders and kept walking. "Let's find a place," he said. But they couldn't. Finally, they settled for high plastic stools at a chicken-take-out stand.

"They're closing Mother Lancaster, Molly." Clay looked jaundiced.

His words didn't make sense.

"Division's done. No more. Kaput. And I'm out of work. I don't have a job. Me." He seemed unable to comprehend what he was saying, and he leaned forward as if trying to catch the real sound of the words coming out of his mouth. "Canned," he said, listening again. "Given my walking papers. I feel dizzy —can't get my balance. I had so many expectations, so many reasons to assume they were sane." He stared at the coffee he had ordered. "I know what you must think of me," he said.

"It's okay." Molly ignored his look of distrust. "It's okay. It's going to be fine." She spoke by rote, falling into the litany women use to heal those in their care. She made promises about a world she barely understood, and she believed them because the important thing was that Clay was letting her close enough to see him at last.

"I feel like a fool. I knew something was screwy. Knew it since November, since I had dinner with Campiglia. But I didn't know what, or how bad. It's felt like a cancer ever since."

She spoke very slowly. "Why didn't you tell me?"

"I thought I was protecting you." He gulped coffee. "I see now I was protecting myself."

"I thought your moods were because of me. I never considered anything else. I thought— Now I feel so self-centered and dumb."

"Maybe if we'd talked, maybe there were different conclusions we both could have reached. It's my fault, but whatever happened, that's the past, all right?"

"Only if none of it ever happens again. Don't lock me out, Clay. I'm your wife, your partner. I want to share your life."

He inhaled in a broken way, grabbing for more air. "Thank God for you," he said softly. She took his hand again. "It'll be different now, Moll. It'll be good."

She believed it. She felt close to euphoric, rebonded. The difficult time ahead didn't frighten her. In fact, it seemed a challenge she could share. She'd be a helpmeet, not a kept woman.

"Anyway," Clay said, "turns out, it's not the end of the world."

"Of course not. We'll find something better. There's lots of local companies. Campbell's, and the ice cream people, and—"

Clay shook his head.

"Well, it doesn't have to be food, does it? You're a talented manager, flexible and—why are you shaking your head?"

"Because I have something more than speculation. Something good. I spoke to Art Baum today. We've talked a few times the last couple of months and he knew about my queasiness. Kept an eye out for me. Anyway, there's something at Kellogg's and he's sure I could handle it, and—"

The light bouncing from the ceiling onto the laminated menus blinded Molly. Fluorescence flooded her, erasing all subtleties, eradicating their walk, the hand-holding, the messages and signals about their future.

Only one thing stood out against the white light. "Kellogg," she said. "That's in Michigan."

"Battle Creek. Yes. And you'd have Joanie, a friend."

"No," Molly said.

The word plopped on the orange plastic counter and dribbled over the sides.

"—challenging position. There's room for growth and even if initially it might be less than I'd hope for, I think my experience would eventually—"

"No."

"—and I work so well with Art, so I wouldn't be in danger of repeating the Campiglia fiasco, so—"

"No! Listen to me, Clay. I'm saying 'no.' No. No."

"No?"

"No. N-O. No."

"How can you say no?"

"Like this." She slowly shook her head. Left to right. Right to left. "No."

"Don't be ridiculous. Look, I'm sure we'll do fine with the house and there are good schools there, and Art says—"

"No."

"No? Molly, I don't have a job. I don't have anything except this chance with Art. I thought you said we were going to share our lives. What was all that about? I'm trying to save us, Moll. How can you say no?"

"How can I say yes? For God's sake, Clay, I feel as if I just crawled onto the beach after almost drowning. And now you decide to dunk my head back under. It hurts me to say no. But it would kill me to say yes."

"You aren't even happy here."

"I'm going to be. I've finally finished with the starting over. And the children, Clay. Your kids. One more shuffling and we're going to have permanent casualties. I can't do it to them."

"I'm not talking about some dumb impulse or mid-life whim, Moll. I'm talking about survival."

"So am I. We can survive other ways. We can rethink our lives. We don't need Mother Megaslop. We need each other, not the big house, the big lawn. I want you, not a job title."

"I need work."

"I need to stay put." She bowed her head. "I can't be Sisyphus, pushing us up the hill again, then having the boulder roll back. This time it nearly crushed me. I don't have a next time in me. Maybe only somebody who hates her life is strong enough to do that forever."

"I'm going outside," he said.

"But you're hungry."

"Not anymore." He left, not even waiting for her.

She ran after him. "I'm right, Clay. I know I am!"

"About what? Not about real life. Listen, Molly, ever since Campiglia's visit I've made discreet inquiries, asked around. There's nothing here for me. But there is a job in Battle Creek. I'm sure, because Art has the final say. It isn't my dream job, but—"

"Art has the final say, but I don't get any say at all? Don't I matter?" Passersby stopped to watch Molly whirl out of control. "Don't I count for anything?"

"Of course you do. Who do you think I do this for?"

"For you! From now on, if you keep with it, then it's only for you. It's destroying the rest of us. Why do you want to be part of it? Look how it treats you. Why?"

"Because I want success!" He looked around him, as if he feared the onlookers would consider his desire a perversion. "Who doesn't?" he asked more quietly. "You're completely unfair. I'm forty-five years old and I don't have a job." He walked briskly while he talked, and now she almost had to run to keep up with him.

"I'm forty and I don't have a job!" she shouted. "And don't tell me it's different. I've been in that hospital for two days, glad that Thea lived the way she wanted to. Because now I know it can end just like that. You're unbuttoning your coat, thinking the rest of the day's waiting for you, and other days, too. And then there's nothing except what you've already done. A person has to grab hold of her life sooner or later. I'm already up to later! I have to start now!"

He finally slowed his pace. Now she didn't have to shout and run to keep up. "I want success," he said. "The good feeling of doing something substantial. Building something. I want to be respected. Is that so bad?"

"Sometimes," she said, "I have the feeling this isn't my real life. There's another, better life I'll get a shot at. Another set of characters, another me, another set of circumstances. Sometimes, I'm ready to just hang around through this life. Just wait for that second chance. That's really scary."

"I think what I mean is that sense of being somebody. Feeling whole. That's success." Clay lapsed into silence for a block or two. When he spoke again, his voice seemed to emerge against his will. "I *need* that," he said.

"I want the same things," she answered. "And community, too. I want old friends. I want to work on a project and see it to fruition. For once, I want to know if the PTA carnival I planned in April made money the following October. I'm sick of not knowing a single local issue when I vote. Of not caring about much except the pattern of my new wallpaper. I want to be involved in the world, not in another new house. I want to stop wandering, want to feel I've reached my destination."

"What are you saying?" he asked.

"I won't be part of it anymore. I hate your job and what it does to people and families. And mostly, to me. I want out. The perks aren't worth the punishments."

He said nothing for a long time. Then he spoke softly. "What are your plans, Moll?"

"For starters, I'm going back into business." It sounded more of a challenge than she'd intended.

"How? Where will the money come from? There's already the loan out West, and—"

"I'll find a way. Besides, Ellen may have a buyer for my share."

She knew what Clay wanted to say as soon as she'd said the words "my share." She tried to say his words, and hers, gently. "I know you loaned me the money and that you want it back, Clay. And now, with your job ended, well, I'm sure you really want it. And please don't think I'm cruel, or selfish, but a good half of that is mine, Clay. Every time we move I improve our houses and we make a big profit. I don't want to sound harsh, but it's literally my sweat that's involved. I want to keep my half and start something new. It's my wages."

"Even if you get your share, even if you keep it all, it's not enough to start another store," he said.

"I'll find more. I'm going to find a way to have a store again. I even think I've found a place, over there, on the corner. I called about it today, and it's perfect. Needs a kitchen, but there's space for it. And there's a fireplace in what could be the eating area, and a dry basement for storage, which is a terrific plus. There's room for extra display cases and—just think, Clay, it'd be so nice for the hospital workers and visitors and outpatients to have something life-affirming where and when they need it most. I can just see it, all wood and warm and—"

"You come alive when you talk about it," Clay said. "I'm beginning to understand."

She filled with hope again. She reached up and kissed him and they stood like awkward teenagers, holding on and kissing in the March night. "I knew you'd understand!" she said. "I just knew it."

"But you'll have to understand me, too. I have an interview in Battle Creek on Tuesday."

There was nothing left to say.

For a long time she stood on the sidewalk, memorizing him. His face was unbearably precious, familiar in all its planes and lines, some of which she'd etched onto it. She knew each layer of skin; the old ones, now hidden, glowed through to the surface for her.

A collage of years whirled before her eyes, picture plastered over picture, glimpses of dresses worn and glasses drunk from, tickets and house keys and street maps and diapers. She saw all the different Clays, all the years, all the triumphs and loving and screaming fights and laughter, and she thought she would die if the picture ended now.

Their lives were on both their faces, their pasts recorded in each other's brain. Separate histories could never be written.

They were more than footnotes to each other. They were joined, and their hands had helped shape each other. The time behind them was so blended the seams were below the flesh and only a terrible rupture would rip them apart. If they parted, they'd take vital pieces of each other with them.

They were married.

They neared the hospital. Give in, Molly, a piece of her cried. Do you want a solitary life? Give in or you'll die.

And she thought of her children walking into yet another unfamiliar schoolyard, saw Joanna neatly excised from Guy, Ben stranded and friendless again, Tony flipflopping. She saw another set of cold rooms whining for her hand, another street map to master, another new start and dead end, and she knew she couldn't survive it.

Give in and you'll die, she amended it.

Either way she lost. All she could do was give up.

"Do you want me to come in and sit with you?" Clay asked.

She shook her head.

He put his hands on his temples, pushing, she knew, at spots he believed capable of preventing headaches. For nineteen years she'd watched him do that. For nineteen years it hadn't worked, but on he pushed. "I don't understand anything anymore," he said.

"You're making a mistake," she said.

He looked as if he might speak, but instead, he kissed her gently, and left.

"You're making a mistake!" she screamed at the top of her lungs. But he didn't turn around.

Her bench was occupied by strangers, a pregnant woman and a grandmotherly type, both in tears. They cried loudly and spoke in a guttural foreign tongue. Only the sound of grief was comprehensible. They made Molly's sounds for her, crying and pulling at their handkerchiefs. Molly herself had dried up.

She saw the hallway for what it was, an endless container of pain for those who cared, intensively. Nothing good except escape happened here. And even then, the jaws, having snapped once, would open and wait again. The best to hope for, for any of them, was a reprieve.

Molly stood, arid and in acute pain. Any moment she would explode with the force of it, break into brittle shards that would impale themselves in the walls and ceiling.

The pain spread until her throat closed and her stomach contracted and cramped as if eating itself. She had lost her husband. He was leaving. This wasn't one of her old songs where boys and girls played games and then made up next Saturday night. She wasn't a kid. She was a woman and love of a serious kind was being trashed. She stood, dry-eyed and in agony, rocking back and forth, her eyes shut tight. She stood so long, she felt herself harden and become fossilized. And still she stood.

And then she heard a cough. A nose being blown. And a voice. "I keep coming here," she heard in a deep timbre that made music of his most ordinary words. "I must need intensive care."

His nose was red and beautiful, his blue eyes rimmed with pink.

"Good thing about hospitals," she said, "is that nobody asks why you're crying. Except me."

"Because I was stupid, that's why." He took her arm and guided her away from the silent station, the wailing women. "When something's as important as you are to me, you don't let go of it. You don't leave it."

She shook her head. That was well and good, but she couldn't afford to be seduced by his eyes and his voice and his love again.

"I drove away," he said. "I knew everything had gone wrong, but I didn't know how to stop it. Then I saw what I was doing —acting as if I was trapped, condemned to more and more of the same even though it hasn't made me happy for a long time. Molly, I don't want to change companies—I want to change lives. We're supposed to be partners. You said so yourself. So —could we be?"

She shook her head. "You're going too fast. I don't know what you mean."

"I mean all the way. All the time. I have severance pay coming. Let's invest it in us, in our own place. I'm not a cook, but I know food—"

"Lousy food," she said, but she could barely contain the smile spreading through her.

"Yeah. But still, I know some things. Marketing and accounting and advertising and promotion. And I can learn. You could teach me."

"You'd really drop out of the whole system? Be happy in a rinky-dink store as a partner, not a boss?"

"Remember what I said I wanted? To build something, make something happen. Why not that? And it doesn't have to be rinky-dink. What about branches in the suburbs? Or what about—"

She laughed softly. "We could do it," she said. "We could do it! My God, Clay, we're going to beat the odds and survive, aren't we? Isn't that incredible—the most ordinary, exceptional thing? We'll break all records, make history, because we'll keep on being happy, stay married, endure."

"You're so beautiful."

She made a face. "Just a forty-year-old broad," she said, "wrinkling up and falling apart."

"You forget. My eyes are forty-five. You look just right to them."

"Listen, Clay, I have a name for it."

"For my eyes?"

"For the place. *Our* place. How does 'Mom and Pop's' grab you?"

He grinned. "I can see it now. History reversed. Mom and Pop stores reappearing on street corners everywhere."

"I'll have to teach you to think small," she said. Then she

reached for him and felt giddy and light-headed as she hugged him and their reclaimed future. She laughed out loud with the pleasure of it.

He put on his most serious Cotton Mather manner. "I don't think we're supposed to laugh in Intensive Care, Molly."

"Oh, Clay," she answered, "what else can we do?"